LEGAL FEES

Travel Brings Solutions
A Money Mystery

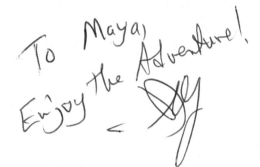

To Maya,
Enjoy the Adventure!

A Book of Fiction by

David M. Melesky

Birch Tree Ranch, LLC

Library of Congress Number: 2018904024
ISBN - 978-0-9894932-2-2

Printed in the U.S.A.

David M. Melesky

TO

THE GANG AT THE RANCH

INTRODUCTION

There appear to be several steps which B.G. Wumpkey, Attorney at Law, keeps in the forefront of his mind when faced with a problem. Whether it concerns something of major proportions with significant consequences, or be it limited in nature to a more simple matter, his recommended formula for handling such invariably seems to begin with three basic steps.

First, you identify the matter that needs to be resolved.

Second, you name the desired resolution that is sought.

Third, you eat a very satisfying meal while you begin to come up with ways to achieve the desired outcome.

To those who have any familiarity with the imposing individual, it is well recognized that the third step is so critical in the process that it cannot be overlooked, which is why it often times must be repeated consistently.

In this fourth book in the B.G. Wumpkey series, the independent minded attorney finds himself meeting up with friends old and new after some highly valued items come into his hands. As the ensuing story line leads him on a trail up and down the east coast which proves to be both complicated and dangerous, our main character has to deal with dilemmas of a mysterious client as well as his own while he persistently tries to reach his desired result.

Of course, all along the way, he makes sure to keep his third step in the process paramount in his concerns, while sharing the delicious details of some favorite recipes encountered in his travels.

CHAPTER ONE

The black leather briefcase that had been left in the law office of Attorney B.G. Wumpkey by his mysterious client on Monday afternoon, was not actually discovered until four days later. This was due to a number of reasons.

First, B.G. acknowledged that the realization that his herd of beef cows back at his ranch had suddenly managed to escape from their fenced pasture had temporarily "thrown him off of his game" as he put it. Whether four black Angus could arguably be called a herd was a point that might bring some dispute from large scale beef cattle operations, but the plain fact that each of the steers weighed upwards of twelve hundred pounds and were in the mood for exploring certainly made Wumpkey feel the term was quite appropriate. In any event, while the foursome appeared to be obviously enjoying their newfound freedom, neighbors and passing motorists alike delivered many reported sightings in backyards, corn fields and woodlands spanning several miles. In each case however, they all turned out to be false leads by the time B.G. was able to arrive at the named location. Thus, the escapees remained "at large."

Ultimately, several days after their extended field trip over hill and dale began, the steers returned to an area about half a mile from their point of escape. It was only then, as the beef cows appeared satisfied with the findings of their expedition, while using the able help of B.G.'s son and daughter (both of whom were visiting from college) and a rancher with experience in such matters that the bovines were coaxed to return to the confines of their fenced pasture.

This was one reason why B.G.'s attention to office matters had been extremely limited during that time frame.

The second reason that the briefcase was not discovered until four days later may well be attributed to the fact that it was left behind a desk in the front office area where it was partially obscured. After some reflection, and for reasons which were soon to become evident, B.G. concluded that the concealment clearly had been intentional.

*

As was his habit, whenever B.G. had matters of a very serious nature to review, his first action was one of a well practiced routine. Thus, he automatically went into the building's entry area and proceeded to lock the door.

Next, he picked up the briefcase and carefully brought it into the inner room of his office. Turning the window blinds down to further insure his privacy, he then walked behind his large desk, placed the briefcase upon it and sat down in his high backed office chair. As an afterthought, he put his ear to its flat surface. He heard no sound.

Then, he studied it carefully for several moments.

What he immediately observed was that the brief-case was constructed of fine leather, had a sturdy carrying handle and numerical combination locksets next to each of the two closing buttons and tabs. The numbers were turned to show matching triple combinations of 3-3-3. In addition, he had concluded from carrying it that it was not empty, as whatever its contents were, such had quite a substantial weight.

Of course, all of this only added to his building curiosity.

Taking a deep breath, B.G. shrugged his shoulders and smiled. Then, he put his thumbs in place and prepared to very carefully move the left brass tab to the left and right brass tab to the right.

CHAPTER TWO

In order to better understand what B.G. may have been about to get himself involved in, just before opening the briefcase he paused again momentarily to quickly review some of the background that had led up to this. In doing so, he recalled the following events.

*

When B.G. came into his office that previous Wednesday morning, he had a voice mail message waiting for him that was recorded the previous evening.

The message was short and a bit vague. In essence, however, it informed that the man calling had been referred by a mutual acquaintance, that he needed to meet with the attorney, and was hoping to do so in the next day or so, preferably in the morning. Before hanging up, the man had added simply that it was "about an important matter that is extremely time sensitive."

The man had not left his name nor his telephone number and the "caller id" screen was no help, having indicated that the previous incoming calls had been either toll-free numbers or otherwise "unknown."

Obviously, this was a bit intriguing to B.G.

Years of experience had taught Wumpkey that such calls usually proved to be significant, insofar as they generally represented a situation in which the caller or his or her associate had two significant characteristics. First, they typically were in a serious bind of some sort, and second, they almost always knew that they would have to pay someone handsomely in order to help deal with it.

Wumpkey had further come to realize that in order to best handle such situations, he had to be in the proper frame of mind. And, pursuant to his years of experience and related research, he had also found that certain rituals best served that purpose.

And so, with such thoughts in mind, B.G. decided that he needed to take certain preparatory steps as he awaited the expected telephone call from his prospective client.

*

One hour later, Wumpkey was seated in his office with an especially broad smile on his face. Placed on the gleaming wooden desk in front of him were a frosted chocolate cupcake and a small glass of milk.

Brimming with gleeful anticipation, B.G. lifted the cupcake and momentarily observed it.

Curiously, it was just as he took his his first large bite, that he heard the distinctive sounds of two barks of a dog followed by the ringing of his doorbell.

*

The older gentleman with a head of bushy white hair was of average height and weight. The only immediately distinguishing factors were a length of scars on his left hand and forearm, which appeared to be the result of some sort of burn injury.

12

"Good day, sir. I called yesterday and left a message, but since I wanted to meet with you right away, I thought I'd stop in and see if we could set up a meeting."

"That may be possible. I'm B.G. Wumpkey, at your service."

"My name is Kurt. Kurt Koppy. And I want you to meet my friend Jack."

Looking over his shoulder and seeing no one else, Kurt then called out, "Hey, come over here."

At that moment a very, very large dog with bushy black fur walked from the reception area into the office.

"This is Jack."

*

About an hour later, having set up an impromptu consultation, B.G. seemed to have a rough idea of the essential elements of this client's particular situation. Recognizing early into the conference that this in fact was the same person who had left that somewhat mysterious message, B.G. also came to arrive at certain conclusions.

First, Mr. Koppy clearly wanted to have an attorney - rather - this attorney, handle his financial affairs, effective immediately, should the need arise. Second, Mr. Koppy had some unknowns in his situation that he was unwilling to fully disclose at this time.

Third, and perhaps of special significance, as a sign of his appreciation for seeing him on such short notice, Mr. Koppy had volunteered to pay generously for B.G.'s time and advice, which he did so from a large wad of cash that he took from his jacket's inside pocket.

The general scenario seemed to be well suited to have a Power of Attorney prepared for Mr. Koppy, and when B.G. mentioned such, Mr. Koppy greeted the recommendation most favorably. Although such typically required at least one more office visit by a client to have such a document properly drawn up and finalized, it was at Mr. Koppy's polite yet persistent requests that a blank draft copy of such a document was presented to the gentleman for him to take with him to review. However, in doing so, B.G. was certain to make very clear that such paperwork had certain requirements for its proper completion which should be completed with legal assistance, to which Mr. Koppy indicated that he fully understood.

It was at that point in their meeting, B.G. was later recalling, that Mr. Koppy informed that he wanted to go out to his vehicle to get his card for Mr. Wumpkey, when he took the blank paperwork and briefly left the office. Just before making his exit, the new client had encouraged Jack to come over and visit with B.G., which time they both seemed to enjoy.

A few minutes later, B.G. had heard the front entry door open and close, and after a brief pause he saw Mr. Koppy return, with a card in hand, into the back room of the law office. At that point, the two had exchanged business cards. Shortly afterward, while promising to be in touch with Wumpkey again very, very soon, his new client and the furry companion had gone outside.

*

As he looked back on these events and gave the matter more thought, Wumpkey soon realized that it was when Mr. Koppy left and then returned, while Jack and B.G. were still in the back main office, that the briefcase must have been quickly and strategically placed in a spot that would not have been immediately noticed, and where it had in fact remained unobserved until now.

CHAPTER THREE

There was a layer of newspaper, from Tampa, Florida that covered the contents of the briefcase. The date of the newspaper was from a month ago. On one of the inside pockets of the briefcase's top cover, there was also a manilla folder which appeared to have some papers in it.

He'd get to that later.

As B.G. gently lifted the newspaper (the pages were from the classified section, he noted), his eyes widened.

"Wowsy!" he said aloud.

Underneath the newspaper he saw cash, neatly stacked in small bundles.

A lot of it.

U.S. currency, larger denominations, layers and layers of it.

B.G. would get to counting it later, but for now his estimation was that the total amount of money in all these bills had to be into the six figures.

But there was still more to see.

In the inside leather pocket of the briefcase, behind the manilla folder, there were cardboard squares, with circular openings having clear plastic covers. And through the clear plastic he saw that each piece of the cardboard sheath had a coin in it. Picking one of them up, he noted that it was both shiny and heavy.

Gold.

He'd need to verify this of course, but they appeared to be authentic gold one ounce coins. Some were the American Eagle, and some were the Canadian Maple Leaf. While B.G. had in the past taken a passing interest in these commodities, as they were sometimes called, he had recollected that the valuation of such seemed to range in recent years from a high of nearly two thousand to a low of around one thousand, being dollars per ounce.

Carefully, he counted out thirty-two of the individually wrapped coins.

Two pounds.

That accounts for some of the weight the case contained, he thought.

Next, it was time to bring his full attention to the manilla folder. Taking it out of the briefcase, he placed it on the desktop in front of him. There were no markings of any kind on the folder, on either of its sides or on the tab on the outer edge.

Of the two sheets of standard eight and one-half inches by eleven inches, unlined white paper, only one of them had anything on it.

Looking at the one, B.G. was astonished to see that it contained his name in bold print.

The wording, in neatly printed letters after showing today's date, read as follows:

"AGREEMENT

Effective this date, entire contents of items which have now or shall be delivered to law office are to be divided in accordance with these terms:

To Attorney B.G. Wumpkey One-third (33.3%)

All remaining amounts to be distributed and disbursed by said attorney pursuant to further instructions.

By: Kurt Koppy"

Next to Mr. Koppy's printed name was also a written signature of the same.

*

A few minutes later, having once again gone over the contents of the briefcase, B.G. did some thinking out loud.

"Well, it certainly appears to be a fee agreement of some sort...sparse though it is. But then, what are these legal services for which I am being hired to perform?"

CHAPTER FOUR

A partial answer to B.G.'s puzzling situation was presented to him the next morning.

After a breakfast that was unusually light for him, he had headed out a bit early to his law office for a couple of reasons. The breakfast of a bowl of oatmeal and a piece of fruit was hardly the repast to start the day that he was accustomed to, but it was one which the newly health conscious Mrs. Wumpkey had felt was necessary as an introductory effort both to improve her husband's eating habits and also to keep his tendency to have an expanding waistline somewhat in check.

Subsequently, with the thought of reviewing the matter of the briefcase, B.G. was now also intending to visit the newly opened bakery that was located just a block away from his office, which was in the small city of West Paradise. While situated in western Pennsylvania, B.G. had often thought it a curious fact that there was no East, North or South Paradise nearby, nor any other named Paradise to his knowledge in the area, and wondered how such a specific designation originated.

Twenty minutes later, after parking his car, he approached the front door of his law office building with a small bag, which held two freshly baked donuts. Before he had a chance to enjoy them, however, he had an unexpected situation to deal with.

As he walked up the three steps of the covered entrance to his office, he saw a familiar figure standing in front of the door.

It was Jack, wagging enthusiastically, with a long leash that had been looped around and attached to the front storm door's handle. Looking around, B.G. didn't see Mr. Koppy, nor anyone else. This seemed a bit strange.

Then, just as B.G. was reaching to open the outer storm door, he noticed that between that door and the inner heavy oak door, for which he held the key, there was an object.

It was brown, rectangular, with a metallic handle. Another briefcase, this one a bit larger than the other.

Suddenly, off in the distance, something caught B.G.'s attention that made him turn around quickly.

He heard three distinctive blasts of a horn, and then saw a vehicle that was in a church parking lot about two hundred yards from where he stood, turn onto the road and drive away. As it moved out of sight he noted only that it was a small recreational vehicle, a gray colored motor home, and appeared to be a newer model, but other than that it was really too far off for him to distinguish much else.

Had someone been waiting and watching him from that distance?

Apparently so.

As he thought over these events, his attention

was brought back to the present by a nudge that he felt. It was on his leg, and came from the head of the large black dog that was now looking up at him expectantly.

Jack smelled the donuts.

*

Once inside his office, B.G. brought both Jack and the briefcase past the reception area and into the back room where his desk was located.

He waited a few minutes at the front door, expecting Mr. Koppy to show up momentarily, but he did not.

After twenty minutes, B.G. locked the door and returned to his desk, where Jack was already settled and comfortably stretched out on the carpet nearby.

B.G. ate one and a half donuts, with a glass of milk from his refrigerator in the kitchen. Jack had the remaining half. Already, it was clear that the two had a lot in common.

"Wowsy, again!" came B.G.'s excited voice as it broke the silence in his office.

The second briefcase, now opened before him, held what appeared to be an equal if not greater amount of cash than its predecessor. In addition, B.G. also carefully counted out another sizeable number of what appeared to be similar gold one ounce coins.

"Forty-eight more coins in this one," he stated aloud.

B.G. paused, and then looked at Jack.

That makes three more pounds. Five pounds altogether, he calculated.

Then, within the confines of the interior pocket of this briefcase, he saw the additional papers, neatly folded and in a brown envelope. These had a lot of printing on them.

A few minutes later, he had confirmed what his initial impression had been.

This was the Power of Attorney document that he had given to Mr. Koppy last week, for him to review and get back to him.

However, to his surprise the document had already been filled out and completed. And from what B.G. observed, it had all been done correctly, and properly signed, initialed, notarized and witnessed where designated.

"Well, well, well," ruminated B.G. as he looked at the items on his desk.

So, now there was this to try to understand as well as the whole matter of the two briefcases...along with the very large dog.

And what made the situation even more puzzling for the moment, was that by virtue of these papers, Mr. Kurt Koppy had legally named B.G. Wumpkey as his duly authorized Power of Attorney, effective immediately.

CHAPTER FIVE

Three hours later, there had been no other sign of the elusive Mr. Koppy, and B.G. was starting to get hungry. During that entire time, Jack had gotten to his feet once, moved over to the opposite side of the carpet in front of the desk, and gone back to sleep.

While what was contained in the briefcases kept returning to the forefront of his thoughts, when Mr. Koppy had neither appeared nor called, B.G. began to consider how this man might be contacted directly. And that was when he remembered that they had exchanged business cards.

The card that Kurt Koppy had given to B.G. did not have his name on it. Instead, it had a colorful emblem, and the name "Blue Ribbon Enterprises," along with a telephone number. There was no address.

Recognizing the number as having a Florida area code, he reached for the phone on his desk and dialed it immediately. Much to his disappointment, a recording informed that the number was no longer in service.

So then, this Mr. Koppy was proving himself to be

quite an interesting character. Clearly though, the man must have his reasons, and his actions, while mysterious, had shown themselves to be well thought out thus far. With no other options coming to mind, B.G. decided that his best procedure now might well be simply to wait to hear from his new client.

That is, providing his new client, wherever he was, felt the same way.

With his furry companion still snoring peacefully at the side of his desk, and B.G.'s increasing appetite reminding him that it was now well into the noon hour, he picked up the telephone again and made a call.

When his wife Carol answered, he told her that his plans had changed. Instead of having lunch in town, he would be coming home shortly.

Hearing her cheerful surprise, he added that he would also be bringing a friend.

*

Wumpkey's decision to bring Jack back to the ranch over the lunch hour brought some unintended benefits. Carol, in expectation of a two-legged guest for lunchtime, had prepared a repast that was far more in line with B.G.'s usual dietary preferences than the type of extra healthy morning meal she was encouraging her husband to try to make a part of his daily regimen.

The hot roast beef sandwich prepared from the grass fed black Angus raised on their own land was both tender and juicy. The mashed potatoes and gravy along with a fresh garden salad complete with a vinegar-olive oil-herbal dressing provided just the right touch. The added fact that the amounts prepared had been for three expected diners made Wumpkey's offering to consume the remaining portions to avoid leftovers seem reasonable.

Once the revelation that Jack was the one and only guest and that B.G. was merely temporarily taking care of him at a client's request was briefly explained and made clear that such would in no way otherwise interfere with Carol's luncheon preparations, after their own meal was finished, she proceeded to locate some beef trimmings along with a meaty soup bone. Seeing these put for him in a bowl on the outdoor porch, the large dog's attention was soon fully occupied while the sounds of his contented gentle gnawing carried over into the kitchen.

Some time later, B.G. informed that he would soon be going back to the office just to check on a few things. He was pleased to observe after his wife sat down in her favorite chair on the back porch with a book she was reading, that Jack, who had been stretched out comfortably on the floor close by, proceeded to begin calmly resting his head upon his wife's foot. While he had expected to have their guest remain with him for the afternoon, upon seeing that this new friendship was already well established and progressing nicely on the porch, B.G. opted instead not to disturb the moment of relaxation between the two and thus to return to his office alone.

*

As most individuals with knowledge on the subject would generally agree, in its most basic terms a Power Of Attorney is a legal document which, by the authority of one person to act in place and stead of another as and in the capacity of their attorney in fact, is described and set forth by the terms therein.

The actual description of the type and terms of

the authority is all important, and it can vary widely from document to document. As but a few examples, the authority can be long term, short term, or just for a specific date or transaction. While it can be revoked at times by certain steps, or specifically limited at its inception, it can also be set up in a way to be continuous and kept in effect for the duration of one's lifetime. Another type is a so-called Health Care Power of Attorney, that has as its intended effect only the power to make health care decisions for another, which is often brought into play when an individual faces some severe illness or incapacity.

Although a Power of Attorney most often can work smoothly to achieve its desired effect, there can also be instances where the person may acquire the authority by deception or ruse, and in these or other, sometimes initially well intentioned cases, the authority may later be misused or even abused to the extent that some or all of the financial resources of the unsuspecting individual are dissipated, squandered, or improperly spent altogether for the personal gain of another. For these reasons, the first choice of deciding to make a Power of Attorney, and the next one of selecting a worthy individual to carry out the extensive authority it grants, are ones of extreme importance and consequently deserving of much care and consideration.

With such background knowledge well established in his own mind, it was with more than a bit of curiosity that B.G. Wumpkey picked up and began to once again review the Power of Attorney that had been signed by Mr. Kurt Koppy and recently left at his office.

*

One-half hour later, B.G. had verified his first impression that the document was both properly executed and legally enforceable. To arrive at such a conclusion, Attorney Wumpkey had read it over carefully line by line. Then, he had also taken a few more minutes to locate and review the latest statutory updates concerning the specific laws relating to a Power of Attorney.

Basically, the only significant changes in the state law in recent years had related to the execution or completion portion of the document. Now, along with the requirement that the person granting the authority to another sign the document and have it notarized, Pennsylvania law included a provision whereby the individual being given the authority to act for another (referred to as the "Agent"), also had to sign in a separate part of the document and then have a separate acknowledgment by a notary public of that signature as well.

Kurt Koppy had properly signed and then had notarized the Power of Attorney granting B.G. Wumpkey broad powers to handle, manage, give, sell or otherwise dispose of his real or personal property. While the language therein did not apply to health care decisions, the wording in this particular document was broad enough to include most everything else. The powers designated to B.G. Wumpkey were not limited in duration, and therefore as written were to be effective immediately. These powers as described furthermore included the ability of the Agent to give away all of the person's property while he is alive as well as to substantially change how the property is distributed at the time of his death. Importantly, from his past experience with other cases B.G. recalled that a Power of Attorney's authority becomes invalid upon the death of the individual who granted it, and that there are specific requirements that the Agent act in good faith and in the best interests of the person in the exercise of his powers, in order to carry out the person's expectations while having such authority.

Now, having reviewed the document itself as well as related provisions in detail, B.G. turned the stapled pages over and set them on the desktop in front of him. It was as he did so, that he happened to notice some handwritten words that had been printed on the back, blank side of the last page.

There, neatly printed in black ink was the following inscription:

"Mr. Wumpkey:

I know that this all may seem a bit unusual, but there are some factors which are difficult for me to explain right now. Please recognize that you were recommended by a mutual acquaintance. So that there is no misunderstanding, you are to distribute any and all of my assets delivered and entrusted to you as you see fit, to those deserving, as soon as possible. I have faith that you will make the right decisions."

The note bore the clear signature of Kurt Koppy.

*

With this last and latest bit of information before him, B.G. decided that this was no time for hesitation. After locking up his office, he proceeded to the bank across the street where he met with a curvaceous lady who was a notary public whose services he used frequently. He signed the document, had it notarized and walked out of the bank.

Now it was official that Kurt Koppy had designated B.G. Wumpkey as his duly appointed Agent pursuant to the authority of the Power of Attorney, and that the Agent had accepted his duties.

CHAPTER SIX

Once back inside of his office, B.G. locked the doors and then closed the window blinds.

With a wide smile growing across his face, he paused as he sat down behind the desk. He took a moment to go over his situation.

"Let me look at this matter rationally," he said aloud. Putting his hand to his chin, it didn't take him long at all to simplify the facts, tailor them a bit to appear in the most favorable light and come up with a preliminary plan.

He wasn't sure how all this would eventually unfold or end up. Certainly, there were some questionable aspects with possible negative or serious ramifications. But he didn't want to speculate. Therefore, he concluded he would maintain an optimistic perspective.

Since the elusive client had demonstrated full faith in his attorney both in person and in separate writings, then entrusted him with valuables, and had not only proposed a fee agreement but then even paid him, albeit a bit unconventionally, in advance for his services, B.G. decided that without further delay he should proceed to take the next logical step.

So, let the fun begin.

It was now time to count the money.

*

B.G. certainly hadn't expected it to take him nearly this long.

Although he quickly realized that due to the volume of the amount of money he was dealing with his first run through would have to be considered a preliminary one, it still surprised him to find that even this task took him several hours.

And that time didn't even include the multiple breaks that he took to have some pieces of chocolate cake and a couple of glasses of milk from the kitchen refrigerator.

To further insure himself of complete privacy, even though the office doors had been locked and the window shades closed, he decided to conduct the operation in the pantry off of the kitchen in the back of his law office. The pantry room was a separate space that had been originally designed for storage of food supplies, having multiple shelves and a small counter area. What Wumpkey especially liked about the room was that in addition to having its own interior door which could be closed securely, the room did not have any windows at all. Thus, he felt it was the ideal spot to conduct this rather unique inventory process.

*

He had to admit that the afternoon's activity was the most fun he had experienced in recent memory.

Periodically, he would find himself giggling uncontrollably.

Moments later, he would notice that he was sweating profusely.

And all the while, the number he was counting just kept getting bigger and bigger.

*

Really, it was quite astounding, Wumpkey mused as he closed and locked the larger of the two briefcases that was placed next to the smaller one on the pantry shelf.

The total amount of cash in the two briefcases was somewhat more than six hundred and forty thousand dollars.

And that did not include all of the gold coins, which by his basic calculations, he figured would easily surpass at least another one hundred thousand in value.

With that preliminary answer of a total amount of the contents of the briefcases now ascertained, however, immediately came more questions to the forefront of B.G.'s thoughts.

Why hadn't he heard back from Mr. Koppy?

And what should he do if Mr. Koppy did not get back in touch with him soon?

By taking on this case, was B.G. possibly putting himself in some unforeseen danger?

Could he follow his client's instructions and start deciding now just how to distribute the proceeds?

And by the way, what was one-third of about $740,000.00?

CHAPTER SEVEN

Meanwhile, at the same time in a location some twelve miles from Wumpkey's law office, the following events were taking place.

It was fifteen dollars an hour, cash, under the table money that the man was paying Merle on weekends. The man, Mr. Shipton, was an independent investor who was in the house flipping business. Mr. Shipton liked that Merle knew his way around the drywall part of construction, and that he could make unfinished or old walls and ceilings look just like brand new.

Merle liked Mr. Shipton because he let Merle work on his own hours, on the honor system, which allowed for Merle to pad his time by adding a couple of extra hours each weekend to those that he actually worked. Merle also liked that by working on his own he could play his loud music, drink his favorite whiskey and bill Mr. Shipton for a take out pizza as part of the deal. Merle had agreed that he only had to be sure to have the pizza delivered to his work site (by not leaving the premises this reduced extended lunch breaks) and that he would provide a receipt for the cost of the pizza.

Mr. Shipton knew how Merle was over billing, and that he had a love of the bottle, but he was pleased overall with the work Merle did. He came to recognize that as long as Merle didn't work for more than six hours any day, which really meant five hours, Merle's work was above average. Any shift longer than that would show the effects of the booze, which had been the cause of Merle's loss of regular employment on multiple occasions.

The house Merle was starting to work on this Saturday morning was a newer one that Mr. Shipton had just acquired in a distress sale. Like many in the area, this was a modest single story ranch home with an attached one car garage. The old walls had been damaged and then torn out by the prior owners, but never replaced or finished. Since the framing studs on the walls were all exposed and the new drywall boards and buckets of drywall patching plaster had already been delivered and were in the garage, all this made Merle's project easier. Consequently, he was in an especially good mood as he started the work bright and early at ten o'clock.

The only thing that caused him a slight bit of concern that morning was the fact that Mr.Shipton had told Merle that due to a rodent problem that had been the result of the prior owners not removing their garbage, he had left his girlfriend's two pets in the house overnight to help eradicate any remaining pests. After telling Merle the names of the pets, Mr. Shipton had then assured Merle that they were both very friendly and that he would get along well with them.

Mr. Shipton's assurances proved to be only partly correct.

*

The cat's name was Elvis. The dog's name was Spike.

Elvis, although nearly full grown, was young and playful. Spike was older, rather plump and more laid back, but still he retained an extraordinary curiosity from his youth. This had often been displayed when Spike was calmly napping in the corner of a room and had been awakened by nearby laughter or the like, when he would immediately jump to his feet and move to join in the others excitement while wagging enthusiastically.

"Spike sleeps a lot, but is really sociable and he always likes to be part of the action," was how Mr. Shipton had explained it when he had given Merle the keys to the property with instructions on locking it up when he was finished for the day.

*

The temperature this summer morning was already climbing, and Merle was glad he was wearing only a pair of Bermuda shorts, open sandals or "flip-flops" on his feet and a loosely fitting t-shirt. While the heat might get a bit uncomfortable if he kept at it later into the afternoon, he figured he would reach a stopping point around two o'clock, when he would order the pizza. What was good about this kind of weather was that the drying time on his project made his progress appear quicker than on cooler days.

With the music turned up from his boom box, Merle then reached into his duffel bag and unwrapped his sweatshirt and removed the quart of whiskey that it had concealed. Taking three ample gulps, Merle took a deep breath and smiled.

Now he was ready to begin.

*

About three hours later, Merle's steady effort was already showing some real signs of improvement. He'd hung the large boards of Sheetrock on the walls, and was now set to begin putting on the tape and then applying the drywall plaster or "mud" on the screw holes and seams. The application of the mud, which generally required three coats along with a drying and sanding process over several days, was where Merle was able to pad his work the most.

After he took another belt from his bottle, he finished the process of putting the drywall tape on the new wall boards. He then began applying the first coat of the mud. Merle had told his friends at the bars that this part of the work made him feel like an artist, because he was able to transform something unsightly and dark into something that would become bright and beautiful.

Merle had just finished the first coat on one of the walls when he noticed that Elvis seemed to be taking a real interest in what he was doing. As Merle took the tool for the corner application of the mud, he placed the larger flat trowel he had been using onto the pass through bar and shelf that served as a divider between the kitchen and the dining room areas.

It was at that point that Elvis jumped up on the bar, stretched and then playfully pawed at the larger drywall trowel. Elvis then bit the handle of the trowel.

Merle noticed what Elvis was doing and thought it was funny. He went over and scratched Elvis under the chin, which made Elvis roll onto his back and start to purr. That made Merle chuckle.

Meanwhile, Spike was in the far corner of the adjoining room, snoring peacefully.

When Merle had finished the corner work, he then moved to the wall where the bar was located. Merle gave it a quick look over, and was pleased to note that this one would be easy because instead of a solid wall much of it was open space as a divider between the rooms.

It was just after Merle had picked up the bottle when he noticed that a piece of the drywall tape above the bar was loose. While holding the bottle in one hand, Merle reached up over the bar and onto the wall to smooth out the uneven piece of tape with his other hand.

They say timing is everything, and what happened next clearly illustrates that maxim.

As Merle was stretching to smooth out the uneven tape, Elvis, while now on his back, took a playful swipe at the drywall trowel.

A trowel is a very effective tool. While the one that Merle was using today could also be used for smoothing cement, he was very adept at using this particular one for drywall jobs as well. Typically measuring about five inches by ten inches, this type of device is made of lightweight metal, having a heavier handle in the middle. The edges of it are thin and sharp, which by design make the application process of the mud easy and smooth.

While Merle watched the following events, they all appeared to him to take place in slow motion. This may have been due to the whiskey or to the totally unexpected nature of the occurrence, or more likely to a combination of both.

With both hands fully occupied, Merle glanced down at the cat just as it took the swipe at the trowel.

Merle saw the trowel slide off of the bar, and start to fall. While it descended, Merle noticed that as the trowel was falling it was in a line directly above his right foot.

The trowel was falling in such a position that as its sharp edge was heading downward, it was also to all appearances very straight.

This was not good.

As the trowel proceeded in its downward trajectory, before it hit the floor it met up with Merle's baby toe, that along with his other toes, was fully exposed due to the flip-flops he was wearing. Then, upon impact, with the efficiency of an experienced surgeon, the falling trowel quickly, neatly and cleanly cut off Merle's baby toe.

As the blood spurted from the open wound, and he saw his little toe now on the floor separate and apart from his foot, Merle's eyes widened and then he began to scream. The screaming made the cat upset, and it leaped from the bar and ran into a closet.

The screaming also got the immediate attention of Spike, and caused him to jump to his feet and enter the room where the commotion appeared to be occurring. Once in the room, Spike seemed to get a handle on what was taking place, immediately, and he acted as though he knew exactly what to do in such situations.

While Merle continued screaming, at one level, what he observed next caused his screaming to increase to an even higher volume.

Spike, never one to hesitate in times of crisis, in one swift movement, walked up to the severed baby toe, took a sniff and then ate it.

*

It took a solid hour before Merle, in his understandably agitated state, was able to contact someone who would agree to drive him to get medical care. Since Merle did not have a valid license, nor a car, it took some explaining as to why his need for help was so urgent.

The first two calls he made were to friends of his who happened to be visiting separate taverns that afternoon. However, after the details of his situation had been presented, his requests were each time greeted by howls of laughter followed by the hanging up of the phone.

These reactions did not help Merle's demeanor.

Approximately ninety minutes after the unfortunate event in which the playful cat had caused the unexpected falling of the tool that had cut off Merle's baby toe which in turn had resulted in the awakening of the sleeping dog that had arrived from the next room and, with curiosity piqued, then proceeded to eat the freshly severed member, Merle felt that he was at last making some progress. Seated now in the back of a lady friend's minivan, he had his wounded appendage resting up on the cushioned upholstery as he stretched out sideways. While the bleeding at the end of his foot had stopped, the level of pain was now increasing dramatically. And it hurt even more whenever he looked at it.

Sheila, the operator, was driving and seated next to her in the front passenger seat was the ever agreeable Spike, now taking the position of co-pilot. Spike's presence was felt to be most necessary for this hasty journey, since at least for the time being, he was also now serving as an evidence locker.

As Sheila proceeded on the highway towards the nearest medical facility, she offered some well intentioned advice.

"You know, Merle, you may not want to think about all this right now, but you really need to see Mr. Wumpkey."

"What are you talking about? Who is this Wumpkey guy?"

"You know, that guy who really helped Irwin. B.G. Wumpkey, the attorney. You really need to talk to a lawyer about this."

Merle's response to this suggestion came rather quickly from the back seat. In light of what might be called by some his agitated state at the time, it also came in what could best be described as in a voice that was on the highest volume.

"A LAWYER ? I DON'T THINK SO. BE-CAUSE WHAT I REALLY NEED NOW IS A DOC-TOR. AND UNFORTUNATELY, IT SEEMS...THAT I ALSO NEED A VETERINARIAN!"

While it may have been mere coincidence, nonetheless at that precise moment Spike's tail thumped enthusiastically against the inside of the vehicle's front door.

CHAPTER EIGHT

One week had passed since B.G. had tallied up the amounts of the valuables that Kurt Koppy had delivered to his law office. In that interim, although having high expectations that he would be contacted by Mr. Koppy again, B.G. had received no communication from him whatsoever.

B.G. had just decided to give that client three more days before taking further action on his own.

Now, as Wumpkey walked towards his office door in the middle of the morning, he was met by a man who could best be described as looking a bit rough around the edges, who approached him while moving very slowly. Appearing to be about thirty-five years in age, the man was unshaven, and wore jeans and a faded blue flannel shirt that had a torn front pocket. Of average height and well above average weight, by his halting movements it seemed evident to Wumpkey that the man was in some amount of pain.

"Hey!" the man said as Wumpkey was unlocking his office door.

"Hey to you too," replied B.G.

"You're the lawyer guy, right?"

"That's me - B.G. Wumpkey, Attorney at Law. Can I help you?"

"I sure hope so. You see, it's kind of an unusual situation."

*

A few minutes later, Wumpkey was at his desk and getting some basic information from the man sitting across from him.

"That's Merle-with an e at the end. You got the last name right, and my address and telephone. But don't call it for a few days, because it's out of service right now."

Although as an experienced attorney he had heard of a large number of strange cases over many years, as Merle described in detail exactly how he had been injured and the developments that ensued, it caused B.G.'s eyes to grow wide with amazement.

"Now let me get this straight. The cat knocked the drywall tool off of the bar, and then it fell directly onto your bare foot because you were only wearing those plastic flip-flop sandal things. And the blade of the tool actually cut off your toe?"

"That's exactly right, it cut my baby toe completely off of my foot. And I have to tell you that's not a pleasant thing to experience. And if that wasn't bad enough, what happened right after that made it all even worse."

"Why, what happened next? " B.G. inquired a bit hesitantly.

"Well, that's when the dog came over, from where it had been sleeping in the next room, and it came over, and right as I'm looking at my foot in one place and my toe separate and apart from it lying on the floor, and all the blood spurting out, then I see the dog rush over real fast, get up close to me... And then the dog, it takes a quick sniff and then while I'm watching all this, the dog goes and eats my whole baby toe."

"The dog actually ate your toe?" Wumpkey's voice sounded incredulous.

"That's what happened, and I saw the whole thing happen and believe me it's quite upsetting just to think about it again. Not to mention the pain that I've been going through from the physical part of it all. It still hurts a whole lot just to walk. And the bills."

"From the hospital?" B.G. inquired.

"Well, there will be those coming, as well as the doctors. And the vet."

"The vet?"

"Yup, we stopped at the vet's also to see if there was any chance of getting my toe safe and sound out from the dog, but it turned out that both the surgeon and the veterinarian said that was a lost cause, especially by the time they saw it. But even so it doesn't seem right to me but the vet charged for that as well."

"Well, there certainly are a lot of twists and turns to this all right. I'll need to review some things and if you have any other..." B.G. began.

"I've got photos, and the names of the owners of the house, the cat and the dog along with the first of the bills they sent me already."

"Those would be very helpful for me to look into and evaluate your situation."

"No problem. I can get a ride again in a week or so and bring them to you."

"That would be fine," B.G. responded.

"What time do you open up anyway? I got here at nine, but you didn't get here until ten, and that other guy was wanting to see you before me but he left after about a half-hour, said he couldn't wait any longer, had to go out of state..."

B.G. suddenly sat up very straight and leaned across the desk toward Merle.

"Other guy? What guy?"

"The older guy, white hair. He said to tell you to proceed with the plan, whatever that means. Made me repeat it so I said it right. Be sure to tell the attorney that Kurt said to proceed with the plan."

"Did he say anything else? Anything at all?"

"Not really. But it seemed like it was pretty important to him, so much so that he actually gave me a fifty dollar bill just for doing him the favor of passing that message along to you. I promised him I would, so now I did. Sure seemed like a nice enough gentleman, but a little nervous, kind of like he had a whole lot on his mind. Anyways, then he walked across the street, got in that compact motor home and just drove away."

CHAPTER NINE

It was that night back at the ranch during dinner when the conversation entered into a subject that for the past week B.G. had so far been deftly avoiding.

The primary focus of the subject at the time was located under the dining room table and had just started snoring.

"He's really a wonderful companion." Carol was saying as she passed B.G. the salt and pepper shakers.

"And honestly, with the kids still away at college, having Jack around the house just seems to make the place seem more of a home. I mean well, for one thing that dog is so friendly and always in such a good mood that it would have a positive impact on any property. And because he's always so interested in what I'm doing in the kitchen, well it makes me feel like cooking more. Anyhow, by the way you spoke at first I felt you'd have the dog for just one afternoon. But it's been about a week or so already. So now, let me know, what's going on with the client who asked you to look after him?"

Under normal conditions at the home front, B.G.

had always felt it the better route to try to keep the details of the matters he was handling at the law office separate and apart from his personal home life. Aside from the confidential nature of his work, he had always also felt a more important obligation to keep his family protected from some of the information he became privy to in the course of his work. So typically, he would as a rule just talk in general terms about the nature of a particular case he was handling or what he was helping a client try to accomplish.

However, this time he was admittedly dealing with a most unusual situation, due in large part to the simple fact that the unexpected appearance and continued presence of the one hundred and sixty pound furry guest could not be easily overlooked.

In addition, there was another element which at this particular time made B.G. seem a bit more inclined to revealing information than was customary for him, in his response to Carol's pointed inquiry.

In short, this was because B.G. at the moment was now in his most vulnerable state.

After all, the plain facts that it was dinner time and B.G. was ravenous, were significant on their own. However, added to that baseline was the quality and quantity of the meal that his wife had prepared and just put on the table for the two of them.

This evening, it was a treasured recipe for homemade lasagna handed down from relatives now deceased, and it was so delicious that whenever B.G. was able to partake in such, it honestly could bring tears to his eyes. The blending of the layers of al dente pasta, with the rich tomato sauce, the ricotta cheese, the spices, the mozzarella cheese, the garlic, the parmesan cheese, the onions, the meatballs, the sausage, the mushrooms and olive oil and a few other tightly held secret ingredients all created a magical finished product that could serve to reduce a normally strong willed man like B.G. Wumpkey prone to revealing national secrets, if he had any, in very short order.

And clearly, Carol knew this very well.

"Well dear," she was saying now as she looked at her husband with compassion, "Do you think you'd like another portion now before you tell me all about it?"

In a hoarse voice, that bespoke of utter helplessness, he softly answered, "Yes."

And then, as the wafts of the delectable aromas rose from the large steaming portion that had been served upon his plate, through misty eyes B.G. decided then and there that he would tell her everything.

*

Afterward, nearly an hour later, he was glad he had done so.

And whether it was because he was feeling the contented after effects from the sumptuous meal, or that it was just the sharing of these most interesting yet confidential details with someone he could trust which added to his excitement, in any event Wumpkey had to admit that he now held an overall feeling of assurance that things were headed in the right direction.

It did, however, come as somewhat of a surprise that the facts of the situation did not seem to create any special level of concern or anything approaching alarm or apprehension in the least to his wife, after B.G. had presented such to her.

Carol's reaction also caught him a bit off guard when, just as B.G. was about to tell her that after counting the contents of the briefcases, that his preliminary estimate of the total worth of the valuables was...

"Stop right there," she had suddenly interrupted him before he was able to finish his sentence.

"What?" asked Wumpkey with puzzlement, thinking that he was reaching what was probably the most interesting part of his presentation.

"No, don't tell me the amount of the valuables. I don't want to know yet. Right now I know that there is a lot of cash involved, along with some precious coins. That's enough. If you tell me an amount it will taint my perspective. I want to sleep on it and let my subconscious and inner spirit give me direction. Then, sometime tomorrow I will have my answer about what you should do."

At first, B.G. took this reaction in silence.

"Really?" he asked a moment later, just to be sure.

"Yes," Carol answered with a fixed look.

Then she broke into a mischievous smile. "But I do have to admit, it is all wonderfully intriguing..."

*

The next morning, when B.G. awoke, the scent of something wonderful that seemed to be coming from the area of the kitchen downstairs caught his immediate attention.

Shortly afterward, while sitting at the breakfast table, he came to fully recognize that he had a very strong and invaluable ally now in the house.

"Well, after I let Jack outside early in the morning, when he came back in he seemed very interested in the apples that were on the counter. I don't know why, really, but that got me to thinking that I hadn't made a fresh apple pie for quite a while. And wasn't I surprised when I was peeling the apples, that Jack loves to eat the peels and the cores as well! So, making the two pies was quite easy, and there really was no waste whatsoever."

The sight of the pies, coupled with the fact that Carol had seemingly overlooked the previous thoughts from earlier in the week of a minimal breakfast and had instead prepared one of ham, eggs and European dark rye toast put Wumpkey in an especially good mood.

What added to that even more was when Carol had put a slice of freshly baked apple pie, with a slice of sharp cheddar cheese on top, on a small plate in front of him.

"Try that and tell me if you think it came out okay," she said.

After happily consuming it and voicing his full approval, Carol went to the living room to answer the telephone.

With the kitchen now to themselves, B.G. roused Jack from his sleeping state where he was stretched out underneath the table.

Calling him over, after watching the dog give a long yawn, Wumpkey put his head down close to Jack and looked intently into his eyes.

"Keep up the good work," Wumpkey told him with a grin.

CHAPTER TEN

The car that B.G. Wumpkey had been driving for the past few years was distinctive, and in many ways was a good match for him. However, really ever since he had bought it the vehicle also had been developing an increasing amount of unusual problems. Although many might call these problems serious, nonetheless B.G. maintained an altogether different perspective and did not allow them to interfere with his daily use of it whatsoever.

It was an older Cadillac Sedan De Ville, a large spacious luxury automobile that had expansive, sturdy and extremely comfortable leather seats. The car also had a smooth and powerful engine that was surprisingly fuel efficient, plenty of head room which was important to a person of Wumpkey's height and girth, as well as a top quality radio and sound system. The body's exterior, still solid and unmarked, when properly washed and waxed bore the shine of a much newer vehicle to all observers.

The fact that the car had no working reverse gear

made Carol refuse to drive it anywhere, and somewhat reluctant to even ride as a passenger, but it had instead given the vehicle much added appeal to Wumpkey from the very onset. Initially, that flaw had enabled B.G. to purchase the car from the owner at an extremely low price, in a deal which left the seller and the buyer quite pleased with the outcome. After that, B.G. had relished the opportunity to drive it anywhere, even for long distance excursions. To those who knew of this car's particular peculiarity, and who inquired with incredulity at why and how he could continue operating it, B.G. had explained simply that he loved the fact that merely getting behind the wheel posed a continuous challenge and furthermore that whenever driving it, such required him to always think ahead.

While driving a powerful luxury car that was unable to back up was something that B.G. had become quite accustomed to, his inclination to routinely park at the far end of parking lots be they for courthouses or shopping malls would be looked at with occasional curiosity, in those rare instances when he was actually asked why he did so he would alternatively reply that he wanted the extra exercise or that his car had no reverse, depending on to whom he was talking and his particular mood at the time.

Of course, the truth was that he parked in such a manner simply to avoid getting blocked in by another vehicle, an occurrence which could prevent any exit and forward proceeding indefinitely.

Approximately six months ago, there had been another problem with B.G.'s favored mode of transportation which developed, that had not only added further complications to his operation of it, but that had also, painful as it was to consider, made B.G. come to grips with the fact that a replacement automobile might soon become necessary.

While he hadn't told anyone, even his wife, about this latest complication, he realized that it was probably something that he couldn't keep from her much longer.

After all, to drive a car with no reverse was one thing, but to drive a car with no reverse that had the added drawback of being limited in its ability to make right turns well was quite another thing entirely.

It was this more recent development in the car that had led B.G. to seek out the trusted opinion of an expert in the automotive repair business, namely his old friend Shooter.

Shooter was a tall, wiry man in his early sixties, who ran a garage, tow truck, and junk business out of an abandoned general store in a run down part of a small city in Ohio. The location was just over the border from the Pennsylvania-Ohio line, and about a half-hour's drive from Wumpkey's ranch. Because his business virtually straddled the border between the two states, Shooter routinely handled car repairs and deals with vehicles from both Ohio and Pennsylvania.

While many assumed that his nickname was due to his accuracy with a handgun, which he had demonstrated to several ill-advised burglars one evening years ago, the moniker actually came from his natural talent to be able to consume vast quantities of beer with accompanying whiskey chasers in a shot glass (called "shooters"), which ability was held in esteem throughout many taverns in the area.

B.G. had first become acquainted with Shooter some years ago when he was representing a client in a criminal case in Ohio. When Shooter, who was there to serve as a witness in another matter, saw this extra large lawyer involved in a courtroom shouting match with both the prosecutor and the judge while defending his client, he took an immediate liking to the man. That liking turned into a deep respect for the man, especially after he learned that B.G. had eventually won that case by having illegally obtained evidence thrown out and deemed inadmissible.

Along with his mechanical skills, Shooter was also a part-time fence. This meant that he was occasionally the go-to man by those adept in the nighttime trades, for acquiring at reduced rates certain items that had been relocated without an owner's approval.

This morning as he drove his Cadillac into the unpaved parking area, B.G. recognized the familiar figure of Shooter looking under the hood of a late model pickup truck. And on the ground underneath the truck he saw what appeared to be Shooter's assistant with socket wrench in hand.

One particular trait about this friend that B.G. had found to be admirable was the fact that Shooter had consistently demonstrated that he was an equal opportunity employer. Not necessarily in the traditional or politically correct sense, but by his own set of standards. Because Shooter's auto repair shop was known to be the first stop for someone with basic mechanical skills and a desire to work who had just been released from jail, regardless of the length of their recent prison term. As long as he felt comfortable after interviewing the person (Shooter avoided the term convict), if they needed a few months to get back on their feet, Shooter would provide cash payments, under the table of course, in exchange for a fair day's work at his garage and was even known at times as long as the weather was still warm to allow a wayward soul to sleep in the back storage room of his place of business in special circumstances.

A few minutes later, after exchanging greetings, B.G. described the latest problem with his Cadillac. Both Shooter and his assistant named Andy, who had recently completed a jail sentence for unapologetically breaking the arm of a neighbor who owed him money, then agreed to take the car for a short test ride around the block.

With Wumpkey in the back seat and Shooter behind the wheel, the car was driven out onto the street with a roar. Accelerating quickly on the straight roadway, it shifted smoothly as it reached high speed.

"Nice power still for an older one," the driver was saying.

Less than a minute later however, as they approached an intersection, his tone changed rapidly. "But Jeez... Oh my gosh this steering is a lot worse than you described it."

"But it's only difficult when you need to turn right, and not all the time. Maybe three out of four times, though, it does get pretty hard to turn the steering wheel," B.G. explained.

From the front passenger seat came a giggle from Andy. "So, like only one out of four times you can make a right turn?"

"Well, I suppose that's one way of describing it," B.G. acknowledged.

" Yeah but instead, look at it this way," Shooter added practically, "Maybe all these years you've been going the wrong direction and now the universe is telling you that you need to change your ways and start making a lot more left turns."

*

Back at the garage, B.G. was disheartened when Shooter told him that to correct the problem was a major job. And when reminded that the car's transmission still lacked a working reverse gear, his assessment was short and to the point.

"Now I remember, when you bought it that you said it had no reverse. But I thought you were going to put in another tranny. But face it, you can't back up, you can only turn right once in a while. You need to start thinking of selling this...like yesterday. Even for parts...just with those nice leather seats you'll probably get back what you paid for it."

*

To soften the blow of the negative diagnosis, Shooter invited B.G. to go with him for lunch to a favored tavern just a mile away. Realizing that a good meal might change his somber mood, he accepted the invitation.

"It'll be be good for you to see Henry again. He asks about you a lot. Plus today they're roasting a pig on the spit."

Henry was a man of great knowledge and experience. He was a decorated war veteran, who had chosen to buy and run a lumber yard instead of using the law degree he had earned earlier. He did so for a decade, and when the lumber yard burned to the ground, (Henry said with a wink that it didn't bother him too much since it was very, very well insured), he joined up with some attorneys he knew and began to practice law.

He did that for several years, and then when an

opening arose to run for the position of a local municipal judge, he did so and was easily elected. (Ohio was one of the states where state or local judges ran for office, whereas in some other states they are appointed positions usually made by a sitting governor.) Henry was a well liked and efficient judge to the public at large, but his tendency to favor the defendant over the prosecution in criminal cases and his obvious inclination to feel that insurance companies should promptly pay in injury cases made him less than the golden boy to both the police and the insurance lawyers.

Although it seemed likely that he would have won another term if he ran again, Henry decided he'd gotten bored with the job, didn't like the system and instead went in another direction entirely.

He bought a bar.

*

The food was delicious and the attractive, full figured waitress seemed to recognize immediately that Wumpkey was a man who had a healthy appetite. With a pleasant smile, she kept bringing him one plate after another for him to enjoy. About an hour later, the lunchtime patrons started to thin out. When Shooter got a call to tow a car and said his goodbyes, Henry came over to visit, with two desserts in hand.

"Wow, been busy back there. The roast pig today or chicken on the grill later in the week usually brings them in. But hey, it's good to see you here again. And now that the rush is over, I wanted to catch up on things."

*

It had not occurred to B.G. that Henry's wide ranging knowledge might be of some benefit in relation to the current events at his law office. In fact, with his thoughts initially more concentrated on the prognosis of his beloved old Cadillac, B.G. had not even expected to be seeing his old friend this day until Shooter had presented the invitation for lunch.

However, after the two had enjoyed their respective servings of rice pudding, it was Henry who set the stage for such when he asked B.G. if he had any interesting cases going on at the office. While considering that any input the former attorney and judge turned tavern owner might share could be helpful, at the same time B.G. didn't want to come to any premature conclusions in what he was handling, since he himself still wasn't exactly sure how to describe the whole situation.

"Henry, I'm going to tell you about something, to see what you think, but at this stage it's all just a hypothetical, Okay?"

Henry licked the last of the whipped cream from the remains of his dessert. Then he looked across the table and smiled.

"Sounds familiar," Henry stated in a matter of fact tone.

"What do you mean sounds familiar? I didn't even tell you about it yet."

"I know you didn't. But the name is the same-maybe a relative. I represented a lot of Mr. and Mrs. Hypotheticals back when I was practicing."

It took only a short while for Wumpkey to describe, in general terms the essential elements of the matter in which he was dealing with currently. Applying the rare combination of his sharp mind, his legal experience, along with his street smarts and common sense, all of which B.G. had come to admire in his friend, it took virtually no time at all for Henry to get a full understanding and then render his opinion.

"All right, this sounds like a good one. A mysterious client comes in, wants you to be his Power of Attorney, then drops off some valuables and skips town. The valuables, you haven't told me any numbers, but let's just say you find out it's a substantial amount. And the client already gave you your fee, along with instructions to distribute the entire remaining amount as you see fit... Is that an accurate summary?"

B.G. thought it over for a few seconds, then agreed.

"Okay then. Here's my take...Nothing local and no paper trail. Go far away to handle it. And no receipts no matter what. In this situation, you want to be able to account for your own actions. You have your client confidentiality to fall back on, but if it gets sticky and there's an investigation you can be squeezed. So keep it simple. Some guy comes in, asks you for a Power of Attorney and then disappears. That's all you know. To you, the valuables don't exist. What valuables? All you ever got was a document."

B.G. looked at Henry. "Go far away to handle it, huh?"

"Absolutely. Take a short vacation, maybe also use as an excuse as a start to go to one of those boring legal education seminars someplace that you have to take every year. And be sure to have a little fun along the way as well, because these kind of opportunities well, they won't come up again, you understand...So, sound good?"

"Yeah, I see what you mean. But right now I've got another problem with the Cadillac so as far as..."

Henry shook his head and laughed loudly.

"Man, don't forget, I know you. With what I

think you got going in this, you could buy a lot of new Cadillacs and still have plenty left over. And not only that, if you do it right, you can make some people real happy along the way."

B.G. paused, and took a long drink from his glass of beer.

"So you think that's how to best handle it."

"Without a doubt," Henry said. Then he added with a wink, "Hypothetically, of course."

*

His ride back to the office went smoothly, and the one right turn he had to make was a gradual one so he maneuvered it without any difficulty at all. And as there were no telephone messages, no notes, letters or new briefcases waiting for him, he decided since it was already later in the afternoon that he would return to the ranch.

Carol was pleased that he came back a bit earlier than usual.

"You know, this afternoon I felt a little drowsy, and though I don't do it often, I took a short nap. Probably seeing how much Jack sleeps during the day gave me the idea without realizing it. Anyhow, you know, it was the best thing, because after that I felt so refreshed and clear headed. On top of that, that extra rest time let my thoughts come together. And I now feel comfortable in telling you my feelings about that whole matter with the mystery man client of yours."

After she'd put out some tea and cookies for them to enjoy on the back porch, she shared her conclusions with him.

"Well, there may well be something fishy about the source of the things he left for you to distribute in those briefcases, but I don't think you should look at it that way. It could also all be completely above board. After all, we always hear of some eccentric wealthy person who had all sorts of money and things stashed in odd places for personal privacy.

In any event, this client did the proper thing for you to be able to handle his affairs legally, and specifically authorized you to complete certain matters for him. So, I think you should do just what he hired you for, and take steps to distribute whatever he wants you to without any delay. And be sure to be extra careful and keep quiet about it, which is your normal custom anyhow, but even more so in this case. Keep a low profile about the whole thing. After all, you know how you've found that very often when other people or even authorities get involved they can take forever and then not really accomplish anything, and usually they can make the situation more complicated...or even make valuable things disappear."

B.G. looked at his wife with a mixture of both surprise and admiration. It wasn't the words of guidance he had expected from her. But deep down he knew it was what he had been wanting to hear.

Once he let her words settle over him, B.G. proceeded to tell her about his visit with Henry, and the recommended advice, in essence, to do nothing locally and have no paper trail when carrying out the client's instructions to make distributions. He also told Carol how his friend advised him to keep in mind he was being given an opportunity that only comes along once, so he should be sure to have fun along the way.

Her response provided a blend of encouragement and caution he welcomed.

"Well I certainly agree with Henry's advice. You've often said that he has a lot of real world, practical experience, so follow his recommendations closely. And you know, I also have no doubt that you can make it enjoyable. In fact I'm absolutely certain that you will. Just be extra careful, because my intuition tells me there is danger somewhere behind all this."

CHAPTER ELEVEN

There were a few things that Wumpkey wanted to check out before making any definite travel plans.

The Power of Attorney that had been left off at B.G.'s office showed that Kurt Koppy's signature was previously acknowledged by a notary public in the appropriate section. It was only after he had received and reviewed the document that B.G. on his own had then gone to the nearby bank to have his own signature notarized in the separate section of the document.

But the names of the notaries were not the same.

In fact, the individual who signed and sealed, so to speak, the signature of Mr. Koppy was not a name that was familiar to B.G. Of course, that was not unusual, since there were many notaries just in the local area and B.G. knew only a few of them.

However, it was a recent document, and since B.G. was now bent on learning as much as quickly as he could about his client, he decided it would be a good idea to try to locate and talk with the person who he knew for sure had met, however briefly, with Mr. Kurt Koppy in relation to the Power of Attorney document.

Surprisingly, it didn't take him very long to locate her. After a couple of phone calls and some quick research, he had an address and was on his way to meet the lady in person.

She was a retired real estate sales person, and had kept her notary credentials up to date to help out a few friends with local businesses, and at the same time to earn a little extra money on the side for her services. Her name was Monique, and she had a desk with an older computer on it, in a porch that had been enclosed and made into a comfortable office space in the front of her home.

Monique remembered Kurt after a moment, and verified that she had met with him. She described him as a polite gentleman who had asked her to notarize a document for him early one evening about a week ago.

She did remember that he was driving a "camper vehicle" as she described it, and when she remarked that it looked like a newer model to Kurt he had spoken very proudly about it, saying it ran like a clock, was very easy to drive, and got good gas mileage.

As it was getting dark when Kurt was there, B,G. asked her if she noticed anything else about the small camper-motor home. She said she thought the plates were from out of state, and they looked like the Florida ones that her relatives who came up to visit had on their car, but because of the darkness and the distance she really couldn't be certain.

One thing that B.G. made sure to clarify was if Monique had taken any information from Kurt to verify his identity, which most notaries routinely do. She said that Kurt had produced a license with a picture id, but that all she honestly recalled was that she thought it was from out of state somewhere, and she had not recorded any of the numbers since it was not her custom to do so. Unlike the notaries at a bank and many other businesses, Monique was relaxed in her duties and kept no written records of her acknowledgments. At her stage of life, she told Wumpkey, the twenty-five dollar cash fee she charged was really all she was concerned about. As one other point crossed his mind before leaving, B.G. asked Monique if she had any video surveillance or similar type of security system on her property. That question made Monique laugh out loud.

"Mister, the only type of security I have out here is my little Pekingese, and she's even more retired than I am. And other than the occasional notary work, I don't really socialize at all. I never listen to the news, I don't buy any papers. I just read my books, tend to my tomato and pepper plants and spend my time thinking of new dessert recipes to try."

B.G. expressed thanks for her information before he went back to his car. As an afterthought, B.G. looked again at the document that Kurt Koppy had signed and Monique had notarized about a week ago. Not surprisingly, he noted that only the name of the local town, county and state where it had been notarized were shown next to Kurt's name.

Well, well, well.

B.G. was now quite certain that Kurt had located and selected this retired, part time notary out in the country intentionally, since she provided just the type of low key services he wanted.

And for now, B.G. still had no address, no history and no idea of the man's current whereabouts.

No tracks.

It seemed like this mysterious client was now following his friend Henry's advice as well.

*

When he was driving back to the office, he had another idea that he thought might be worth pursuing in his effort to learn a bit more about the gentleman who had entrusted him with a not so small fortune.

Since the notary had indicated that the vehicle Mr. Koppy was operating might have had Florida plates, B.G. felt it was at least worth looking into. So, after locating the state telephone number for the licensing bureau, B.G. eventually made three separate calls.

His first contact with the bureau had him speak with a lady who had a heavy southern drawl. When B.G. politely stated that he was calling just for some basic information concerning the status of a person's operating license, before he could even give a name he was curtly informed that such information was not available to the public and his call was promptly disconnected.

He waited another half hour, and then tried again. This time he was informed by a recording that his call was very important to them, but that all attendants were currently busy and that his expected waiting time was eight minutes for the next available attendant to speak with him. One hour later, while still on hold and just when B.G. was reaching the point when he thought the canned music on the recording would drive him insane, he inadvertently hit the disconnect button and thereby lost all chance of preserving his place in the alleged waiting line, if in fact there ever was any.

Not one to be discouraged easily, two hours later he made one more call to that state office number. This time, he was greeted by a young lady's voice that was overflowing with such kindness that B.G. was certain he had dialed the wrong number.

Much to his pleasant surprise, she not only looked up all that he requested but even voluntarily provided additional information. So helpful was she, especially in contrast to his previous attempts, that when the call was almost over, Wumpkey was seriously considering sending her flowers.

He learned that a man by the name of Kurt Koppy did indeed have a valid Florida driver's license. He also was given not only Kurt's date of birth, but his license number. In addition, he was provided with an address that was on the license. Lastly, he was also told that there were no motor vehicles registered in the name of Kurt Koppy.

However, some time later, after calling reference librarians and a post office, he was informed that the address he was given was now in fact just a vacant lot that bordered a shopping mall.

Feeling that he had made progress, albeit limited, B.G. decided that he would call it a day without doing any more investigating. After all, at least now he felt he knew a little something more about his client than he had before.

While driving home, however, he was disturbed to realize that he could not get that unpleasant music from the telephone recording out of his head.

CHAPTER TWELVE

After having a very satisfying dinner, B.G. found that he was feeling unusually restless.

Since it was late summer and the daylight was still plentiful, he and Carol went outside and took an after dinner stroll. Carol had suggested it, having noticed that something was bothering him, but saying only that it was especially good for the digestion to walk for a while after a meal. Jack accompanied them, moving slowly as they crossed the wide backyard and approached the fencing that marked the beginning of the pasture area where their black Angus beef cows were grazing in the distance.

Seeing that view, with the expanse of green grassland bordered far away by a large hardwood forest on two sides as they stood under the row of mature apple trees at the end of the lawn, somehow always made Wumpkey feel better. It reminded him that he'd made a good decision buying the ranch some years ago. And the beef cows, who overall were calm (except for the rare occasion when they broke a fence) and simple to care for, served as a frequent reminder that sometimes just taking things easy was the best way.

Being out in the fresh air and enjoying the scene before him, made him relax and it wasn't long before he broke the silence.

"It's the thought of travel and the car that's bothering me. I love driving it, but there are some more problems, and I'm not sure it would be the best choice to use now. But that Cadillac and I have been through a lot together."

After learning exactly what had been weighing heavily on her husband's mind, Carol felt it was an opportune moment to present her feelings on a subject that had been concerning her for too long.

"You've certainly got your money's worth out of it. But you become so attached to these vehicles. It's as though they develop into a personal friend, instead of just a machine that takes you places. Maybe it's time for you to be a little less sentimental and instead think of what's best for your own safety and well-being. You know very well that it makes me uncomfortable just to ride in it, and I certainly won't drive it if I can help it. I realize the car still looks really nice and it is spacious for a man of your size. But honestly, it's gotten to the point that now with all that's wrong with it, just by you being able to drive it anywhere and then come back safely every day, well it makes me think you deserve an award."

They smiled at each other and then both began to chuckle.

Jack walked between them and proceeded to sit on Wumpkey's foot.

One of the beef cows mooed in the distance.

*

A bit later that evening, B.G. announced that he wanted to take a short drive and buy a newspaper, and use the time to try to come to a decision about a few things.

Carol thought that it was a good idea, adding that she knew he had a lot to think about and that sometimes just a change of scenery can help put things in their proper perspective. When he told her he'd be back in about an hour she said she'd have some apple pie and ice cream waiting for him.

*

The sequence of events that followed created some lasting memories. In fact, it is fair to say that what actually took place over the next hour was completely unexpected by all parties who had any role whatsoever in the occurrences.

*

As he turned left out of his driveway, B.G. stomped on the gas pedal and enjoyed the simultaneous roar of the engine and the vehicle's rush of acceleration in speed it produced. He headed west, and was traveling past the Pennsylvania line and into Ohio in a few minutes, driving towards the Warren and Youngstown area.

There was a convenience store and a gas station across from a well-known truckers restaurant that B.G. was headed towards. It was about twenty miles away, and the route that he took allowed him to exceed the speed limit while encountering little in the way of traffic.

He was a recognized customer of the store, and recalled that a former client had worked there behind the deli counter in the back. Occasionally he would purchase some cold cuts and various types of cheese from her, because they carried a wide selection of each. Tonight, though, rather than thinking about salami, capicola, muenster cheese or the like, he resolved that he was going to reach a decision about the car he was driving.

It didn't take him long.

After just twenty minutes of smooth operation along the highway while having the radio's volume turned up to hear the music, he stated his feelings aloud to the Cadillac.

"All right old friend. We both know you've got some health issues. But we have a real bond together, that goes back a ways. So, with that in mind, I've decided that I'm going to spend whatever it takes to put you back in tip-top shape. I know it will be costly, but we make a good team."

Feeling good about his decision, B.G. then reached over and gave an affectionate pat to the car's dashboard.

*

Ten minutes later, he drove into the parking lot of the convenience store. Ever mindful of the fact that he had no working reverse gear, he positioned the car so that it was out of the way of the gas pumps, in order to insure that no other vehicle would block him in.

He then went inside and bought a newspaper. As he was only going to be in the store for a moment, and he had a full view of the car through the glass doors, he kept the car running.

Just as he came out of the store, a very large black sport utility vehicle with oversized chrome wheels and music blasting, drove into the parking lot. Although it had tinted windows, he could tell there were a number of people in the front and back seats.

At the same time, noticing that it was now getting dark, B.G. had decided that he was going to use the long handled sponge mop in the washing solution tub near the gas pumps to clean off his car's dirty windshield.

He had just picked up the squeegee mop when a lady and a man that had stepped out of a pick-up truck asked him if he could help them with directions. B.G. noticed that their truck had Texas license plates on it. He made some small talk with them, and explained courteously how they could best get to where they wanted to go.

He was only about twenty five feet away from his car at this time.

Meanwhile, Nicky and Maurice were two of the five people who were in the large black SUV. Nicky and Maurice were feeling emboldened, partially because they were naturally cocky but more so because they each carried a loaded nine millimeter handgun and were both high.

Seeing the people near the store entrance changed their initial thoughts, so they instead made a split second change of plans.

As it turned out, that new plan wasn't a good one.

*

B.G. never did get to wash the windshield on his Cadillac.

It all happened in about fifteen seconds.

As B.G. was finishing his short conversation with the people from Texas, he heard a familiar noise from behind him, but it seemed not to register immediately as it was out of place.

He saw the couple he was talking with look over his shoulder and watched their eyes grow wide.

As B.G. turned his head to see what was going on, he recognized the familiar roar of his car's engine and watched the Cadillac being driven out of sight with two people in its front seat. The black SUV then sped out quickly behind it.

"Hey, is that your car?" the woman from Texas yelled as she pointed in the distance.

B.G. paused for a second to let all that had just happened settle into his thoughts.

Then he gave a small smile, and said with a surprising air of composure, "Yes it is, and I think they may regret that decision."

*

The store clerk had seen the whole thing and was calling in the report of the car theft to the police even before B.G. had a chance to do so.

Then, some more unexpected events took place.

While B.G. was waiting for the police to arrive to provide his information, the lights in the convenience store suddenly all went out. So too did the outdoor lighting in the parking area, and the Texas couple said that the restaurant across the street had gone dark all at the same time.

*

Speeding down the road, with Nicky behind the wheel and Maurice riding shotgun, they were screaming and hollering with excitement. They had the Cadillac up to ninety miles an hour in no time, and they could tell the car still had a lot more power in reserve.

Their plan was to drive for ten minutes to an abandoned warehouse where they would store the car

74

until they sold it. They had several options with chop shops and salvage yards with which they had done business before. With their friends in the SUV now providing secure back-up from behind, this, they knew, was an easy score.

They had traveled only a short while when they saw some blinking lights starting to appear in the darkness. A cop had pulled over a vehicle that was traveling in the opposite direction. Although it was still some distance away, they could see the officer standing next to the driver's side window talking to the operator inside.

Nicky and Maurice did not want to go near that cop right now. Although their direct route to the warehouse was to stay on that road, they felt it might be too risky even if they slowed down.

"What do we do?" yelled a frantic Nicky.

"I know right where we are, it's okay, we can take another road. Just calm down and up ahead make a sharp right!"

*

Much to their surprise, they didn't make the right hand turn at all. In fact, it wasn't even close.

When the car careened off the road, hit the telephone pole and ended up on its side in a ditch, the impact momentarily knocked the two unconscious.

During that brief time frame, two more significant things occurred.

The police officer who was in a kindly mood having just finished giving the operator a warning, was more than a little surprised to see the car approaching at a high rate of speed from across the street not make the turn and instead go off the road and snap a utility pole that had a transformer on it. In no time at all he had called in the accident and driven the short distance over to the scene.

Another police car, whose officer had also learned of the stolen vehicle report, was already approaching, with lights flashing on the distant horizon.

Seeing these unusual developments unfold before their eyes, the three occupants in the black SUV made a very quick decision, and continued on past the accident and drove out of sight.

Nicky and Maurice were not seriously injured physically, but their pride was definitely hurt. No one seemed to even listen to them when they tried to explain that the car acted weird when they tried to turn. Of course, the fact that they each had a criminal record, were carrying loaded weapons, had just committed a car theft and in the process caused a major power outage didn't help them at all in their attempt to present an explanation.

At first B.G. was crushed when he learned that his beloved Cadillac had been demolished. But then, the more he thought about it, he felt it was perhaps a good sign, and thereafter acted as though his friend had died a hero.

*

The car had to be towed someplace, so B.G. gave the flatbed operator specific directions.

The next morning when Shooter saw the crushed Cadillac being brought to his parking area, he recognized the car and the rear license plate immediately, and at first thought the worst.

But when the truck's driver told him it had been stolen and the owner asked that it be delivered to Shooter's while he figured things out, Shooter was visibly stunned.

And then he just laughed and laughed and laughed.

*

A few hours later in the morning, B.G., now driving his wife's compact sedan, arrived at Shooter's.

They looked over the car together, and Shooter was already making plans.

"Well, the leather seats are still in real good shape, but that's probably about the only thing left that's worth much now. But hey, you are going to make out great in this. The insurance will cover it, the book value is still good and those clowns who stole it will get what they deserved."

"Yeah, I guess you're right."

"Of course I am. I told you you needed to get rid of it just the other day, and now it's all been handled for you. Pretty nifty outcome, you know. But now you are going to need another car."

"I know, another thing to have to deal with."

"I may be able to help with that. Consider this for a minute. I've got a vehicle I've been planning to use as a loaner when a customer leaves their car for repairs. It's that light blue SUV over there. The engine is strong, and it's really comfortable. It has lots of room and I think you two would get along."

"So, you want to sell it to me?"

"Not just yet. I tell you what. It will take some time for me to try to get the best deals on selling these seats and parting out whatever is left. And I know it takes some time to get the insurance matter settled on this. Why don't you just drive it for a few weeks, and see how you like it? If you decide it's a good fit, we'll work something out between the Caddy parts, the insurance and whatever... Sound good?"

"Just one thing. You mind if I travel any distance?"

"No problem. Go wherever you want. I know that the longer you drive it the more you'll want to buy it."

"But what about the paperwork?"

"That's all set. Registered, insured, and I've got dealer plates on it. You, especially, would probably like that so that if you want you can be a bit more anonymous when doing what you do."

Ten minutes later Wumpkey was sitting in the front seat of the large, light blue sport utility vehicle.

He closed the door and then put down the window.

Shooter gave him a long look, then yelled out, "I gotta admit, you look good in it!"

CHAPTER THIRTEEN

Since he was in the area, after figuring he could have his wife drive him over the next morning so he could pick up his soon to be new-to-him set of wheels from Shooter, B.G. then drove over to Henry's tavern.

He was told that Henry was out until later in the day at a dentist appointment. While he thought he'd have lunch there, but now with his new vehicle situation seemingly solved and Henry being away, he decided to return directly to the ranch.

He found Carol in the kitchen, where she was reading a book about health foods. She told him she was glad he came back for lunch, and that she had a new recipe that she wanted to try with him. Twenty minutes later, she called him to the dining room.

"Now, I know you will probably give me some resistance about this, but please just do me the simple favor and try this and tell me truthfully how you like it."

She then placed a large glass with a thick green liquid in it on the table.

B.G. studied it for a moment, then proceeded to

look at Carol and pinch his nose.

"It looks like some type of wallpaper paste. And frankly, I think it stinks."

"Now how can you say that? In the first place it doesn't stink, it only contains fresh fruits, vegetables and herbs, and in the second place you haven't even tried it."

"Yes, but I'm a pretty clever guy."

"Just take a drink of it. I think you'll be surprised."

"That's what I'm afraid of."

They stared at each other for a moment more. Then B.G. reached over, lifted the glass to his mouth and drank down the entire contents.

"See that ---it wasn't bad at all. Tell me how you liked it."

"Before I do, are you making me drink this as some sort of punishment?"

"Nothing of the sort. It's just the opposite really. I want you to be healthy."

"But I am healthy. I have a good appetite, I'm strong, and I still get exceedingly angry at the reporting by the mainstream media on the national news. Those are all the signs of a very healthy, active man."

"These drinks are called smoothies." Carol went on to explain. "I make them in a special blender I bought, that chops and cuts and blends all the healthy ingredients into a consistency that makes it easy for the body to absorb all the nutrients that we need quickly. And I can do the same with another kitchen appliance called a juicer, that makes drinks that aren't as thick. Either one, the smoothies or the straight juice mixtures provide large amounts of wonderful vitamins and minerals to give our bodies just what we need, in a way that allows us to absorb all that goodness virtually immediately."

"All right, I have to admit it wasn't quite as bad as I expected. But now, can we have lunch? I have some good news on the vehicle issue to tell you. Right now though, I'm really hungry."

"Oh, but you don't understand." Carol said with a puzzled look. "You see, that was lunch."

CHAPTER FOURTEEN

Wumpkey spent the rest of the afternoon in his home office, a large room with an expansive view of the pasture where his "beef cattle herd," of four head, grazed peacefully. There were no telephone messages left in the voice mail at his law office, so he was investing some time to do a little independent research on a subject that might be useful.

Although much of what he came across was vaguely familiar, his review was informative, but yet at the same time increasingly aggravating.

The Bank Secrecy Act was a far reaching federal law that was enacted, purportedly, to protect the public from criminal activities. In reality, however, Wumpkey interpreted it as yet another part of the government's continuing war on cash.

Among that act's many provisions were the efforts to monitor and mandate reporting of certain transactions which converted cash into other forms. In essence, the Act requires financial institutions as well as some businesses, including but not limited to car dealers, jewelers and the United States Postal Service, to complete and file a transaction report whenever a cash transaction meets a certain amount. The report is to be filed with the U.S. Treasury, and typically applies to purchases of three thousand dollars or more in money orders made in one day.

Other certain post office transactions of lesser amounts, which range from one thousand dollars to two thousand dollars, have similar disclosure requirements including the name address, date of birth from an approved photo identification card, along with a social security number. His reading also showed that a customer must fill out a form with similar information whenever cashing money orders of higher amounts.

Wumpkey's research, while in general reinforcing what he basically already knew, was at the same time in its specifics making him a bit upset. And the more he read, the more annoyed it made him.

Asset forfeiture laws by federal, state and local governments have been used increasingly to confiscate sizable amounts of cash. In fact, in many instances the person from whom the cash is taken has not even been charged with any criminal offense, but their cash is labeled as having an involvement in criminal activity, and it becomes the burden of the owners of the cash to demonstrate that they are the legitimate owner.

"But it is their own damn money!" B.G. exclaimed aloud.

Banks too are at the core of this type of monitoring. In fact, banks have been given lists of businesses that the federal government have designated as so-called high risk, which in essence have banks divulge specific information related to the finances of any customers who match the lists, and then even to close out the bank accounts of those determined by the banks to be involved in "suspicious" actions.

Consequently, in such instances wherein government policy may take away a small business's ability to maintain bank accounts, the business may have to be forced to operate in cash in order to survive. But by doing so, at the same time such actions may become reason enough to arouse suspicion and bring such activity within the cross-hairs of the government's eager desire towards undertaking asset forfeiture of that very same cash.

The government has been requiring for over forty years that the banks report any cash deposit or withdrawal in the amount of ten thousand dollars or more. In addition, more recently an associated criminal offense labeled "structuring" was enacted. That offense means withdrawing or depositing some amount less than ten thousand dollars, but with the intent to avoid having the transaction being reported to the government. Along these lines, banks also have requirements to report certain financial actions or behavior which may be regarded as being unusual or suspicious in nature. Banks face the real possibility of punishment under current regulations should they fail to report certain information accordingly.

After reading much of this, Wumpkey found that he had become engrossed in all the specific restrictions that the government has been gradually imposing on an individual just for using cash. But it had only caused him to be more angry with what he was coming to recognize as an overbearing, authoritative, and bloated government system.

"And to think that all these limitations are put on

a person's ability to possess or use their own money. But perhaps even worse, these limitations that are enacted and enforced are all carried out with, and imposed using the taxpayer's money as well!" Wumpkey fumed aloud.

Numerous persons he had known, ranging from family, friends and clients over the years had good reasons for not wanting to entrust their personal assets, be they large or small, by placing them in banks or similar entities. Many of these people still carried with them the bitter memories of how years ago banks had closed, and those with money in accounts were simply out of luck. Although more recent regulations and insurance were supposed to eliminate such risks, there were still real concerns by many which gave them reason to want to possess cash or other valuables for their own peace of mind.

And the thoughts of safety deposit boxes, the types which are kept secure in a bank, nonetheless were too looked on with skepticism by some others due to certain restrictions, including but not limited to that full access was not always available and some reporting requirements were sometimes still applicable. For those and related reasons, a large number of other individuals still kept much of their valuables under their own control so as to safeguard them and have them accessible at all times as a precaution in the event of disaster, natural or otherwise, which could, for example, cause extensive power outages or travel restrictions and otherwise prevent access.

And yet these laws, by their nature, made such conduct suspicious!

In essence the overall message that B.G. was left with after his extensive reading was one that he was able to summarize. Cash is anonymous, and for that very reason the government doesn't like it.

*

This revisiting of the laws and restrictions on the use of cash or similar valuables by Wumpkey took a lot of time, but he didn't notice just how much. In fact, it surprised him greatly that it was already early evening when Carol came up to see if he was ready for dinner.

After briefly explaining some of his findings to her, he realized that he needed to change his state of mind, because at the moment it was simply too maddening for him to dwell on such matters any longer.

What he needed now, he realized, was a good hearty meal to provide him with enjoyable sustenance. Unfortunately, instead what was waiting for him once more was, brimming with healthy ingredients, a somewhat pink-colored meal in a glass.

"This has a base of carrot juice, as well as cucumber, orange, kale, celery, and ginger."

"I was really looking forward to something a bit more traditional," Wumpkey said with obvious disappointment. "I mean, is this all there is?"

"Oh no, there is enough for another full glass for each of us. I tell you, with all this weighing on your mind, with this case, and the Cadillac, as well as because you are probably having to do some traveling soon, I want you to be as healthy and strong as possible once you begin. And considering everything you have been dealing with, well it takes a real toll on a person, whether you want to admit it or not. And after all, we both know that the food that you will most likely end up eating when you are on the road is usually not very good for you."

While she was explaining her concerns, B.G. had

been looking at the glass intently, with the beginning of a scowl.

Undaunted however, Carol continued.

"Really now, I just want you to be in your best of health, that's why I am doing this. And these drinks are so beneficial and powerful. For instance, did you know that as soon as you start taking them they will help eliminate all the harmful extra toxins in your body?"

"Well, that's not a problem with me."

"What on earth do you mean?"

"I mean that I am quite sure that I have just the right amount of harmful toxins...Not too many, not too few. In fact, if ever there was a person with the proper amount of toxins, it is yours truly. And I must add that I feel very confident about that."

It was at this point when a noticeable period of silence ensued, accompanied by a bit of what might be best described as a short term staring contest.

This was broken only when Carol picked up one glass and put the other in the hand of an obviously reluctant Wumpkey.

"Bon Appetit!" she said cheerfully, as she reached over and made their full glasses clink.

CHAPTER FIFTEEN

The next morning B.G. and Carol drove over to Shooter's and picked up the SUV that was to be the replacement, for the time being if not longer, for the crushed Cadillac. Carol appeared to be very pleased with the look of the vehicle and the overall arrangement, and also seemed less than saddened when she saw the corpse of the Caddy near the garage. She did wince though, as the impact was described to her and she saw the results of such on what remained of the car.

Before heading back to the ranch, B.G. tried again to meet up with Henry. When he went into the tavern, he saw his friend behind the bar. But it appeared that Henry was about to be leaving. The waitress explained why.

"His dentist had an emergency come in yesterday, so they rescheduled him for this morning. He had a root canal, got back a half hour ago and he's in a lot of pain. He just took a few shots of whiskey in addition to what the dentist gave him. We told him to go home and sleep, since we can't understand what he's saying anyway."

Henry had overheard what was being said, and nodded slowly in agreement. He was quite pale and didn't look good at all.

Nonetheless, he came over close to B.G., leaned over and whispered in his ear.

Henry then shook his hand and on somewhat wobbly legs walked out to his car and drove towards his home.

Watching him leave, B.G. was a bit confused.

In the parking lot, Carol asked him what it was that Henry had whispered to him.

"Well I'm not quite certain, really. He said a few sentences that I just couldn't make out at all. But then he ended it by saying what sounded like either 'Good---luck---hypothetical'...or else it was 'Wood---duck---highly ethical.' Either way though, I could tell he was being sincere."

*

Back at his law office later that afternoon, B.G. did have a message. Merle, the client with the missing toe, had telephoned. His message was simply that he keeps getting more medical bills in the mail, so he was going to wait until he figured that he had received most of them before coming back to meet at the office. That pleased B.G. since with all that was going on in his own thoughts, he wasn't ready to start on a new case right now.

Before leaving the office that afternoon, Wumpkey did take certain steps. After performing his routine of locking the doors and closing the blinds, he made sure to secure the two briefcases, in a well-hidden, confined spot that he realized even he would have some difficulty getting to subsequently. Just before doing that, however, he also carefully removed his one-third agreed upon fee and put that in another location which was equally well hidden and secured in the building.

With that done, he felt an inexplicable sense of relief come over him.

B.G. understood that the only individuals who knew the precise amount of valuables that were involved in this matter and delivered to his office, were, to the best of his knowledge, just B.G. himself and Mr. Kurt Koppy. Nonetheless, with B.G. planning to do some traveling, if he wasn't going to have the entire amount with him, he wanted to be certain that the remainder was kept protected and secure. And it gave him added pleasure to realize now that he alone was the only person who knew the exact whereabouts of the valuables.

*

That night back at the ranch, B.G. was extremely disappointed to find that the only item on the menu happened to be dinner in a glass once again.

However, not wanting to create unnecessary tension when he knew he might be traveling soon, he tried to keep his objections to a minimum. And, as he drank down the container of a gray, lumpy liquid, the thought of a pending road trip was certainly becoming more and more appealing.

CHAPTER SIXTEEN

A good night's sleep helped his swirling thoughts become formulated into the framework of a plan. And then, two other unexpected developments made him put his plan into action.

B.G. had found a legal education seminar (some of these were so boring that he felt they should be more aptly called illegal seminars) in the more central part of the state which was being offered twice this week on two different days. As each one was to be incorporated into a noon time lunch event, and either would only last two and one- half hours, this seemed to be workable for him. It wasn't overly expensive, it wouldn't be so lengthy that it would put him to sleep as these programs often did, and as it could entail an overnight stay, it would present a legitimate reason as to why he was out of the office should anyone ask. The only uncertainty was that he still didn't know in what direction he would be heading when his travel plans began. However, for now that part of Pennsylvania, with its relative proximity to major highways going north and south and east and west, seemed for the moment to be as good a starting point as any.

Most of the day passed quickly while B.G. made general preparations for a short trip. With Carol's help several items of clothing, including one sports jacket and tie with dress slacks and freshly shined shoes (the lawyer's attire, should he need to assume that role), as well as several more casual outfits with more comfortable walking footwear were packed. For some reason, his bathing suit and his extra large beach towel were also included, although he wasn't sure if such would be necessary. Along with all this were also boxes containing numerous bottles of water, along with some fresh fruit, packets of salted peanuts, cans of tuna fish and pineapple, packages of beef jerky, potato chips and various types of so-called granola bars.

All tolled, B.G. figured that if for some unforeseen reason he had to, he could probably sustain himself on these provisions alone for about three days. In packing these, the objective was to have a supply of prepared food items that would not spoil and could be eaten without cooking. Thankfully, Carol agreed with B.G. that the freshly prepared smoothies and juice drinks that had been the mainstay of his diet over the past few days would not meet these requirements.

B.G. had recently purchased a new handgun and he gave some serious thought about bringing it along as well. After some deliberation, he opted not to and instead included a large hunting knife along with a retractable fishing pole and a small tackle box. The more he thought about it, the more he came to the conclusion that if he were to be carrying large amounts of cash, while a gun might at some point be necessary, its negative connotations outweighed the likelihood of him having to use it. This, in his mind, was to be a pleasure trip, one in which some scouting and preliminary work could be accomplished as well. He didn't want to elevate it into something more dangerous without reason.

As one more afterthought, B.G. also put a rolled up sleeping bag, a pillow and a very lightweight nylon two person camping tent into the SUV. While he had no intention of doing any camping, it was after all summertime, so he felt it wouldn't hurt to bring these along.

While the Cadillac had certainly been a spacious car as far as sedans went, the amount of items he was packing would have filled up a lot of that car's trunk space and overflowed somewhat into the back seat area. Now, however, with the abundant size of this sport utility vehicle, B.G. became immediately impressed to see that there still remained plenty of empty and open interior space even when all of the goods they were packing had been placed inside it.

Having been so absorbed in these preparations, before they knew it, they saw that evening was already approaching. Back inside the house after washing up, Carol started to head towards the kitchen. Before she did so, now from his back office B.G. asked her to turn on the local television news in the living room in order to see the projected weather report for the next few days.

However, because of another breaking news story, the weather report, when it later came, was entirely overlooked by both of them.

CHAPTER SEVENTEEN

"I think you had better come and see this right away!" came Carol's loud instructions from the living room shortly after the television had been turned on.

The lead news story described the discovery of the body of an unidentified man approximately thirty years old that had been found that afternoon on the side of a road, in a town that was about twenty miles east from where the two were now watching from their ranch.

That in itself, however, was not nearly as alarming as the rest of the report. The newsman went on to say that police were at this time regarding it as a homicide, but were releasing no further information. In the meantime, authorities were following up on the report of a witness who had led them to believe that the driver of a compact motor home with out of state plates might have important information and was at this time wanted for questioning.

Carol put the volume on mute, and looked directly at Wumpkey with sudden concern.

He answered her question before she had to ask

it.

"Well, it certainly sounds like the same type of vehicle as my client's, all right. And although I never confirmed it with my own eyes, it was my understanding that he probably did have out of state plates. Not only that, but when they say that a person is wanted for questioning, it generally means they have a lot more in mind than just a casual chat over a cup of coffee."

*

With the details of the evening news report going through his head, Wumpkey without much at all in the way of protest somewhat absentmindedly consumed the latest dinner in a glass health mixture that Carol had just prepared. This one, B.G. did notice in passing as he drank the last of it, was a light colored green.

"What about that notary that you went to see... do you think she will raise any problem in all this?"

"You know, I was just thinking about her. She's a very kindly older lady in her eighties, I think, and she made it pretty clear that she likes to mind her own business about things. Plus, I distinctly remember her saying that she never listens to the news or reads the papers, and that she mostly just likes to read her books and tend to her garden. And she likes to try new dessert recipes...No, although she's really the only possible link between that client and me, I don't think she'll learn of any of these reports. You know, honestly, even if she did, she's not the type that would want to get involved.... And actually, come to think of it, I made it a point to not even tell her my name."

"Well, that honestly makes me feel a little better. I mean if you're away, I don't want to be wondering if the police might show up and ask what you might know about the person."

"Rest assured, I'm pretty confident that won't happen. But even if by some chance it did, you know enough from the many cases that I've handled and that you've heard about over the years, to simply say that you don't want to talk to them without me."

Carol nodded in agreement.

B.G. paused, then continued sharing his thoughts with her.

"Somehow, I really can't picture the older man I met with as having anything to do with a suspicious death. Nonetheless, people can fool you. Still, I just wish that I had a little more to go by, even a little other background that was positive about this mysterious client. Something that at least would encourage me that my plans to quickly carry out his instructions is the right thing to do."

They discussed the matter a bit more, and completed adding a few provisions which they packed with the other boxes into the vehicle.

One hour later, the telephone rang.

*

Carol answered the call. She then came into the living room to inform of the following.

"It's not a clear connection. But there's a guy on the phone who says he tried to reach you at the office yesterday and today but just kept getting a recording and he didn't want to leave any message. He says he thinks you'll be happy to hear from him, but he didn't want to tell me his name, because he'd rather surprise you. He said he's a former client and an old friend. And his voice sounds kind of familiar, but with the static on the phone I just can't place it."

*

Wearing a look of puzzled interest, B.G. went to the adjoining room, picked up the telephone and said "Hello?'

"Is this Mr. B.G. Wumpkey, the world famous attorney and all around hero?"

It took just a few seconds for the unmistakable gravelly voice on the other end of the conversation to register.

Then as he unexpectedly broke into a wide grin, came his return response.

"That depends. Is this that world renowned artist and traveler extraordinaire, who goes by the name of ---Irwin?"

*

It was fair to say that Irwin was certainly one of Wumpkey's most memorable clients. And in part because of some assistance that B.G. had provided, he was now also one of the wealthiest.

A few years ago Irwin had sought B.G.'s assistance on a seemingly simple minor drug possession charge. In short order, what developed from that was a complex scenario in which Irwin's life was being threatened, but which ultimately resulted in the whimsical artist, who was struggling at the time just to make ends meet, being the unexpected recipient of a very large inheritance. After that, when the artist realized the threats were eliminated and he could actually pursue his art work without financial worry, he had become forever gratified for Wumpkey's counsel.

Although B.G. had not heard from Irwin for more than a year, he had been pleased to learn several months ago that Irwin's work was gaining recognition by some museum directors and art dealers across the country. Last he knew, the artist had relocated and was living comfortably in Florida, still doing his oil painting, and fully enjoying his new lifestyle.

This evening, the upbeat tone of the raspy voice indicated that Irwin was both happy and healthy. After they gave one another an update on their current news, Irwin's call took on a more serious note.

"Okay, Mr. W., I'm glad to hear everything's going well for you and I apologize for not being in touch with you sooner. Believe me, though, you are in my thoughts a lot. Now, I want to tell you about something, and it's one of those situations that like you used to tell me when we had some things to deal with, let's just keep it in general terms. So here goes."

B.G. was intrigued. "All right, I'm listening."

"Now first of all, this doesn't involve me directly at all. And still keeping it real general, well, let me get right to it. You see, I have this friend that needed some help, and he has bushy white hair and a real big black dog. Sound familiar?"

CHAPTER EIGHTEEN

They spoke for over a half hour. Part way through the conversation, Carol took Jack outside to go for a walk. When she came back into the house, she was surprised to hear that they were still talking.

Some time later, B.G. made it a point to repeat certain numbers that he had written down before their talk was being wrapped up. When the telephone call was finally over, Carol noticed that B.G. now had a determined and focused expression on his face. It was a look she had come to recognize which signified that someone needed his help and he was anxious to face the task.

She poured them both a drink before he began to explain.

"You remember Irwin, of course. Well, now that I think about it, Kurt Koppy had, either when I saw him, or else in his handwritten note, made mention in passing that we had a mutual acquaintance. And guess what? That person is Irwin. But all during our call, Irwin was smart and he never even used Kurt's name. But it's a certainty that we're talking about the same person."

"Really! So Irwin knows all about the situation?"

"No, that's the thing. He only knew a little of what was going on, and when Kurt mentioned to him he had a real situation, Irwin said if anybody could help him work it out it would be this attorney he knew and trusted. And that attorney is yours truly. But that was well over a month ago, and Irwin has neither seen nor heard from him ever since."

B.G. went on to explain that as Irwin put it, Kurt felt he was on a mission to accomplish something positive out of something that was negative. Kurt had headed up north, he told Irwin, to get out of the area and also to avoid Florida's summer heat. He intentionally got rid of his cell phone, so he can't be contacted. And Irwin forewarned B.G. that the guy is really good at disappearing. Irwin had also said he actually saw Kurt throw the phone right into a campfire. He added it was really something to watch it melt and that he's been working on a painting to show it.

At this point B.G. paused and finished his drink.

He then continued to summarize their conversation with the following details:

"Anyway, he gave me these numbers. One of them is a friend of Kurt's. Apparently the friend will never answer the phone for anyone, but if arrangements are left on the voice mail he should cooperate. The other number is Irwin's new one...he moved to another area in Tampa Bay and figured he'd get a new cell phone at the same time. Irwin said he has access to a bunch of Kurt's possessions that are in storage, but that he really doesn't want to get involved on his own. To tell you the truth, even though Irwin stressed that Kurt is a good man, he sounded like he's a little leery to find out what's there. But then he invited me to come down and said we could go through the stuff together. By the way, he said I'd really love his new place. And Kurt does have Irwin's new number---he got it before he headed north."

Carol had been watching him closely. She could tell he was becoming energized by these new revelations.

B.G. reached down and patted Jack fondly on the head.

"Oh and you know what else? Kurt's friend, the guy whose number Irwin just gave me...Well, that guy is now living in Maine."

*

It took a bit more time to absorb and apply what he had been told by Irwin. While many questions remained unanswered, what he had learned however, was extremely helpful.

B.G. at least now had the framework of some background information to support what he had been tentatively planning to accomplish. His mysterious client was a real person, now corroborated by someone he knew and trusted, who had not just randomly left a large amount of valuables at his office after executing a legal document, but who had instead done so because of and based upon a personal recommendation.

While B.G. acknowledged that this client might have troubles ahead of him, upon recalling Irwin's reference to Kurt as a good man, he decided to ignore the dark implications of the news reports from earlier in the evening.

He would help this man.

He would start tomorrow.

It was time to move.

CHAPTER NINETEEN

He left early the next morning.

With the large sport utility vehicle holding the provisions he'd packed, he lingered a bit as he and Carol shared a tender goodbye. Although she had insisted that in order to maintain the benefits of the diet of smoothies and juices he needed to have just one more as his breakfast this morning, and B.G. had grudgingly coalesced, as it turned out there was a consolation prize for his cooperation.

Just as he was getting into the vehicle, she presented to him a large plastic container with a snap-on lid. It was a peace offering of sorts, in the form of two dozen chocolate brownies with walnuts that she had baked for him very early this morning while he slept. Feeling it was a good sign to the start of his journey, he accepted it gratefully with his assurances that he would be returning some time soon.

Before going on to enter the interstate highway, B.G. made one stop. Entering his law office, he performed the now common ritual of locking the doors and closing the window blinds. He then proceeded to where the smaller of the briefcases was hidden, being the same from which he had earlier separated and secured his agreed upon fee into yet another part of the building.

Opening it, he began to make a calculation based upon information he had once learned from a savvy banker friend. Closing his eyes, he paused for a moment, trying to remember.

As best he could recall, he'd been told that a strap of cash is a term used for a band holding a certain number of bills together. B.G. was also pretty sure that another term, a stack, specifically refers to a sizable number of straps.

Now, without making any breakdowns or tallies, from his earlier tabulations as well as his passing glance at the moment, B.G. already knew that the briefcases contained a whole lot of what most bankers would call straps, and that when added together the abundance of which were more than enough to make numerous stacks.

Reviewing these large numbers in his mind, he decided there was no reason to be hesitant.

B.G. removed a small portion, and then carefully returned the briefcase to its well hidden location.

He had decided to view this trip as a preliminary exploratory venture, but at the same time he wanted to be somewhat prepared for what he was intending to accomplish.

After he locked up the office and was driving towards interstate eighty, he had a feeling of warmth and contentment envelop him.

This was in part because he had on the seat right next to him the still warm container of freshly baked brownies. It was also due to the fact that under his seat in a very large padded envelope he had fifty thousand dollars in cash.

*

Several hours later, B.G. had just entered the building where the legal seminar was to be given. As he registered at the front door of the room where the program was to be presented, however, he quickly came to discover that he had made an error in his plans, and that he was soon to be suffering from its consequences.

Pennsylvania, along with many states, has as part of its requirement for attorneys to keep their law license current, made mandatory the taking of a certain number of continuing legal education seminars on a yearly basis. Apparently, these are supposed to keep their members up to date on new developments in the law while providing an opportunity for networking at the same time. B.G. however, in large part, found these presentations to be not only costly, but exceedingly dull and not worthy of the investment of time and money.

B.G. had found one position to support these programs to be rather preposterous.

Occasionally, there would be the news story of a certain lawyer who had stolen money or real estate from a helpless elderly person, by forging documents or committing similar swindles and who would frequently attempt to blame such crimes on an addiction to alcohol, drugs, or gambling. In response to such heinous acts by a professional who was entrusted to help someone in need, the likes of which B.G. could not comprehend nor tolerate, those who were in charge of or gave these seminars would often tout the claim that if only Lawyer X or Lawyer Y had just taken one more credit of ethics courses in these seminars, that would surely have prevented such misconduct.

Of course, B.G. personally regarded these claims as being utter nonsense. If a guy or gal was going to steal from their own client, a classroom instructor briefly stating that such action was really naughty would do little to thwart such thievery. Nonetheless, that was in part the justification which was given to make mandatory the taking of these annual courses, which incidentally were huge revenue makers for the organizations that promoted them.

This morning, the mistake B.G. recognized by attending was twofold. First, he was immediately bothered to find that the lunch to accompany the program he had paid for consisted of only a small sandwich and a beverage of choice. And second, he realized that he had mistakenly signed up to attend a program that was not live, but was previously videotaped, which incidentally, B.G. had learned from experience, made it even more sleep inducing.

There were only three attendees. One of them read a mystery novel throughout the presentation. The other was soon fast asleep while remaining completely upright in his chair, a feat which B.G. noted with admiration was one requiring exceptional balance. B.G., being the third, after consuming the light lunch, soon after put his head down on the table in front of him and unintentionally followed the lead of the second in attendance.

*

He was awakened by the squeaking of chairs being moved on the floor and of brighter lights being turned on in the room. The seminar was over.

It was only after he was leaving the building and

entering his vehicle that he looked at the papers he was carrying, and was reminded that the topic of the program had been the Laws of Charitable Giving. The irony was noteworthy.

He laughed aloud.

Because in this case, having that client's direct approval, Wumpkey was now going to follow his own rules.

*

The time he spent at the seminar had, he noticed, served to make him feel refreshed. He thought this strange at first, considering his aversion to these programs, but then he realized it was because he had been asleep through most of it that it had produced such a positive effect. Perhaps he had found a way to make these seminars beneficial after all.

In a short time he was back on interstate eighty. He drove for two hours, before he stopped at a truck stop. There, he filled the tank with gas, and then went inside where he ordered a hot turkey sandwich. It was very satisfying.

Before leaving the restaurant, he located a pay telephone. These had become a rarity with the advent of more modern communications, but the anonymity they offered had always been attractive to many. This particular truck stop actually had several separate booths, each with a wooden door that could be closed for added privacy, which made them even more appealing. And they were obviously still being used by customers. Locating one that had just become empty, after closing the door and depositing the requisite coins, he made a call.

Back on the highway, B.G. sat up straight and

looked in the mirror. He liked what he saw. With the open road, the powerful and comfortable vehicle, and a satisfied stomach he felt very good about the direction in which he was heading.

B.G. hadn't had some good seafood for a while, which made his choice to drive to Maine make even more sense.

*

Having practiced law in Maine for many years before his wife and children had relocated with him to the Pennsylvania-Ohio border, B.G. was quite familiar with the state. They still owned some property there, with a small, rustic cabin in the woods which made for a welcome summer getaway.

Just after ten o'clock that night, B.G. turned off of the unpaved road, and drove into the narrow, bumpy driveway. Within a half hour he was in the cabin and snoring under some blankets.

CHAPTER TWENTY

To those who have any real knowledge about the subject, Young's Lobster Pound on the water in Belfast, Maine is regarded as the best place for fresh seafood on the entire east coast.

Located off of Route 1, the family owned establishment has been serving happy customers from far and wide for generations. The drive down to the two-story restaurant was a familiar one for B.G., as he and his family had been frequent patrons there for years. One thing that he really liked about the place was that it was comfortable. Having solid wooden picnic tables, they were arranged inside and outside to afford a lovely view of the waterfront, where modest boats ranging from those owned by working fishermen to large masted sailboats and huge private yachts all combined to form a scenic panorama.

And in the summertime the place gets really busy. This afternoon, having parked his vehicle in a spot near the big boulders on the edge of the water, B.G. took note that there was a new table set up near the walkway at the side of the building.

The table had a sign draped over it that read, "Author" in large black letters.

As B.G. approached the main entrance, the table with the sign to the right drew his attention, and he walked up to investigate.

Arranged neatly on the table were a half a dozen or so books, each having colorful covers and with separate titles.

Seated behind the table was a middle aged man, with wild windblown hair and a moustache, who was reading a newspaper at the moment. Walking towards the man, B.G. couldn't help but think that he looked familiar.

As he looked over the titles of the collection of books, he was intrigued. Still reading, the man behind the table had not noticed that B.G. was standing there for a minute or so. When he did, he immediately folded the newspaper and rose to a full standing position.

"Good afternoon, sir," the man greeted B.G.

This was followed by a strange period of silence as they each looked more closely at one another.

The similarity between the two was striking. Both were very large men. Both had dark brown hair that was unruly and out of place due in part to the afternoon sea breeze that was blowing. And both had a long dark moustache.

"You know the author?" B.G. asked the man.

"Even better than that...I am the author."

In response to B.G.'s obvious interest, the man proceeded to give a brief description of each of the books. Some, it turned out were a series of humorous fiction, while others were entertaining and gripping works of non-fiction.

"Well," said B.G. after hearing him out, "I think I want to buy some."

"You know what I think?" the man replied with authority. "I think you should buy a lot of them."

It turned out that the Author Man was a lot of fun to talk with, and also very persuasive.

They spoke a bit longer. And the more B.G. thought about it, the more he liked the idea.

Before long, the two shook hands and shared a warm laugh together. Shortly afterward, the man had opened the trunk of his nearby car. He then proceeded to carry over three boxes of books to the SUV, which in total contained ten copies of each book. Just before they parted, B.G. was handed a business card that had only the single word "Author" along with a website that read "www.dmmbooks.com."

"I"m giving you this to be sure you'll have it when you want to order some more. And remember, it's real simple ---dmmbooks.com."

B.G. looked at the card for a moment, after which he gave a quick wave of acknowledgment and tucked it into his shirt pocket.

Next, B.G watched with interest as the "Author Man," having apparently sold out the inventory he had in his car, then went inside and purchased a box of lobsters to go.

*

Exactly one hour later, the telephone call B.G had made bore some fruit.

The day before, at the truck stop B.G. had called from the pay phone and left a message at the number Irwin had given him. The message was that B.G. would be at Young's Lobster Pound over the next several afternoons. He had hoped that it was received and understood.

Just as B.G. was finishing his second lobster, a small, older man with a baseball cap came over to the table where he was sitting on the outside upper deck.

The man seemed to know B.G. immediately.

He sat down across from him.

Since the lunch rush was now over, there were only a few customers still eating, and none were close to where they were sitting.

"Got your message," the man spoke to B.G. directly. "And this was a good place to meet."

"They do have great seafood."

"Oh, it's the best around," the man said with a quick smile.

*

A short time later, B.G. was looking at his third order of the afternoon. This one was a lobster roll, the basic recipe for which was a lot of tender lobster meat mixed with mayonnaise and celery in a fresh roll of bread. He ordered one for the man sitting with him as well, who so far had remained nameless.

Quietly, while looking out at the boat traffic in front of them, they then each ate the lobster rolls with obvious enjoyment.

B.G. was in no hurry.

This was due to the fact that had often been demonstrated to him after years of personal research, which was simply that good food puts people in a good mood. And when people are in a good mood, they like to talk.

"So, now can you tell me---any news from our

friend Kurt?"

"Well, yes and no. Kurt---the nickname I know him by is Foto---and I happened to speak this morning. When he heard you had left a message, he asked for me to meet you."

"Was that difficult for you?"

"Travel wise, not at all. I've been living about an hour from here for the past year."

"Have you known him long?"

"Our friendship goes back decades. Anyway, he wanted me to tell you a few things. He said you needed to be reassured."

"Please continue," replied B.G. with interest.

"Well, first of all, he said to tell you to proceed with the plan. He said that he'd left word of that through another guy a while back. He wanted to make sure you understood that he was very clear about that. 'As you see fit'...those were his words."

"Do you know about that plan?"

"Only in very general terms."

The man in the baseball cap paused thoughtfully, as if considering what to say next.

"I will share this information with you. Foto---Kurt--- is a real decent man. But a while ago he had some things develop that put him in kind of a tight spot. I don't know about all of them, but I'll tell you about part of it...See, he owned this empty warehouse in Florida and was renting it out to a guy last year. The guy led him to believe that his business, which was buying used furniture from estates when the owners died, and then reselling it at a nice profit to snowbirds who wanted to furnish their vacation homes, well it needed a lot more storage space."

A very large sailboat came into the bay in front of them, and they watched it silently until it passed out of view.

"Anyway, the guy was behind on his rent, and was ducking the payment. Well, one afternoon ---Kurt--- is driving to the warehouse to try to catch up with the guy... and he sees there was this bad accident. Lo and behold, he comes to find out it was a hit and run, and the dead victim lying there now is literally...his deadbeat tenant!"

This term made the man chuckle.

"So what happened next?"

"Kurt goes to the warehouse, thinking he wants to see if the guy happened to leave out the rent money in an envelope like he had promised, but of course he had not. Kurt pokes around the warehouse and comes to find out that the guy was running a meth lab in there. The furniture business was just a cover to have a lot of stuff to conceal what was really going on. Kurt looks into it some more, and then he finds money...lots and lots of money."

The man looked away for a moment, had a funny look come over his face, and sneezed loudly, before returning to his story.

"Kurt figures that the guy owes him money, first of all. Then he realizes that with the guy dead in the street a few miles away, word is going to get out and somebody is going to be coming to the warehouse to get what they can real soon."

"So, Kurt gives it a little thought. It becomes real clear to him that the amount of money he's finding is huge, way, way more than the overdue rent. He's thinking that maybe the place was being used as a sort of pick up and drop off point for cash deliveries as well. He also realizes that if the others involved in the meth business don't show up soon, the cops probably will because they'll find out that was the dead guy's nearby place of business. Either way, if the official bad guys get it, or if some un-official bad guy cops get their hands on it, it's quite likely that the money will rapidly disappear."

"And so, Foto---Kurt---does the honorable thing."

"Which was..." B.G. prodded, now on the edge of his seat on the picnic table.

"He takes all the money, and then he torches the place."

*

As it was described, it really was ingenious. Meth labs are widely known to cause fires. The warehouse was a run down building and it was not insured at the time. So there was no insurance fraud claim to investigate to cause more problems. Besides, even though no number was ever stated, it was very clear from the description that the vast amount of cash that was taken far exceeded any value of the building.

The warehouse is totally destroyed, just a pile of rubble left. Kurt took off, and already sold the property for a song to one of the neighboring owners.

"And all that missing money?" B.G. inquired.

"Well, the hope is that those involved will assume it all got burned up in the fire."

*

His guest was now getting ready to leave. The hot late summer sun was coming at them from over the skyline of the small city in the distance, and it made them both squint as they looked at one another.

"Two other points. The first is, Foto wanted me to tell you that there is another situation, entirely separate, that involves a substantial amount of cash as well. Personally, I don't know anything else about that one, but he wanted me to mention it to you. And let you know that it may come up at a later date.

The second point is there may have been some news reports in your area. He wanted me to tell you specifically that even though he was there, he didn't do anything wrong."

B.G. allowed those last words to settle over him, as he thought he began to understand.

"Well, that's it. Thanks for the lobster roll. Kurt will be glad we were able to meet."

"When you see him tonight be sure to..."

"Oh I'm not going to see him again anytime soon. As we speak, by now he's already out of state. But he seemed to have his thoughts together when I saw him this morning."

B.G. felt a connection with this man, and had known enough people like him so that he was not going to pry. He did, however, politely ask for his name.

"January," the man said.

B.G. gave him a puzzled look.

"You ever know anybody named January?" the man asked him.

"No," came Wumpkey's immediate reply.

"Well, now you do."

*

Before he left, B.G. told the man to wait just a minute right there, as he had something for him. Returning soon afterward, he was very pleased to give a present of six brand new books to the man called January.

CHAPTER TWENTY-ONE

Wumpkey remained in Maine for another four days. This allowed him to rest a bit from the long drive up, and to enjoy some more of the delicious fresh seafood that was readily available in the area.

He also used the time there as an opportunity to experiment with various approaches to hone his skills in the art of giving.

To distribute substantial sums of money without divulging its source might seem like a simple task, but the more he looked into it the more he realized that it wasn't as easy as one first might think.

To begin with, one who attempts to do so to a complete stranger, he found, may immediately be regarded with suspicion. This was shown to be true in several instances even though B.G. never got around to mentioning the amount of any possible gift.

One person he spoke to said that the donor should first meet with both their lawyer and their doctor before the person would even consider accepting such a gift. What made this somewhat astonishing was that the man who made such demands had just been released from prison.

Another, expressing disbelief as to the validity of any such offer, looked around her several times and said, "I'm being videotaped for a reality show, right?"

So, B.G. began to understand certain parameters for his task.

He would not mention an amount to a potential recipient, but would make that determination on his own in each individual case.

He would advise any recipient, although it was probably to have only a temporary effect, that if and when financial help was to be given it would have to be kept quiet, as the source of the present demanded to remain anonymous.

Whenever possible, B.G. also determined that he would be well advised not to remain in the area once a gift had been made. Such conduct, he concluded, would avoid further questions and any possible involvement with inquisitive newspaper reporters, law enforcement or other third parties that might cause complications. Furthermore, with the source of the gift having mysteriously disappeared, it would add to the overall joy of the recipient.

He felt good about these guidelines he was developing, but at the same time he also realized that this was no doubt going to be a project that would remain open to further modifications.

Recalling that the instructions from his client had been to carry out the distribution "As you see fit," he gave that part of his task additional deliberation. Ultimately, he reached the decision that he would conduct a sort of informal screening process, which could be very short term in nature, to assess the qualifications of a candidate.

His purpose in doing so was to avoid the compounding of problems which an individual might be going through. In particular, based on his experience as an attorney in the court system of several states, he had seen how a person in the midst of having substance abuse, gambling or related problems could fritter away vast amounts of money in short order, without any real benefit to themselves or others. He wanted to steer clear of these problematic situations.

The help he was going to provide to people would, he hoped, be to those who were in his eyes deserving of such.

"As I see fit," B.G. said aloud with conviction, giving special emphasis on the pronoun, to further reinforce his feelings on the matter.

*

His first successful experiment in giving came about quite by chance.

He was driving in an area where he hadn't been for several years, on a back road that was about a half-hour from his cabin. A lady about thirty-five years old was standing outside of her car, which was emitting large amounts of smoke from underneath the hood.

B.G. pulled over behind the car, went over to her and asked if she needed help.

The woman was pleasant looking, but now obviously distraught. She told B.G. that a cop had just come by and they had arranged for a tow truck which was on its way and set to arrive in forty-five minutes. The cop had given her a warning for having no brake lights, which she had to have corrected. After sending a receipt for such, she was told, the warning would disappear. Although it seemed like a minor fix, she explained that the car's engine also may well have to be rebuilt, and the cost would be more than the car's value.

As she finished telling him this, she began to cry.

Without prodding, B.G. learned a little about her. She was recently put out of work when her employer went through a period of downsizing. Not long after that, the same employer went bankrupt. She was struggling to make ends meet. Although she had another job prospect, as it would require a daily commute of thirty minutes each way, she needed reliable transportation. She was single, living alone and had no current boyfriend and no children. Her parents were no longer alive.

B.G. inquired as to how much a used car of the type she was in need of would go for these days. She told him she had just finished making the final car payment on this last month, which made this breakdown even more painful. She added that she didn't want anything fancy, just something for a couple of thousand dollars that would stop and go when she wanted it to. B.G. got the immediate impression that she thought he was trying to sell her a car, which seemed of interest to her.

He looked at her with a serious expression. Then he excused himself for a minute and walked back to the SUV.

When he returned he asked her if she could keep a secret.

Her answer, a bit hesitant, was affirmative.

B.G. said he had something for her, but that it had to be kept confidential. He also requested that she follow his exact instructions. With growing curiosity, she agreed.

"Sell this car for scrap...you can get about three hundred dollars for it. Buy another car, for not more than the two thousand dollar price range that you mentioned, from a private party, someone with whom you feel they know a bit of the history of the car. A used car dealer won't usually have that. And one other thing---don't buy it on credit---pay for it in cash, so you won't have any monthly payments hanging over your head."

The woman had been listening intently up to that point, but when she heard the last sentence, she started shaking her head, saying "But there's no way that I can afford..."

That's when B.G. Wumpkey smiled and reached into his pocket.

"Do you have a purse?" he asked.

She nodded and retrieved it from the front seat of her still smoking car.

Now, he read her thoughts, she believed he must work for some kind of loan company and that he was going to give her an advertising brochure with a card.

But when he gave her a small envelope that she could see was full of cash, her eyes widened with amazement.

"This will help, with a little extra to get you back on your feet. Remember, keep the secret and follow my instructions. I wish you well."

B.G. then turned and began walking back to his vehicle.

"Wait!" he heard her yell from behind.

He turned around to see her eyes full of tears, but this time she was smiling, too.

"Can I please give you a hug?"

*

Although she introduced herself, in spite of her own polite pleadings, he chose not to tell her his name.

As he reached to open the door of his vehicle, she said some words that stuck with him.

"Everything always goes wrong for me---how can this really be happening?"

B.G. saw the tow truck slowly coming over the hill in the distance.

He decided to say nothing at all, but just gave her a broad smile with a knowing wink. She would soon find out that she had seven thousand reasons to help shape a more promising future.

And at that moment as he drove away, a newly discovered feeling of gratification arose from within him.

CHAPTER TWENTY-TWO

B.G. came to recognize that he liked calling this work to carry out the authorized distributions of money with a new title, one that he had already begun using unintentionally. By giving the work its own distinct and official designation in his own mind, it gave him a sense of a loftier purpose in what he was seeking to accomplish.

Thus, his efforts to achieve those ends from that point on became known to him, simply, as The Project.

"The Project," he said aloud in a deep voice brimming with reverence and respect, that afternoon while he was smoking a cigar and relaxing in a chair on the cabin's back porch.

Yes, he definitely liked the sound of that.

*

The next morning he decided to treat himself with a full and favorite breakfast.

After getting the coffee prepared, he proceeded to mix together the ingredients for one of his most basic, yet consistently prized additions to a homemade breakfast menu.

It was, however, only after he had fried a generous amount of thick sliced bacon in his treasured black cast iron fry pan that he began with the special recipe.

Locating the proper amounts of flour, baking powder and salt, he then mixed them into a small stainless steel bowl. Adding just enough water to create the desired consistency, he knew from experience when it was ready to separate into four sections. He then placed each section into the warm fry pan, and heard the familiar snapping sound as the bacon grease met the doughy mixture.

The tasty staple was handed down in the Wumpkey household from a long deceased family member, but this particular recipe was one that was treasured indeed.

Called "bannock," it was a quickly and easily prepared fresh bread substitute that had as one distinct advantage the characteristic that it could be cooked in a frying pan. It was known from pioneer days and reportedly had been a favorite of miners in the west who longed for a fresh tasting bread or muffin, but who didn't have the time or ovens to prepare any of the traditional recipes. And preparing this simple serving from olden days seemed especially appropriate to him this morning, while spending time at his rustic cabin in the Maine woods.

As Wumpkey turned the four golden brown portions over and later removed them from the pan, he looked at them with what could be described as adoring eyes.

While they were cooling somewhat on their own separate plate, he cracked three eggs and cooked them slowly. Having an inkling for variety this morning, he broke the yolk of one, and left the other two with their yolks in tact. A little later, he turned over all three and when they had reached the desired consistency, he placed them onto a large plate spaced alongside the bacon. After that, he cut a thick slice from a juicy beefsteak tomato, lightly fried it in the remaining grease and then carefully transferred it from the pan to an open location right between the bacon and the eggs.

With the bannock still warm, B.G. then sliced each portion in half, lengthwise. Next, with tender loving care, he spread butter on each half, after which he drizzled some honey on top.

Sitting at the table, as he looked favorably at the properly sweetened mug of coffee, the full portion of bacon and eggs next to the bright red tomato slice, and the freshly prepared bannock with melted butter and honey, he suddenly felt very pleased with the decisions he was continuing to make.

*

That afternoon, B.G. explored a bit of the area. He noticed that some new houses were under construction, and saw some "for sale" signs on properties with dense woodland. There were some signs of improvement in this part of mid-coast Maine---but the overall conditions of most of the roads, being still rough and bumpy, remained as he remembered them from years past.

He stopped to fill the gas tank at a general store, which as a reflection of the local economy, he recalled had been periodically closed and then re-opened again in recent years. B.G. prepaid for the fuel, and also bought some Smith's Log Smokehouse beef jerky as a snack, which he recalled was a long time favorite especially when driving lengthy distances in Maine. As he was standing at the counter, he noticed a headline on the weekly newspaper which described a large fire that had taken place in a nearby town.

While he was dispensing the gas, he heard two men at the adjacent pumps talking about what turned out to be the same fire, saying the remains were still smoldering somewhat, nearly a week afterward. Based on what they were saying, the fire destroyed a new barn but had not done any damage to the owner's small house that was next door.

He wasn't sure just how it occurred, but a short while later he found himself driving on the same road where the fire had taken place. And it soon became readily apparent that he was approaching the property as it had been described.

Looking back on it, B.G. would not even have slowed down if he had not observed something a bit unusual.

A man was walking up the dirt driveway towards the interior part of the property. He was carrying some envelopes in his hands, which seemed to be just retrieved from the mailbox on the road. As B.G. drove closer, he saw the man stop walking, and proceed to tear up a particular envelope he had been holding into small pieces which fell to the ground.

B.G. slowed the vehicle to a stop. Putting it into reverse, he backed up to where the mouth of the driveway began. After a momentary pause, he drove in.

The man was nearly on his front lawn before he noticed that there was a vehicle coming up his driveway. As B.G. stepped out of the SUV, the man walked directly over to him.

"Listen, I told the lady at your office when I called yesterday, I won't be able to..."

B.G. held up his hand with an explanation.

"Excuse me, but I believe you have mistaken me for someone else. I only stopped because I happened to be driving by and then thought this was the place that had the fire."

The man took a careful look at B.G.

"You're not with the collection agency that sent those papers or the fire marshal or the zoning..."

"No, no, nothing like that at all. However, I suppose you could classify me as more of a nosy neighbor, although I live a few towns over from here."

An expression of obvious relief came over the man. It was clear to B.G. that he had been through a lot.

*

They talked for at least a half an hour. As was shown by the printed letters on both the mailbox and the letters he was carrying, the man's name was Andrew. He had moved here three years ago from the Midwest. At the age of fifty, he gave up his job as a computer technician and decided to pursue his dream of making and selling his own pottery while living near the ocean. His girlfriend had moved here to Maine to join him shortly afterward.

According to Andrew's brief account, which he seemed quite anxious to share with someone, his business had been struggling but was showing signs of a promising future when the kiln that he used to bake his pottery had somehow caused a fire and entirely destroyed his newly constructed workplace. Along with the building, also went his supplies, his packaged inventory, equipment and much needed paperwork. The only thing positive was that his house, a very small but comfortable looking structure that appeared to have been a unique do-it-yourself project, was not harmed. B.G. noticed a huge amount of firewood, this coming winter's supply, that was stacked neatly a short distance away from the house. Seeing the house's chimney it was evident that this home, like many in the area, used a wood stove as the primary source of heat to deal with the often prolonged, sub-zero temperatures of wintertime in northern New England.

B.G. let him finish before he took a moment to speak.

"So, kind of a neat idea, moving from the Midwest---to the Mid-coast...of Maine that is. How has your girlfriend adapted?"

"She moved out right after the fire. Said she just couldn't bear the idea of starting over again. The fact that the job market here isn't that great didn't help. I mean, she has a master's degree, but the only work she seemed to be able to get was as a waitress, and even that wouldn't last long after the summer tourist season."

B.G. kicked a small stone in the driveway and watched it roll into the woods.

"You had insurance to cover the damages, though, right?"

"Nope. I built this whole thing myself, a little at a time, as I could afford it. It took twenty-five thousand dollars from all my savings and a lot of sweat equity to get it done. You understand, I didn't want to have the extra expense of insurance until it was all finished and some of my business prospects were rolling in. And the way things were looking, that was to be in another couple of months. I had really only completed the building this spring, even though the construction had been going on for over a year."

Andrew looked sadly towards the rubble that was still smoking. That had been his dream, and now it was gone.

*

When B.G. told him that he would give him something, but on one condition, the man was clearly puzzled.

A few minutes later, just before handing Andrew a brown paper bag with the top twisted to conceal its contents, Wumpkey first made him promise that he would never leave it near the wood stove.

This time, while he again chose not to give his name and requested that his visit be kept a secret, Wump-key also specifically asked that the bag not be opened until he was out of sight. While he didn't share this fact, if used wisely the amount in the bag would enable the building of a new barn, along with some extra as well.

Upon reaching the end of the driveway, he glanced back to where the barn had been, and where the smoke from the remains still wafted upwards. At that moment, the recollection of the story from January describing another fiery event which led up to the situation in which B.G. now found himself, came to mind.

"Ashes to ashes," he said aloud, while slowly driving away.

CHAPTER TWENTY-THREE

On the day he began his return trip back to the ranch, B.G. left at sunrise.

Although he was bringing along some seafood in the form of three pounds of uncooked steamer clams and a one pound container of cooked lobster meat, these were packed on ice and reserved for later consumption. The thought of such being close by did cause his stomach to begin growling loudly just after he crossed the bridge from Maine into New Hampshire. By the time it was mid-morning, he felt it necessary to stop for some sustenance, and chose a well known delicatessen in Massachusetts. There, he enjoyed immensely the large and delicious dill pickles which were always served along with the hot pastrami on rye.

Two hours later, he found himself at a small but very busy restaurant which had a prominent sign stating that it had been voted to be the best sandwich shop in all of Connecticut. Eating the overstuffed "grinder" that he ordered, containing an abundance of various cold cuts, vegetables, olives, cheese, with a special sauce packed onto a large section of thick fresh bread, it quickly earned his high praise.

As he left the restaurant, located at the far end of the lot where he had parked, B.G. noticed a group of six young men and women. As he drove up to them, he observed a forlorn look that they shared.

"Can we wash your car, mister?" one of the women asked.

Recalling that the dusty, unpaved roads in the area of Maine where his cabin was located left a film of dirt on any and all vehicles passing through, he thought it to be a favorable idea.

"All we ask for is a donation. It's for a good cause," another one in the group informed.

B.G. stood nearby as the four women and two men began their work. With buckets, large sponges and brushes having long handles they soon had the vehicle covered with a soapy mixture.

They explained that they were students at a local community college, and were members of a foreign language club. A small but dedicated group, they were trying to raise money to enable their club to take a trip to New Orleans to study and experience the variety of foods and languages available there.

When B.G. asked how the plan was going, the group showed a grim expression.

"Well, if it tells you anything, we were here all day yesterday and today, and so far you are our only customer. Mrs. Bigelow, our adviser, she went to school in New Orleans so she knows the city real well, she said we had to have all the money to make the reservations by the end of this week to get the reduced travel deal, but..." the woman's voice trailed off with disappointment.

"Anyway," one of the men added with a more hopeful note, "even if we can't take that trip, whatever amount we raise will help the club for some local activities."

As they worked steadily, B.G. asked the group if they knew where the nearest post office was located. They told him there was one about a mile away, on the same road.

When they had finished washing and rinsing the car, B.G. gave them a warm smile. He then got into the SUV, and told them he would be right back.

All in the group watched him with both disappointment and disbelief as he drove away. He could tell that they did not expect to see him again.

However, ten minutes later, he returned.

B.G. got out of the SUV and with his hands behind his back, he approached the group of young men and women who were now all looking at him with a note of curiosity.

As he walked over to them, he motioned for them to all come closer.

"Now make sure to stay in a nice place and have plenty of crawdads and gumbo," he said as he handed them a bulky postal mailing envelope, that was sealed shut.

On the outside address portion of the envelope he had written "Bon Voyage."

Before they could react, B.G. was back in the newly cleaned vehicle and after giving them a big wave, drove away.

The nine thousand dollars, he felt certain, would provide the group with a safe and memorable trip.

*

The rest of his travel went smoothly. The SUV provided a very comfortable ride, and the radio had a fine sound system that had long range reception. Hearing the stations from different metropolitan areas was entertaining, and made the time pass quickly. Before he knew it, he was through the state of New York and entering Pennsylvania. Although he still had another five hours or so to travel before he reached the ranch, he felt pleased with the time he was making. Still, the drive was a long one, and the trek was always tiring. He had made the trip in all seasons, but during summertime it was the most pleasant, due to the warm temperatures and the noticeably extended hours of daylight.

Once on Interstate Eighty, he was able to drive steadily without much concern about his exact location, since that route eventually brought him very close to his home.

As he drove, B.G. reflected on what he had accomplished in this trip. It had been very productive, he felt. Certainly, the fact that he had met up with the man who knew a lot about his client had provided a sense of verification and further explained the work that B.G. had been asked to undertake. Of course the delectable seafood, some of which he'd consumed and some of which was on ice in the container next to him, was an added benefit.

His time in New England had also allowed him to experiment and create a framework for how he was going to continue his work. Already, in his own mind what he had done so far had been educational, and he felt was successful as well. Recalling the looks on the faces of those he had made distributions to, he felt proud about what he was doing.

And while there was still much more to do which he understood, he was also mindful that unforeseen complications might arise which could present some challenges in the coming days.

Nonetheless, The Project was already underway.

*

B.G. pulled into the driveway at the ranch just as the sun was starting to set. The lurid colors on the horizon blended in such a way to put the property in a light that made it seem especially welcoming.

Carol was thrilled to have him back and she made no mention of any more dinners in a glass for the immediate future, which B.G. found to be encouraging. Jack too seemed to have been expecting him, and was extremely enthusiastic in his greeting.

While Carol told him there had been some news that would interest him, she also indicated it was not urgent and was resolute in her decision not to discuss it until the morning. For now, she told him, she just wanted to be sure he had a warm meal, got comfortable and enjoyed a good night's sleep after his long trip.

CHAPTER TWENTY-FOUR

After breakfast the next morning he caught up on the current events.

Merle, with an "e" had called, and said he had some more medical bills now and he could arrange to show them to the lawyer. Carol remembered that he specifically had noted the spelling of his name ended in that letter.

Irwin had left a message for B.G. to give him a call, but said it wasn't anything urgent.

There had been a few other inquiries from people needing to hire a lawyer for various matters. Carol had taken the initiative and on her own returned their calls but urged them to look elsewhere. Just with what she knew about the ongoing situation, she didn't want B.G. to have any more on his plate.

But there was more to tell.

*

While he was out of state, the local news reports had been steadily covering the story of the body that had been found and the operator of a compact motor home that was wanted for questioning.

The alleged facts that were being released had now been increased. The public was being asked to provide any information relating to the scene, the vehicle or the body that may be helpful to authorities in the investigation. Without making any conclusions, a police spokesman stated the coroner's report indicated that the man had died as a result of blunt trauma to the skull and they were continuing to view this matter as a homicide. The identity of the victim had not been released. Apparently, there also was now a witness who reportedly had seen the body being dumped from the vehicle which the authorities were still asking for help to locate. That vehicle was repeatedly being described as a late model, compact motor home.

These new revelations served to put a cloud over B.G.'s cheerfulness about returning to the ranch. To gain a different perspective, later in the morning he went to his law office.

There, he found that nothing was new either in the way of mail or messages.

While sitting at his desk in deep thought, he did take a phone call.

It was Merle, informing that as he could get a ride over the noon hour, if it was possible he would like to meet with B.G. and have him look over some of the medical bills.

B.G. agreed, and about ninety minutes later while behind his desk, he was looking at Merle sitting across from him.

"To tell you the truth, I'd be happy if I didn't have to be talking to a lawyer about this whole toe episode. But Sheila reminded me about how you had helped

Irwin, so I figured if I have to have a lawyer it might as well be someone that I'd heard good things about."

These words came as a surprise to B.G.

"You know Irwin?"

"Yeah, sure, Irwin the artist guy. We used to go to the same bars, before he got mixed up in that whole mess. But then he fell in to a lot of money, with your help I heard, and he moved down south someplace. I haven't seen or heard from him since, we weren't real close, but he was a fun guy to spend time with. I remember telling him that when I did the drywall work it gave me the feeling like I was an artist, and he said he knew exactly what I meant. His paintings though, man they were really something-that's a guy with talent, all right."

Hearing this information, B.G.'s level of interest in the man sitting in his office chair rose considerably.

Some time later, B.G. had written down the details of Merle's lost toe ordeal and perused the initial medical bills that were now on his desk. While noting that there were more bills and records he'd have to go over, B.G. proceeded to explain the terms of the contingent fee agreement that he used if he decided to represent Merle. Merle was anxious to know if B.G. was definitely going to take the case. B.G. said it looked like he would but that he wanted to learn a little more about Merle's prognosis first.

After explaining in basic terms that in this type of case the contingent fee agreement provided that the attorney's fees are based on the amount recovered for the client, he gave the often repeated example that if for instance he were to get ten dollars for his client, that the attorney's share in this matter would be one-third

or three dollars and thirty three cents, plus certain expenses.

"But you think you can get more than ten dollars
for my case, right?"

"Well, I wouldn't take a case unless I felt it would
be worthwhile. In your situation, the injuries you suf-
fered appear to be clear, but the big problem may well
be trying to establish liability---in essence, how to get
someone to pay."

B.G. then told Merle that unless something out
of the ordinary came to light, that once he had the full
medical reports, bills and related information from the
doctors, he would have Merle sign a fee agreement based
on the terms he had presented. Even though nothing
was finalized, Merle seemed pleased that this attorney
he had come to know would probably be his advocate,
and equally so with the part about the contingent fee,
providing that he wouldn't owe legal fees unless there
was an amount actually recovered for the client.

With that much explained, B.G. was nearing the
conclusion of the meeting when he presented a question
that, from years of experience, he had learned was far
too important to overlook.

"Is there anything else that you haven't told me
that I should know about? Because if there is, good or
bad, I'd want to hear it from you now rather than be
surprised later to learn it from the other side in this case
later on."

Merle looked sheepishly out the office window
and was silent for a moment.

"Well you probably already figured that since I
say I can get a ride that I don't have a driver's license.
It was suspended a few years back, too many speeding

tickets. And then I drove while it was under suspension, so that was another offense, and after that to try to get it back was a lot of trouble, so I never did. But you know something---not having a car or a license saves me a lot of money. I mean, forget the reinstatement process and the fees for that---but then when you consider the insurance which would be really expensive for me, the registration, buying the car and then the repairs... well when you add it all up it's a big cost. So, I just said the heck with it, I'll get by without it. And so far I'm okay with that."

B.G. studied Merle as he paused.

"All right, so you have some criminal driving records. Is that all?"

Now it was Merle's turn to look intently back at B.G. during a momentary silence.

"Actually, there is another thing. And I guess you'd be hearing about it sooner or later anyway if you go ahead with this case. You see, a little over a year ago, I had this other criminal thing, and as part of the deal I've been on probation. But the good news is, as of yesterday, I'm all done with it. So the probation is all over and finished now."

"Just what kind of a criminal thing was it?"

Merle wasn't thrilled with the idea of revisiting this, it was apparent. But, he had decided to be up front with this lawyer, so he might as well continue.

"Okay, it was a theft thing."

"All right, what kind of a theft?"

"A theft...a theft of letters," Merle finally got the words out.

"Oh, I think I follow. So you stole these from a post office?

"No."

" A mail delivery truck?'

"Nope."

"Someone's home mailbox?"

"Not that."

The effort to sort this out and understand what was at the bottom of such was becoming painstaking. Nonetheless, after taking a deep breath he pushed onward, holding a belief that he was close.

In a way, B.G. felt as if he were mining for gold.

"Theft of letters from the mail is a federal offense, so..."

"It wasn't a federal case."

"But letters from the mail..."

"No, it wasn't like that. It was a different kind of letters."

"All right then. Why don't you tell me how these letters were different?"

Merle squirmed a bit in his seat. He reached down and tied his shoelace. Then, with a sigh and a shrug, he provided further explanation.

"The theft wasn't of letters like that are in envelopes and sent by people. This was a theft of actual letters. To be precise, one in particular."

"I still need a bit more clarification," B.G. replied, "Maybe if you just..."

"E." Merle said loudly.

"What?"

"E. The letter 'E.'"

"What about the letter 'E'?"

"That's what I stole. The letter 'E'...But it was lots and lots of them, actually."

B.G. let Merle's words hang in the air, and a brief

silence followed.

Then, recognizing his breakthrough, he smiled, because even though it wasn't in full view yet, B.G. now knew that he had, so to speak, hit the mother lode.

*

It was a crime that B.G. had never heard of, and over his many years in the courts, he had heard of a lot.

Merle had over a period spanning some eighteen months, undertaken a stealthy project whereby he would remove from outdoor signs, his favorite vowel.

And not just once. He had over those many months acquired such an extensive inventory that businesses as well as churches in the area were noticing and reporting the shortage. Merle's ambitious business plan had been to make it so that particular letter, having become scarce at best, was in highest demand. And Merle was amassing a healthy quantity, of sizes, styles and fonts, including capital and lower case.

As he gained a more complete understanding of the criminal enterprise, B.G. presented to Merle a question.

"So tell me. With this whole plan to get all the 'E's...was it ever profitable?

"Well, it was just starting to get rolling when I got arrested. But really, I was already doing okay by it. And it's a basic concept that was driving my plan."

"What concept is that ?"

"It's real simple. If you've got an outdoor sign, you are going to need an 'E'."

Always being one who had respect for entrepreneurs, B.G. had to admire the obvious pride which the man exuded while describing his work from days past.

*

It had bothered Merle a lot that he had gotten caught for his misdeeds, but it upset him even more that the prosecutors had, as he put it, "made such a big deal out of it".

Apparently, wanting to send a dual message to the community, being that the businesses and houses of worship were going to be protected and that such outrageous criminal conduct would not be tolerated, Merle's sentence included fines, restitution and a year's probation.

"And that probation is completed now, like I was telling you earlier. By the way, while I was there for my last meeting, what I heard makes me think that the guy who was here the last time I came by, the one who left before you came, it sounds like they sure want to find him."

B.G. suddenly took a deep breath.

"What do you mean?" he asked.

"You know. That guy who wanted to talk to you and gave me the message, to proceed with the plan or whatever it was. When I was at the last probation meeting, a cop came in and talked to the head probation man, and then he gathered us together and said they were looking for this guy who had a small motor home. The cop said it was a very serious matter, and he wanted to know if any of us knew anything that could help them. The cop said if anybody hears of anything, they would be very appreciative...like it could help them and they'd return the favor."

"So what happened?" B.G. heard his voice crack with the question.

"None of the other people said anything and neither did I. After what the cops did to me about that theft thing, there's no way I'd want to help them. Hey, my probation is all over now anyway. Besides, that guy who was here, I don't know what his deal is but I bet they're just trying to pin something on somebody quickly to make them look good. And frankly, in these kind of things, I naturally root for the guy to get away. Not only that, it was real nice of him to give me that fifty dollars, so I'm on his side anyhow."

Having taken all this in, when their conference wrapped up, a short while later B.G. was walking Merle towards the office door. Still limping somewhat, and using the cane for assistance, B.G. was looking at him with a new found respect.

In parting, he told B.G. that he'd call again either after his next doctor's appointment or when he got some more of the bills in the mail.

And then Merle, with an "e," the man with the missing baby toe, carefully walked out of the office and flagged down his ride that was waiting across the street.

CHAPTER TWENTY-FIVE

The next morning Wumpkey was outside just after breakfast, surveying the back pasture at his ranch. Periodically, he had come to learn since his herd of four black Angus beef cows had escaped earlier in the summer, that it was a wise practice to walk the perimeter of his fencing, in order to check for possible breaches.

This morning it was quite humid and already warming up quickly. Because of the heat B.G. found the walk to seem longer than he had recalled it from when he had previously done his last inspection.

The cattle were spotted in the far corner of the fenced pasture, under a spot that was always shaded by the nearby maple and oak trees. They took little notice of him as he approached.

Although he found several spots where the top portion of the woven wire fencing had been bent by the leaning and pushing of the twelve-hundred pound bovines, he saw nothing in the way of broken posts or dislodged staples. Sometimes, he had come to learn that the cows used spots in the fence for an itching post, which conduct left tufts of their black fur stuck in the metal fencing. This morning, he saw several telltale signs of that fur lodged into the bent woven wire. B.G. patiently spent some time repositioning these twisted portions of the fence so that when he was done they appeared mostly straight and true again.

As he rounded the back line of the fencing and turned the corner to head back towards the house, he made a mental note that there were already several areas where some more of the brushy saplings would have to be trimmed again to keep the walkway that bordered the fence area clear. It was a constant task to keep the fast growing wild mixture of trees and shrubs at bay.

Approaching the back side of the house and barns, he saw the open blue sky, the expanse of green lawn, the large garden area and the row of healthy fruit trees. From the far distance, B.G. took a minute to take in the full view of the scenic property. Whenever he did so, seeing that always made him glad to be here.

He knew that some more travel was in his immediate plans and he was in many ways looking forward to it. But he also knew that he would be very happy to return.

*

B.G. found himself taking long afternoon naps over the next two days. Part of this he attributed to the satisfying lunches that Carol was preparing. The other part was simply because he was still resting up after the tiring travel he just completed.

After his second day's nap, he went to the office. There was nothing new there so he left shortly afterward. While driving a mile down the road, he decided to go visit the nearby library.

It was a medium sized facility that had been newly

renovated in recent months. Advertisements on the radio and in local flyers had invited the public to stop in and view the improvements, and it was something that B.G. was meaning to do.

As he entered the new glass doors he saw that the building now had a brighter overall appearance. An older man behind one of the desks welcomed him and directed him to the center of the room where the library staff was offering free tea and cookies. Taking a sample, B.G. made polite conversation with the reference librarian and the library director, both of whom were obviously pleased to point out the new sun room along with various other upgrades in their workplace. Selecting a comfortable chair at a sturdy oak table, he began reading the local newspapers that covered the time period while he had been out of state.

One hour later, B.G. helped himself to another couple of cookies and then after extending his best wishes for the library's continued success, he made the return drive to the ranch.

Before dinner was ready, he turned on the television to see the local evening news. He listened to it all very carefully. After the weather, which reported periods of heavy rain in the forecast over the next few days, B.G. turned to another station. There he watched with interest as an experienced travel guide was showing the favorite foods he had enjoyed from his last journey. That show always made B.G. smile.

Once they'd finished their meal, B.G. and Carol moved to the back porch where they relaxed with after dinner drinks. There, B.G. shared what he had learned over the last few hours.

The newspapers along with the latest news reports had provided some more detail about the events surrounding the body of the man, estimated to be in his thirties, that was found on the roadside. To sum up what the reports agreed upon, the man had died from injuries to his head. A witness had seen the body being dumped on the side of the road. The vehicle in question was a compact late model motor home, being mostly of silver coloration. After the vehicle had stopped and the body was removed from it, the vehicle had left the scene. Although further details were unclear, the reports indicated that the man was already dead well before the body was left on the roadside.

"Of course, there could be another vehicle that was involved, that looks just like the one Kurt was driving," B.G. rationalized before he took a drink from the tall glass in his hand.

"Yes, that's certainly true. But still, those news reports are making the public believe that the person who was driving that small silver motor home killed someone and then threw the body out from the vehicle onto the side of the road like a bag of garbage. And since you have information that can fill in some details, I see why you're concerned."

B.G. took another drink as he looked into the back pasture. The sun was just starting to set, and some rays were shining between the clouds directly onto the area where the cows were now grazing.

" Did that man you met in Maine give you insight on any of this?"

"Yes, but only in very general terms. He told me that as to some reports I may learn about, Kurt wanted me to know that even though he was there, he didn't do anything wrong."

"That's a bit helpful, but clearly it leaves a lot unanswered. It confirms that Kurt was involved, which isn't good. But it says that there is a reasonable explanation."

B.G. shifted in his chair impatiently, then rose to his feet.

"This was all confusing enough just when it was a matter of briefcases with large amounts of cash and gold coins. Now there is a homicide thrown into the mix, and a client who has disappeared after a vehicle matching his own was at the scene where the dead body was dumped. Added to that is a go-between known only by the name of January who serves as a messenger, with word that basically it isn't as bad as it seems."

"I understand the complications," Carol noted calmly. "But you know, even with all that said, you still should look at the bright side."

"Which is?" B.G. asked.

"Well, at least in this case you've already been paid in full."

*

Following somewhat of a restless night, the next morning a large breakfast put B.G. in a better mood.

Not long after he had finished, Irwin called.

*

They spoke for twenty minutes.

After they exchanged warm greetings, B.G. soon noticed that there was an edge in the voice of his old friend and client. While the raspy quality of his tone was the same, there was also a distinct hesitancy and concern, the sounds of which carried clearly through the telephone.

Irwin closed the conversation by summing up the

reason for his call, although he was careful to still speak in the most general of terms.

"Anyway, what I want you to know is that there are some things here, let's say recent developments, which would be of real interest to you. And frankly, I could use your help and guidance now. So I'm going to respectfully request that if possible, you arrange to come down to Tampa Bay and check out a few things. I know that it's the hottest time of the year here, but even so, if it will help, maybe you could call it a partial vacation, and you can be sure that your time and expenses will be covered. Plus, since I haven't seen you for quite a while, it would be a good chance to have some good food and drinks together. I don't want to spring all this without giving you a chance to think about it and talk it over with Mrs. W., but if you could, maybe let me know in the next few days... well, I'd really appreciate it."

After they had ended the call, B.G. looked at the phone and couldn't help but smile. One quality about Irwin that B.G. recalled with affection was that he had always maintained a respectful and courteous tone, even when in the past the situations he was experiencing would have made most others completely lose their composure. It was a remarkable characteristic to have observed, and recalling it served as a reminder to B.G. that Irwin's call and respectful request for a visit in all likelihood involved something of great importance.

"But of course as to just precisely what it may involve, based on what little Irwin told me, well, I have no clue," B.G. later acknowledged to Carol as he was relating what they had talked about.

CHAPTER TWENTY-SIX

The more he thought about it, Wumpkey came to believe that Irwin's call and the respectful request for the honor of his presence by way of a visit to Florida, somehow had a very significant connection to what B.G. had come to call The Project.

Of course, it was feasible that Irwin could have fallen into some complicated situation on his own that was independent of what Wumpkey was currently handling. If such had occurred, it would be quite reasonable for B.G. to expect Irwin to ask for his assistance.

Irwin's use of the term "recent developments" in their conversation also kept being repeated in B.G.'s mind. Just what type of recent developments did he mean? And were they matters that related only to Irwin?

The fact that Irwin had spoken in very general terms, using terminology that could be described as cryptic, was also noteworthy. A few years back, B.G. was the one who had first opened the eyes of the artist and explained to him that most methods of modern communication were not private. That revelation was something that Irwin had latched onto and ever since kept in the forefront of his mind. While protecting one's confidential information was always a wise precaution to take, and was a practice which he continued to recommend, unfortunately it was now also keeping B.G. mostly in the dark about what was going on as well.

And so, after reviewing such matters in his thoughts, B.G. recognized that he would need a little more time to evaluate the situation to consider what, if any, impact it might have on his own evolving plan of action concerning The Project.

*

It took three days for B.G. to reach a decision on what he was going to do next.

On the morning of the third day, with his uncertainty still looming, to help him gain the proper perspective, he started to make a batch of borscht.

The Wumpkey garden was generally productive and high yielding, but invariably there seemed to always be a certain crop each year that was especially remarkable. As this year's award winner, in addition to the always respectable showing of tomatoes, peppers, onions and okra, the top prize recipient went to the high quality and abundant quantity of beets.

Reaching close to near softball size this season, the healthy root crop provided their kitchen with delicious beet greens from above ground which could be prepared much like spinach or swiss chard. Of course, the dark red, rounded beets that grew beneath the greens underground were both filling and delicious on their own whether steamed or boiled, then sliced and served with butter and salt.

To make the borscht, which is a beet soup that is

a favorite among many from Eastern European and Russian backgrounds, is not a quick process. As Wumpkey did it, the all vegetable recipe included a large amount of finely chopped cabbage, onions, and beets, along with certain spices and personally preferred additives. When completed, the beautiful deep, dark, red broth can be garnished with a dollop of sour cream in the soup bowl. What consistently made the recipe most intriguing to B.G. was not only the rich color that can be changed with the swirling sour cream, but the special attribute which makes this a soup that is delicious whether served hot or cold.

Carol, seeing during the morning that B.G. was already engrossed in the preparations, made a most valuable contribution to the recipe that was to be served later that afternoon.

And so it was, even though it was in between mealtimes, that a few hours after lunch and a few hours before dinner, the Wumpkeys sat down to an unexpected but most delicious mid-afternoon meal.

Watching the steaming borscht as B.G. added the sour cream, Carol presented two warm loaves of her freshly baked bread to the dining room table. A short while later, they were silently enjoying the tasty and colorful soup, along with slices of fresh bread topped with thick slabs of juicy beefsteak tomatoes, olive oil and salt and pepper.

It was for that day the perfect mid afternoon repast, and it may well have been the catalyst which prompted B.G. to reach the next decision on his plan of action.

*

"Well, here's how I see it now," B.G. later was

starting to explain his viewpoint to Carol. "I've got this whole Kurt matter to deal with and complete as far as the distribution part of it goes. And then Irwin enters the scene."

"I like the tone of your voice, because I recognize that now you are comfortable with what you're dealing with here," Carol interjected.

"Really? You can sense that? Well that makes me feel even better about it."

"So go on, already," Carol urged.

"Okay. Irwin clearly needs some help with something and he's reached out to me because of how we've worked through some difficult matters in the past. Now Kurt's situation is still a bit cloudy, although I still feel I know what I need to do overall. I need to remember that Irwin apparently referred Kurt to me initially, so there is some connection at least from the inception. But are the two matters as they now stand related at all? I don't know. Actually, perhaps Irwin doesn't even know, and maybe that's why he's calling me."

"You know, that could well be."

"In any event, I don't think that I can find out what Irwin wants or needs unless I go down there, because he's leery, with good reason, to try to tell me about it, whatever it is, any way but face to face. And as far as Kurt's matter goes, well, Henry's good advice, you remember, was essentially 'nothing local and no receipts.'"

"That's right, and you respect what Henry says."

"So, since Irwin's matter requests a face to face meeting, and since Kurt's assignment, as Henry wisely advised, is best if not done locally, I think that I should plan on trying to handle the two situations together, regardless of whether or not they end up having any relation to each other. I really feel that I need to work these things out soon. You're welcome to come along, but I have to tell you I don't know what I'll run into or just how long it will take."

"All right. It might be nice to go with you, but I need to stay here to keep up with the garden and the ranch in general. And with the children coming back soon from their summer jobs before their college classes resume, I'd feel better being here to spend time with them. After all, the last time they were here it wasn't much of a visit since it seemed we spent most of the days trying to locate the beef cows that had gotten loose. Besides, honestly, the heat in Florida this time of year is just too much for me. Okay then, since you are going to Tampa, now you have to be sure to bring back some things that we've been needing around here."

"That I can do. In a way, I'm looking forward to it, but in another way I was just getting comfortable being back here again. And that borscht with your fresh bread was wonderful --- it makes me not so anxious to think about traveling," B.G. said as he looked fondly at what remained from their recent meal.

"Just promise me you will be careful and not take any unnecessary risks. I understand that there are some things you need to finish sooner rather than later. But I really will feel a whole lot more at ease when this whole Kurt-distribution matter is over and done with, and you're back safe and sound."

CHAPTER TWENTY-SEVEN

The distance from the ranch in western Pennsylvania to where he was heading in the Tampa Bay region, they figured, was about eleven hundred miles. It was understood that for many reasons, including the distribution aspect, B.G. would of course be driving the entire way. Although Carol and B.G. were somewhat familiar with the route, looking at the map again reminded them of just how long the trip would take.

B.G. made a brief call to Irwin to let him know of his tentative plans. It sounded as though there was some heavy equipment running in the background at Irwin's end, but it was clear that he was extremely pleased to hear that B.G. would soon be heading his way. It was agreed that B.G. would give Irwin a call when he felt he was a few hours away, so that Irwin could give directions to his location based on rush hour traffic and road repair projects that might want to be avoided depending on his projected time of arrival.

Packing for the trip was made easier by the fact that he had not unpacked most of the items that he'd included on his recent trip to Maine. So, in addition to the already selected supply of food, water, and camping gear, he added certain basics for an extra warm weather visit. After the beach towels, second bathing suit, suntan lotion, shorts, sandals and hats for some comfort and protection from the tropical rays had been located, they were included among the provisions.

Since he had returned from his trip to New England, B.G. had told Carol on several occasions how much he had come to enjoy driving the SUV. Now, as they were starting to pack some more things into the vehicle, he continued to voice his praise.

"And yet, look at that, there is still all that empty space and room back there," B.G. marveled to Carol after they had inserted the additional items into the back of the SUV.

"I see what you mean. But I have to tell you that even more important than how it looks or that it is so roomy, to me is that just simply knowing you are now driving a vehicle that properly turns both left and right, and also has a working reverse gear, has all added a whole lot to my peace of mind. Oh, and by the way, Shooter called this morning and said he hopes you like the SUV and you can keep driving it wherever you want. He said the parting out of the totaled Cadillac is taking longer than he thought but that he has some good leads which should work out in a couple of weeks. He seemed really pleased when I told him that you think it's a very comfortable ride and he's confident that the more you use it, the more you will want to buy it. And oh yes, he also said to be sure to tell you that he and Henry are still laughing about how that whole thing with the car theft worked out."

*

Early in the evening before the day he was scheduled to begin his southbound travel, B.G. made a quick stop at his law office. He brought in with him a large canvas book bag that was carrying several heavy legal textbooks. A half hour later, after locking up when he left he carried the same book bag. Only this time instead of textbooks, it contained three hundred thousand dollars in cash.

All told, the distributions he'd made on his trip to New England left about five thousand remaining from that first fifty he'd taken with him. Now, by deciding to bring with him on this pending journey the contents of the canvas book bag, along with what remained from his past trip, he felt it would make a considerable impact on the total amount that was originally delivered to him, which he was still working with to distribute.

This time, it wouldn't be all of it.

But it would still allow him to make real progress, while at the same time leaving a substantial amount for him to continue to distribute to worthy candidates upon his return.

That night, B.G. and Carol decided that while they knew he would be leaving in the morning, they didn't want to set any alarm clock to dictate his time of departure. Whenever they woke up, early or late, they would have a good breakfast, and proceed to pack any last minute provisions. Then, he would begin his travel.

That plan made for a relaxing and most enjoyable evening. Later on at bedtime, B.G. also came up with a new and most effective way to quickly fall asleep.

Instead of counting sheep, B.G. found his final comforting thoughts before slumber to be envisioning the currency-filled canvas bag, as well as what still remained well hidden in his office, namely the significant amount waiting for distribution, as well as his separately secured legal fees.

He slept quite contentedly.

CHAPTER TWENTY-EIGHT

Morning came quickly.

After a relaxing breakfast which Carol had made to suit his wishes, she added one request of her own. Presented as a way to give him extra nutrients which would help keep his mind sharp and his body strong for his pending travel, B.G. noted that it was a tall glass filled to the brim with a thick, pale green substance.

"One good smoothie for the road," Carol instructed while noticing him begin to wince. But before he could comment, she quickly raised her own glass in a toast and just as the two glasses touched, added "To a successful trip and a safe and prompt return."

Realizing that this was no time to protest, although it took a few minutes, he drank it all.

*

He left the ranch at eight thirty-five. He promised to call Carol that evening to keep her informed of his progress.

The Sport Utility Vehicle was very easy to handle. In spite of its size, he found it quite maneuverable as he approached the traffic commuting to Pittsburgh. The seats were plush and roomy and the radio's reception continued to be clear and strong.

In two and a half hours he was approaching the West Virginia state line. Midway through that state, he stopped to stretch his legs and filled the tank with gas. After that, it was another few hours or so until he was leaving that state and entering Virginia.

The distant mountains in the western part of Virginia, with the rolling open grasslands teeming with beef cattle closer to the highway made for a lovely panorama. Along the way, there were two tunnels that had been carved through the mountains, which caused the traffic to slow and required the eyes to adjust to the change in lighting.

By late afternoon, he had crossed into North Carolina. About two hours into that state, he made a stop at an exit that he had been to several times in years past. With North Carolina and much of the neighboring states having a rich history in tobacco growing, after getting more gas, B.G. made it a point to purchase some cigars at a store that boasted a wide selection. His indulgence of these was typically a weekly occurrence at most, and something he liked to reserve for celebratory events.

He hoped in the next weeks to have special cause to unwrap the plastic and sample some of the selections he bought.

*

As he entered into South Carolina, an unusual occurrence took place.

Proceeding along the interstate, he was noticing that this time of year there were far less of the out of state plates from up north that generally were commonplace on these highways during the wintertime, when so many travelers from the colder climates would be heading to seek the refuge of sunny Florida.

It was just as he was remarking that he had not seen a plate from up north for some time when he saw a sheriff's patrol vehicle parked on the median strip.

He didn't think any more about it until a few minutes later when he saw that the vehicle was directly behind his own.

B.G. checked his speedometer, and confirmed that he was operating within the posted speed limit.

Then, just as he did so, the patrol car slowed down and kept abreast of B.G.'s vehicle for some distance. Not wanting to interfere as he expected the cop's car to pass and turn in front of him momentarily, B.G. slowed down just a bit to allow such.

However, instead of passing him, the patrol car slowed down even more, and was continuing to stay right next to and beside B.G.'s SUV.

At that point, the slowing down of the two vehicles in both lanes was in turn causing the traffic from behind to get much closer to the two vehicles which were now proceeding neck in neck, so to speak.

This parallel pattern continued for a minute more, while the increasing number of cars and trucks behind each of them continued to increase.

B.G. found this action of the cop's car to be puzzling, and so kept his speed reduced with the continued expectation that it would pass and pull in front of him.

But instead, the patrol car stayed right next to him in the adjacent lane, and then even as B.G. slowed his speed, the patrol car did the same.

"Why isn't he passing me?" he wondered aloud.

Then, much to his surprise, instead, after a half minute more, the patrol car pulled in behind B.G. and put on the blue lights. Seeing this, B.G. then pulled over the SUV to the side of the highway.

Having no idea what this action by the cop was

about, B.G. saw the officer approach his passenger side door, and motioned for him to roll down the window.

B.G. complied, and heard the cop ask for his license and registration.

As he was locating it, B.G. asked the cop directly what was the reason for the stop.

The cop said because B.G. kept slowing down and was starting to block up traffic, he felt he might be having mechanical problems.

This puzzled B.G., who then told the cop that the only reason he was slowing down was in order to let the cop pass in front of him, which he did not do.

After asking B.G. where he was going, the cop remarked that he was a long way from Pennsylvania.

The more they spoke, the more the tone of their conversation became cordial. The officer then said he just wanted to make sure that everything was all right with B.G.'s vehicle, and ended the conversation by saying "Have a nice day".

As B.G. drove away, he realized how many times he had handled cases where cops had made a pretextual stop just in order to try to find something to charge a driver with, after which a full blown vehicle search would often lead to more charges.

Reflecting on that, he recognized that what he had experienced was probably just such an event. He had done nothing wrong; there was no reason to slow down and drive abreast of him. He had not been speeding, did not cut anyone off, and there were no lights out on his vehicle. The only reason he had slowed down slightly at first was to allow the patrol car to pass him, which operation was not improper at all.

In short, there had been no legal justification or reasonable articulable suspicion for the traffic stop whatsoever.

However, by merely having a vehicle with out of state plates, which this time of year was more of a rarity, he now believed was the one and only real reason for the stop. Once the two had talked, B.G.'s polite demeanor and questions, he felt, however, told the cop he was someone who had a familiarity with the legal system, even though he never said he was an attorney.

It served to remind him once again, this time first hand, that law enforcement does not always operate within the law.

And then on a more positive note, Wumpkey thought with a smile as he looked in the mirror, it also made him very pleased to be continuing on his way now, without being concerned about an explanation for how he happened to be carrying over three hundred thousand dollars in cash in the vehicle.

CHAPTER TWENTY-NINE

As he drove an hour more further into South Carolina, darkness fell and at the same time B.G. noticed he was getting very hungry.

Reflecting on the recent interaction with a patrol car, and considering the contents he was carrying in the vehicle, he began to think that he should start looking for a motel at which to stay the night. Police officers, he knew from his many years of courtroom experience, seemed to be much more prone to pull over vehicles in the late night and early morning hours. The combination of a vehicle with out of state plates traveling late at night could be even more susceptible to a nosy cop looking for something to do.

There were plenty of motels in the area, and the billboard signs on the highway continued to advertise many with very reasonable rates along the way.

Before making a decision on that matter, he pulled off the interstate and topped off the fuel tank. The location he chose happened to be near a large shopping area, with a mall and a huge grocery and department store which was open twenty-four hours.

While still at the gas station, B.G. saw a pay phone and made a short call to Carol. He told her he was in South Carolina, and was going to find a place for a quick meal before deciding where he'd spend the night. She was pleased to hear he was safe and sound, and urged him to eat something before it got any later.

B.G. drove into the parking lot of the all night grocery and department store. He parked the SUV some distance from the entrance on the far side of the parking lot. In doing so, he wanted to be sure to take a long walk to stretch his legs after all that driving.

As he walked into the store, he noticed that the night air was very warm and humid. He also noticed that there seemed to be about ten cars and trucks, which, like his, were also parked and scattered at various spots some distance from the store entrance. Two of them, he observed, were attached to travel trailers which appeared to have interior lighting.

Once inside the store, he found himself buying more than he had expected. Among a few other items, his purchase included a whole hot roasted chicken, a bunch of bananas, a bag of potato chips, a jar of salted peanuts, and a large container of cold orange juice. He brought these items back to the vehicle, where he sat outside at a nearby bench and proceeded to consume the entire chicken, two bananas and the whole quart of juice.

As he was walking to a nearby trash bin to dispose of the scraps from his meal, he noticed a middle aged man and woman open the back door of their minivan and then both go inside it. The vehicle had Nebraska license plates. A closer look revealed to him that the couple had arranged their bedding in the back of the minivan, and were already lying down stretched out in the back.

"So, they really are sleeping right here, it seems," B.G. remarked to himself.

He walked a bit more, and was feeling much better after having eaten. However, the combination of the warm night air, the full stomach, and the long day's drive was now starting to make him feel a sense of drowsiness and overall fatigue. During his stroll, he noticed that some of the other vehicles that he had seen parked at the far edges of the parking area, like the minivan, also had occupants that were sleeping inside them. But overall, the busier middle portion of the parking lot remained quite full, with customers still coming and going.

Returning to the SUV, B.G. was feeling more and more tired. As he got inside it, he turned to look into the back.

You know, he said to himself, that's not such a bad idea.

Five minutes later, with the back seats folded flat, and the sleeping bag unrolled, B.G. was stretched out comfortably in the back of the SUV. He had assumed that relaxed position only after he'd first checked to be sure that the doors were locked, and had also opened the front passenger side window just an inch or so in order to allow some fresh air to circulate inside. In doing so, he came to notice another positive feature of the vehicle, which was that the tinted windows in the back section made it more private and kept out much of the harsh brightness from the outdoor lights in the parking area.

"There now. This is quite nice. I'll just rest my

eyes here for a few moments before I continue driving," he said aloud.

*

He woke up six hours later. It surprised him to learn that he had slept so soundly and without interruption. Although the sky was still dark, he could see just the beginning of the dawn on the horizon.

Looking around, he noticed that the vehicles he had last observed at the fringes of the parking lot were mostly still there. He also noticed that a truck with a long and quite fancy looking trailer, with two bicycles affixed to the back, had pulled up sometime during the night and stopped across from where he was parked. Evidently, after getting off the interstate, they too may have slept there overnight, he thought.

B.G. took a stroll around the parking lot, and then went into the always open grocery and department store. He brought with him his toothbrush and felt much better after washing up and brushing his teeth in one of the store's large and clean restrooms.

He then bought a container of milk and a box of chocolate doughnuts.

Back outside, he assumed his position on the bench that was near the SUV. There, he enjoyed a very leisurely breakfast of doughnuts and milk as he watched the sun start another day.

As he was finishing up his third doughnut, a man who had been in the minivan that he'd first seen earlier the night before approached him. They exchanged greetings, and began talking about the weather. Some heavy rain was in the forecast, the man told him.

The man was quite open about his situation, and he told B.G. that as far as he knew the store management did not bother any customer who decided to sleep some in their parking lot. Since it was so close to the interstate, the store got a lot of travelers and apparently appreciated their business.

B.G. pointed to a few other vehicles and the man finished his thought by saying that he'd spoken to several of the occupants and they were doing the same thing as he and his wife, heading somewhere, stopped here for a break, and ended up napping for a while or for the whole night.

The man then gestured toward a white sedan that was at the far corner of the lot. It was parked in a spot that had the benefit of two shade trees with a picnic table along with a park bench as well.

"See that car?" the man asked.

"Yeah... it looks like that guy got the best suite in the house," B.G. said with a soft smile.

"Well, you might think so at first. But the guy is in a bad way, got a wife and kid and he's in some kind of a bind, although he didn't give many details. My wife and I talked with him a little when we first got here last evening, and we felt sorry for him so we bought a box of diapers for their baby. If you have a minute, you might want to say 'hi' to him. Looks like he's getting up and out of the car right now as we speak. Anyhow, we gotta get back on the road soon. Nice talking to you and safe travels."

After finishing the last of his donuts, B.G. followed the suggestion, and took a walk towards the white sedan. It was a large parking lot, and to get to the end of it took longer than he expected.

As he got closer to it, he had to stop his walking as a large pickup with dual rear wheels pulling a flatbed trailer turned and crossed his path. The lady driver slowed down as soon as she saw B.G., and then waved at him apologetically before she proceeded to park in the more central portion of the lot.

Continuing towards the white sedan, as he got closer to it he noticed that the older car had a flat tire.

Perhaps it was B.G.'s casual manner of conversing and asking questions which he had refined over the years that put the man at ease, or perhaps it was just that the man had gotten really beaten down by lack of sleep.

In any event, it didn't take long for the two of them to engage in a friendly conversation, from which B.G. learned quite a bit.

His name was Calvin, he was traveling with his wife and his infant daughter from Vermont to Florida to start a new job. Unfortunately, the car's transmission had burned out along the way. The flat tire was just an added complication.

This was their second night that they'd spent in the store's parking lot.

B.G. asked for a bit more information, and Calvin seemed willing to share.

"See, we just got married six months back, and then I was downsized and out of work. We had the baby a few months ago, and it's been really tight money wise. I learned of this work in Florida, and they wanted me to come down for an interview. I took a bus down---let me tell you that's a real treat, took several days with the long stopovers---and the other people who were traveling on the bus weren't exactly the type you'd want as a neighbor, if you know what I mean.

Anyway, I get there, and they tell me as long as I can pass the drug test, I've got the job. And I pass the drug test with flying colors...I'm not into any of that...and next thing I know we've packed up the car and taken our last thousand bucks in savings and are heading south.

Everything is fine and dandy, until the transmission blows, can't move it at all now. We basically crawl into this parking lot, and I'm told to fix the tranny will be two grand, and we need what little we have to get down there and get an apartment. Plus, I'm not even sure the car is worth fixing. As you can see, it's older and has a lot of miles on it. But the biggest problem is, I called the employer, and he's understanding but he says I have to be on the work site...it's construction...in three days because they are already behind schedule. I called a couple of friends to see if they could help with a loan, but I haven't heard back from them, and I don't really expect to now."

As Calvin was finishing his explanation of their situation, B.G. heard an infant crying. A short while later, the back door of the car opened and a lady emerged with a baby in her arms.

B.G. looked at them closely. Setting aside the obvious signs of fatigue, rumpled clothing and disheveled hair, they were a pleasant looking young couple, probably in their mid thirties.

Calvin gestured towards the lady while informing that this was his wife. She nodded shyly, then placed the young baby on the trunk of their car and proceeded to change her diaper.

Seemingly out of the blue, B.G. asked Calvin if he liked doughnuts and milk, and got an affirmative answer, along with a somewhat confused look.

He then told Calvin to wait right there.

"That won't be hard. I can't go anywhere else

right now," came the reply.

*

It took B.G. a little over one hour to get it all figured out. Looking back on it, he would agree that it may have been an example of some of his best work in record time. As it was, he couldn't help but give much of the credit to the unusual breakfast of many chocolate doughnuts and milk.

When Calvin and his wife saw the truck that had hastily crossed B.G.'s path when he first approached them driving up towards the sedan, they didn't know what to think. Then, once Calvin saw the female driver back up the truck and flatbed trailer to within a few feet of the car, he was even more puzzled.

After meeting up with the driver of the oversized pickup pulling the flatbed trailer inside the store, B.G. had found out that she was returning to Florida after delivering a car to New Jersey. With the trailer now empty, she was more than pleased to get some unexpected business for her return travel. Although her destination was another part of the state, to take a little detour to deliver the white sedan on the trailer along with Calvin, his wife and daughter in the four passenger pickup made for a nice fit.

B.G. paid her what she wanted for her services, then gave her a hefty bonus with the request that she be especially nice to the young family in need of a helping hand.

Then he met up again with Calvin. As the truck engine was idling loudly, B.G. took Calvin aside and spoke with him for a few moments. After explaining that they now had a ride, B.G. held out a medium sized shopping bag that had been tied so that it was closed at the top.

Taking care while speaking in general terms to make certain that Calvin would use the contents wisely, and with certain precautions, B.G. then handed the bag to him, and shook his hand.

" I don't know what this is and how...But listen, tell me why are you doing this ?"Calvin asked.

"Simple. Just because you deserve it," B.G. replied with a grin.

As he walked back over to the SUV, Calvin was pointing towards B.G. and talking to his wife who was cradling the baby.

When he saw the white sedan start to be loaded onto the trailer, B.G. beeped the horn of the SUV and waved. Then, he drove away before they were able to see that there was more than just doughnuts and milk in the bag.

*

Back on the interstate, in a short while B.G. crossed into the state of Georgia. There was some heavy traffic in the Savannah area, but after about twenty minutes of mostly stop and go driving, it thinned out. Soon, the flow of vehicles had all resumed their high rate of speed on the flat, straight roadway.

It took him two and a half hours to reach the Florida line. As was his custom from many previous trips, once there he pulled into the welcome center, where he got a state map as well as free samples of grapefruit juice and orange juice.

Seeing the blue sky and tall palm trees as he strolled outside, he felt glad to be back in the sunshine state.

He had made good time and arrived at this point

earlier than expected. But even though it was still well before noon, he quickly noticed that it was already getting really hot.

*

Once he got past the Jacksonville area, B.G. took a smaller but more direct connecting route which eventually led into another major highway that would bring him directly to the Tampa area.

That route went through towns small and large, past numerous fruit and vegetable stands, and several trucks parked on the roadside with signs advertising boiled peanuts. As he proceeded further southbound, he soon encountered some striking horse farms with grand entrances and well maintained fences that seemed to extend for as far as he could see.

In one of the larger towns, he stopped at a restaurant and enjoyed a large serving of barbecued ribs with several tasty side dishes, accompanied by some delicious iced tea. He asked the waitress for a rough estimate as to how long it would take him to get to Tampa Bay, and she told him it was probably another three hours or so.

Feeling very satisfied from the meal, he figured this might be a good time to make a call to inform Irwin of his current location. In the entrance of the restarant, he found a pay phone.

Irwin sounded absolutely thrilled to hear that B.G. was already just a few hours travel time away. He gave B.G. his address, but explained that it would really be the best course of action if they spoke again when he was closer, more like a half hour or so away from Tampa. This, Irwin assured him, would make it much easier to give specific directions for B.G. to follow.

CHAPTER THIRTY

Consistent with his recollection from the last time he had been in this part of Florida, there seemed to be a continuing increase in the number of stores, restaurants and other places of business that dotted both sides of the highway as B.G. proceeded southbound on the interstate.

After taking an exit and stopping for a fuel fill up, he took a moment to pull to the side of the combination truck stop and convenience store's parking lot, just to better observe his surroundings. Getting out of the vehicle, he brought with him an ice cream bar which he had just purchased along with the fuel. As he casually enjoyed the cold sweet flavor, he stood and watched while he felt the beams of the strong midday sun warm his face.

In addition to the flow of various shiny, newer luxury cars, it seemed every few minutes there was another large truck passing in front of his view as he looked on with interest. Some were the recognized tractor-trailers, some were large open-topped trucks, some were heavy duty dump trucks, some were smaller vehicles pulling open bed trailers, and some were pickup trucks with their beds filled to capacity.

He saw trucks carrying dirt, mostly topsoil of one grade or another. He saw trucks carrying massive loads of sod, cut into neat rectangular pieces, awaiting placement on some new or improved home sites.

He saw trucks carrying shrubs of numerous varieties and sizes. He saw trucks pulling long open trailers with very large palm trees, that had been removed from the soil at one place and were being relocated to provide shade, improve the scenery and continue to grow in the soils of a new location.

He saw horse trailers and cattle cars, moving their equine and bovine cargoes from one locale to another, with said passengers appearing to enjoy the ride.

He watched as trucks carrying what appeared to be junk---scrap metal, water heaters and old kitchen appliances, stacked tightly and fastened securely---chugged by him, probably either en route to another home or else to be remade and reborn as part of a system of recycling.

And then, intermingled with the others, he saw lots and lots of smaller cars and trucks, packed to the hilt with combinations of clothes, bicycles, fishing equipment and furniture, along with passengers which often included adults young and old, kids and dogs, all in visibly cramped quarters. These individuals were either taking an extended vacation or else were traveling to start a new life in a new location, and were doing it the old school way, that is of fitting everything possible into your only car and making it work somehow, damn it. And these groups, he knew well from personal experience, were always comprised of hardy souls who would certainly be the most grateful of all when they reached their destination.

He saw refrigerated trucks carrying seafood. Large and small, some brand new and others a little older, with signs on the sides that were either freshly painted, or from sun fading were in need of a touch-up. Each of them touting their contents as being fresh, nutritious and tasty, they too rumbled by, their drivers' wearing expressions which indicated time was of the essence.

He watched as large trucks pulling long trailers full of rocks roared past him. Rocks, in abundant numbers, taken from somewhere, sorted and now hurriedly being moved to somewhere else.

He saw vast quantities of hay being transported as well. Grass, of various types that had been cut, dried and formed into bales, some large round ones measuring five feet by five feet, others smaller, rectangular and tightly packed. Many of these could be coming from a long distance to fill the need that a dry summer here was creating. On trucks and trailers, from one place to another, the movement of this particular product of nature passed by in front of him.

One aspect of what he saw which made him chuckle out loud were the vehicles that motored by him that were quite obviously overloaded. Various cars, trucks, or vans, interspersed with the mainstream of the traffic coming into the area for fuel or food caught his attention by the fact that they would have baggage, freight, or passengers in such an excessive amount that the vehicles would be either sunken precariously close to the ground or else appearing to be about to have some of their cargo shift suddenly on the vehicle in the event they hit an unexpected bump in the road.

The more he observed this spectacle, this colorful, varied, and never ending parade of portability, the more in the way of pure entertainment it provided to him. Everyone who passed in front of him was intent on going, moving, bringing with them things, items, substances, products from another locale. And most of them acted as though they were late and had to continue as quickly as possible.

He returned to the SUV, and proceeded driving along the highway himself, joining in the procession.

Waxing philosophical, he thought to himself that there was a term, a label, a name for all that he had observed while standing outside the truck stop.

After ten more miles of driving, it came to him.

"Rearranging!" B.G. exclaimed in a booming voice.

He smiled at his discovery of the word he had been searching for in silence.

Then, he continued speaking to himself aloud.

"That's it...They are all rearranging! Altering, changing the order or position of something. Taking some of this, that, anything and everything, from here to there. In a madcap sort of way, that is really what much of our lives are spent doing. The rocks, the hay, the creatures from the sea, the livestock, the soil, the shrubs, the trees, their possessions...all these vehicles, all these people, that's what they are doing right now... they are just quite simply involved in a massive, wild task of rearranging."

Hearing his words, and the conclusion he'd reached, made him pause to let this revelation settle in his ongoing thoughts.

Perhaps I'm really on to something here, he mused.

Our life, in large part is mostly an ongoing project to rearrange.

Project.

There's that word which I've been using for another purpose.

Yet, now that I think of it, isn't that also just what I'm doing? I've even given it that title...The Project.

Having gone over these thoughts to himself, he now spoke his findings out loud.

"Yes, when it comes right down to it, it's just what I was hired to do. I too am undertaking, in The Project, my very own effort to distribute, which in this case is precisely the rearranging, of a large amount of currency. I am working to have it transported from one source into various locations so as to be in the hands of and under the control of others. So, like everyone else involved in some type of rearranging of their own, here, there and seemingly everywhere, I suppose I too should proceed towards getting it promptly accomplished."

B.G. gave a triumphant look into the vehicle's rear view mirror, before stating his closing thoughts on the subject.

"Rearranging...yes, that's it all right. And with that in mind, let us now continue, and advance confidently to complete The Project," B.G. announced with a new found enthusiasm, as he gripped the steering wheel with both hands while simultaneously pushing down on the accelerator.

CHAPTER THIRTY-ONE

He drove the next hour and a half in silence, taking in his surroundings with an optimistic perspective. The wide open expanses, the clear sky and hot sun, the occasional horse and cattle farms along with the numerous billboard advertisements indicating what the next exits offered kept him interested and alert. Even though he had spent an unconventional night sleeping in the SUV, he actually still felt quite rested and refreshed considering all the hours he'd been driving.

When he saw an upcoming rest area, he pulled into it. By his rough calculations, after estimating he was about an hour north of where Irwin was located, B.G. decided it was probably a good time to call him again using a pay phone.

Their call was short but enthusiastic. Irwin gave specific directions, and it turned out his place was actually north of the city proper, closer to the gulf side, which would enable B.G. to approach it sooner than he expected. But even though not in the city itself, Irwin told him it was a busy area and that the start of the afternoon rush hour would affect his time of arrival. Irwin ended the call by saying he was cooking up something special for dinner.

Returning to the highway, he was already seeing that there was a lot more traffic. While slowing his speed, he started to recall how he had first come to know Irwin. The crisis Irwin went through and how he unexpectedly ended up coming into a large amount of money was in itself quite a story. B.G. was truly pleased to have been of help to him along the way.

The last he had heard, Irwin still owned a large property back up in Pennsylvania, but had rented it out to a couple he had been friends with for years.

Irwin thereafter relocated to Florida, where he had bought a fine property. Irwin had sent him photos of that home-but had recently sold it and moved into the place where he was now living. B.G. wondered if his new residence would meet or exceed the previous one of which he had seen photographs.

He also couldn't help but speculate on just what it was that Irwin had needed to meet in person with B.G. about, and how or if it had any relation to The Project.

"Well," he said, now voicing his thoughts, "I'll find out soon enough."

*

Even though the actual town where Irwin was located was shown as a small dot on the map, the amount of traffic was overwhelming. While there appeared on the maps to be numerous smaller towns in the Tampa-Clearwater area, the reality is that when driving through that area it seemed to be one immense and continuous connection of urban sprawl.

Mile after mile, shopping malls, smaller plazas,

banks, pharmacies, restaurant chains, huge car dealer-
ships, and large grocery and department stores, seemed
to appear, disappear and then reappear over and over
again. Akin to watching a film loop that continued to
show the same scene, so too did the collection of businesses seem to repeat themselves as B.G. drove on and
on.

If he had not lived in the area in years past
himself, he would not have known from these bustling
surroundings that there were in fact some quiet, lovely
ocean beaches and parks all within twenty minutes or so
from these traffic jammed areas. While the persistent
stop and go rhythm of the drive was at times aggravating, Irwin's closing remarks to B.G. during their last call
were now giving him an extra incentive to arrive soon.

As one who had come to know well B.G.'s love
of good food, it carried special meaning that Irwin had
made it a point to mention that he was cooking something special for dinner.

CHAPTER THIRTY-TWO

Clearly, there must have been some mistake.

While B.G. reviewed the directions that Irwin had given him in detail, and believed he had followed them correctly, he obviously had to have made a wrong turn somewhere along the way.

Pulled over to the side of the road and parked in front of a diner, he stopped to carefully take in his surroundings. Instead of the type of upscale residential neighborhood where Irwin had previously lived, B.G. was now looking at what was primarily a somewhat run down commercial area. On one side of the road was a well known hotel chain, which looked a little shoddy. Opposite that was a large twenty-four hour grocery store. Next door was a used car dealership. There was a second hand shop, which, according to its sign, offered everything from used clothing to appliances and furniture. There was a pizza parlor and a Chinese restaurant. Nearby was a small drive-thru storefront that boasted in large letters on its window menu that it made the best fried chicken. And there were also several taverns, an auto repair garage, a pawn shop, and a health food market.

But no houses.

B.G. looked at the directions and the address Irwin had given him once more. He had driven up and down this road once already, but he decided to do it again.

Slowly, keeping his eyes peeled for the street numbers of the buildings, he drove in the far right lane with his turn signal blinking, so that he could pull over quickly and without much difficulty.

Up ahead, on the right, he saw a chain link fence and a gate. It was open.

The number corresponded to what Irwin had told him, and this was the correct street.

He pulled in, but as he saw the sign he again felt that there had to have been some mistake.

He read the sign once more, then said it aloud. "General Store-It-All."

Behind the secure and tall chain link fencing that surrounded the entire property, there were several very long, single story buildings, with numerous garage doors and no windows.

It was a public storage facility.

Perhaps, B.G. considered, the same address was repeated at the other end of the same road, one going one way and the another in the opposite direction. Like Main Street North or Main Street South, for example. That often happens, he thought, recalling in years past what he'd learned on one of his first jobs from his youth as a part-time delivery truck driver. In that instance, he'd have to travel another couple of miles back to where the numbers got smaller and then where they started over again.

Surely, that must be the case, he thought.

Nonetheless, he got out of the SUV and walked towards the office at the front of the many long buildings to ask for more specific directions.

*

The office door was locked. B.G. saw no signs of anyone nearby. He decided to return to the SUV and then backtrack a few miles to the other end of the road to see if the street numbers there matched the address he had been given.

As he reached to open the door of the SUV, he heard a voice boom out in his direction.

"Hey man, that's a nice set of wheels you got there. But where's the Cadillac?"

It was Irwin, walking around the corner from one of the storage buildings, wearing a white hat and a huge grin.

*

Even though Irwin had given an apparent explanation of this location, B.G. still failed to have a complete understanding of the situation.

While leading him to the backside of one of the long, solid looking storage buildings, Irwin told B.G. that he looked hungry. As they turned the corner, B.G. smelled something cooking.

Irwin led him to an outdoor barbecue grill which had a small amount of smoke pluming from it, and opened the cover to show what was inside.

"You got here just in time. I made some grilled chickens with roasted peppers and onions. Have a beer from the cooler and I'll fix you a plate."

*

Being out from behind the wheel after the long travel, with his feet up while relaxing on a chaise lounge chair, made his stiff body feel much better. And after consuming the grilled chicken, peppers and onions and a few bottles of beer, B.G.'s energy level and state of mind were also noticeably improving.

But he still was not clear on why Irwin was here at a storage facility cooking chickens.

After they shared some more chicken and beer, Irwin presented somewhat of an explanation.

"Now, listen up Mr. W., I want you to know that I really appreciate you coming down here. There are a lot of things to show you and tell you about, but you've had a long drive and I don't want to lay too much on you all at once. So, let me start by just giving you a quick tour of where we are."

Irwin then led B.G. to a spot at the front of several of the long, sturdy looking structures.

Walking over to the side of the building, there was an entrance door with a knob on it. Irwin turned the knob, opened the door and had B.G. follow him inside.

"Welcome Mr. W., to my home sweet home," Irwin said to B.G. as he switched on a light.

*

It was a delicate situation he was dealing with, B.G. thought.

Here was his old friend and client, a very talented artist with a growing renown, who had a few years ago come into a large amount of money, and who had up until recently owned and been living in an extremely nice home in a rather exclusive residential neighborhood near Tampa.

But now, here he was calling a storage unit his home sweet home.

Had his old friend the eccentric artist lost his marbles and gone crazy?

Or was his old friend now completely out of money?

B.G. decided he had to proceed cautiously so as not to offend Irwin, while at the same time realizing that he also needed to know what was going on.

He took a moment to look closely at Irwin.

He hadn't really aged at all since the last time B.G. had seen him. In fact, he looked very healthy now. His distinctive ponytail was neat and clean, his skin was clear and tanned, and he had gained a little weight which actually improved his appearance.

His blue eyes, which were always a little bloodshot, appeared alert and were twinkling.

He was speaking clearly and in complete sentences. In their short time together here, he'd already even made a few jokes, which were quite funny. He seemed clearheaded and logical in how he presented what he was saying.

"But listen to what he was saying!" B.G. said to himself.

Irwin was currently describing to B.G. how he liked the area, and that there was so much all within easy walking distance.

"Pretty much any type of food you want, in a sit down place or take out, you can find close by here. The big grocery store across the street has everything you need. There are some good bars as well, and a branch of a local library is about a mile away. And the best part is that the beach with the warm waters of the Gulf of Mexico is an easy fifteen minute walk, or if you ride a bike or take a car, it's five minutes, tops. But maybe most of all, I like the mix of people that are around here. Really, it's an ideal location for me."

B.G. finished his beer, then looked up at the palm tree he was sitting under.

"How have you been feeling Irwin? You look good, but have you had any health problems at all?" B.G. then inquired tactfully.

"Mr. W., honestly, with all this warm weather and sunshine, I'm really relaxed. I eat well, I've put on some weight, I sleep great and I've never felt better."

All right, B.G. thought to himself. He certainly seems sane all right. Then it must be a money problem.

But after several more beers over the next hour, B.G. was extremely surprised to learn that it wasn't a financial reason that had brought Irwin into this current situation at all.

*

The interior of the storage unit that Irwin had showed B.G. was furnished quite nicely. It measured about thirty feet long and ten feet wide, and at one narrow end there was a closed garage type door which was the same type that the other units seemed to have. Within that space Irwin had arranged his easel and some of his art equipment, as well as a couch that contained a large pull out bed, a dining table with two chairs, several standing cabinets with doors that held clothing, and a couple of bookshelves against the walls. At the opposite end was a large bed with a nightstand and lamp. There was also a smaller upright refrigerator along with a two burner electric hotplate and a few pots and pans on a counter top. In contrast to the hot summer temperatures outside, the interior was cool and very comfortable.

"Climate controlled," Irwin was explaining. "In two of the three buildings the units are all air conditioned."

It was all very pleasant looking. But B.G. noted two things it was lacking.

"Irwin, this is quite nice. But there isn't a window... and by the way, what about a bathroom?"

As with most units here, with just two exceptions, a window was not available in this unit, Irwin explained. But a community bathroom had just recently become available.

"One of the guys who keeps his stuff here used to be a plumber. He added a six foot extension to the main office there, tapped into the water and drain lines, and put in a full bathroom that we can all get to without ever going into the office. It's always open so go and check it out," Irwin added, while pointing towards a door at the end of the adjacent building about twenty feet away from them.

B.G. had taken note of the word "we" that Irwin had chosen in describing the use of the bathroom. Following his suggestion, B.G. went over to it, and found the facilities to be new, clean and comfortable. In addition to a working sink, toilet and tub with a shower, it also had a large counter top with an expansive mirror.

When he returned from using the bathroom, B.G. had another question.

"So Irwin, the owner doesn't mind that you stay here and that a bathroom was installed for general use?"

"That's the beauty of this place. The owner doesn't know about the bathroom or about much else. And he doesn't care at all. He's an investor that lives out of state and travels out of the country a lot, and hasn't even been here for three years. The guy who oversees this is a friend of mine, and he's cool about what's going on here. In fact, he thought adding the outside bathroom was a great idea. The ladies really like it too. The guy who oversees it has been the manager, sort of, for years, and as long as the owner gets his monthly paycheck from the storage unit rentals, he's happy. Unfortunately, the guy who manages it is in and out of rehab, and he doesn't want the owner to know it, so he's been real glad to have me around to keep an eye on the place."

CHAPTER THIRTY-THREE

It took about another hour, and for B.G. to have consumed at least seven or eight beers, before he felt comfortable enough with Irwin to bring up the subject of his friend's current finances, or possible lack thereof.

Irwin was grilling two more chickens when B.G. got up off the lounge chair and walked over to him.

Even though B.G. had eaten a lot of food already, he couldn't help but recognize that the smoke from latest batch on the grill smelled really appetizing.

"So listen Irwin. I'm going to ask you something, and I'm not doing it to pry at all, and I certainly don't want to cause you any offense. But I have to ask you, seeing all this where you are living..."

Irwin misread B.G.'s intentions, and interrupted him with a reply.

"Not to worry, Mr.W. If it's pot you're wondering about, yeah I still partake, but only a couple of times a week, and I'm careful so as not to do it in such a way that will get me in any trouble like I had when I was back up north. And by the way, it's really a lot more common here for recreational purposes. I mean, it's practically everywhere."

B.G. smiled at the response, as Irwin started to turn over the chickens. He noted that Irwin still called him the formal "Mr. W.", and although he had repeatedly in the past said he could use 'B.G.', Irwin had consistently declined. Irwin had stated his using the term 'Mr. W.' sounded more respectful and he liked to hear the sound of it.

"Well, that's fine with me, not a problem at all..but actually that wasn't what I was going to ask you about," B.G. replied in response to Irwin's misunderstood reference to marijuana.

"Oh, really? Okay, then continue and ask away."

"All right Irwin, let me get right to it. The last I knew, you had come into a large amount of money, over a million in cash and property. And then I heard from you that you had bought a real nice place down in the Tampa Bay area, you still had the house up north that you were renting out, and your art work was doing well. But now, when I come down to see you, well, you tell me that your home is in a storage unit...and I, well, I just have to wonder, did you lose all your money and is that why you're living here now?"

"It's a fair question, Mr. W., and I can see why you'd be a bit curious about my situation. But let me tell you, it's not that I have any problem at all."

"Really?" B.G. asked with a hint of disbelief in his voice.

Irwin put down the tongs he was using to turn the chicken, and looked directly at B.G.

"Really and truly, Mr. W. You'll be pleased to know that I took your advice and I was careful not to fritter away the money that you helped me come into."

"Well, that's certainly good to hear."

Before continuing, Irwin got them both another beer.

"In fact, I'm still loaded. And actually, since I sold that house outside of Tampa, I made a good profit, so I now have even more than I did when I first came down here."

B.G. was hearing the words, but still not comprehending the message.

"But Irwin, if that's the case, and you still have plenty of money, why would you be residing in a small unit that is only used for storing people's belongings?"

"Well Mr. W.," Irwin said as he held up his beer, "If you'll join me in a toast to good friends getting together again, I'll start to fill you in on some of the reasons."

*

It took another two beers and a large bag of potato chips, but by the time the beer and the chips were gone, B.G. had a clearer understanding of Irwin's current situation.

Never one to comply with the norms of society, Irwin had nonetheless purchased an upscale home in a well to do neighborhood about two years ago. He had bought it for a good price, and was looking forward to living there indefinitely after he had settled into the place.

However, it soon became apparent to both Irwin and the "uptight neighbors" as he referred to them, that the match was not a good fit. In short, an eccentric artist who has eccentric friends visiting at odd hours was not in keeping with the norms of the neighborhood. As a good example of what was perhaps the last straw, the local homeowners association of the community had lodged a formal complaint against Irwin, for as best as he could describe it, just because late one afternoon he was painting a portrait of a scantily clad couple while he himself was wearing only underwear and standing outside on his own front lawn.

After talking to the realtor who had originally sold him the property and expressing his disenchantment with the community, it turned out that there was a strong market for just the type of house which Irwin owned in that area. In fact, within four months after the realtor listed it, Irwin had sold the property and reaped a handsome profit.

"Well, I'm happy things worked out for you," B.G. later stated before adding, "But I still don't see why you are living in a storage facility after all that turned out so well."

Irwin was pleased to continue his explanation.

B.G. noticed that Irwin was now taking the chicken off of the grill and putting it on a folding table, where he had set up plates, cups and napkins. Wondering why his friend might be doing this, B.G. politely stated that he had really had plenty to eat and that he didn't need any more for the time being.

"Oh that's okay. You see, I figured we'd had enough, but I'm not setting this up for us. It's for the ladies."

While this comment further puzzled B.G., before he could make further inquiry, Irwin proceeded to continue with his prior explanation. At about the same time, B.G. took note that it was starting to get dark already, and saw that an outdoor light above the chain link entrance had come on already.

"Anyway, it's all about eighty dollars a month. That's all it costs for me to live here. Can you believe that? Eighty dollars! Now even though like I said I've got plenty of money, right now after seeing those neighborhoods, I just can't make myself pay a lot for something when I know I can be happier in a place like this for now. Probably some time down the line I may decide to relocate again, but I tell you, at this point in my life, I really like the whole idea of living here. In this place, I can do what I want, when I want. Nobody will complain. And I've already made more friends here than the whole time when I was in that expensive neighborhood. Hey, and speaking of which, I see some of them over there. Yes sir, Mr. W., here come the ladies now."

B.G. looked over once, then turned away, and quickly looked back again.

Approaching him from a distance were two very shapely women, each wearing short skirts, halter tops, and high heels.

Before they got to within earshot, Irwin whispered a bit more information.

"They're hookers. Nice people, and they've been through some rough times. This is on their route one day a week, so I set up a little something for them to eat. Let me introduce you."

Within a half hour there were four more who arrived, making six in total. Irwin graciously introduced B.G. as his friend and trusted attorney from up north, and the reaction couldn't have been more favorable. The ladies were at first kind and courteous, but quickly bawdy and fun loving shortly afterward.

They ate the chicken and had a beer each. They chatted about the area, the best place for this or that type of food, and how some of them were from a different part of the state, while others had moved here from up north.

The ladies stayed for a while longer and then said their pleasant goodbyes.

The rest of the night was a bit of a blur, due in part to the growing weariness that the effects from the long drive had caused B.G. to feel. As a contributing factor, however, no doubt the ample amount of beer along with the tropical heat served to add to his fatigue.

He couldn't remember exactly when, but at some time after the ladies left, B.G. met a gentleman who was another one of Irwin's friends who had stopped by to say hello. Before the visitor left, the three of them had more beer and some fresh popcorn. Afterward, Irwin suggested that B.G. move the SUV to a more secluded spot closer to another storage building.

That other building turned out to be where Irwin showed B.G. the "guest quarters," being a separate storage unit where B.G. was to spend the night. With the door opened, it too looked very comfortably furnished with a large bed, a dining table, and a reclining armchair next to a reading lamp.

Once B.G. had taken a few items from the SUV and put them into his storage unit, he walked over to the bathroom and brushed his teeth. Approaching the mirror, he saw a bleary eyed but perpetually grinning Wumpkey looking sheepishly back at him.

After emerging from the bathroom, a moment later he noticed that Irwin was squinting and seemed to be studying him extra carefully.

"Is something wrong?" B.G. asked pointedly.

"No, nothing at all. It's just that as I'm looking here at you, I'm reminded that you still look in pretty good shape. And for all that you eat, I'm surprised that you haven't really gained much at all in the way of extra weight since I last saw you. You must have what the experts call a good metabolism."

"Actually, although I don't like to boast, I think it's pretty much top of the line," B.G. said with a grin as he finished his beer.

After they said good night, and once he had stretched out on the bed in the "guest quarters," B.G. remembered Irwin saying that he had a lot of important things to talk about in the morning, and that he'd be making steak and eggs for breakfast.

With that in mind, he slept soundly.

CHAPTER THIRTY-FOUR

It took him a while to become aware of just where he was when he woke up.

Since his location was completely dark, due to the fact that it had no window, it added some mystery at first to his slowly awakening thought process. And because of this total absence of light in his surroundings, he had no idea whether it was past sunrise, or even what time it might be.

Gradually, he recalled that he was in the makeshift guest quarters of a storage unit in which Irwin had set up his own residence nearby. As he got to his feet, the feeling in his head also quickly brought to mind that he had consumed a fair amount of beer last night.

B.G. found the door on his second lap around the interior of the darkened storage unit. When he opened it, the harsh light of the midday sun made him immediately wince and retreat.

With the door left partially open, he was able to get dressed and find his toothbrush and shaving gear. Slowly he returned to the doorway and then ambled to the bathroom.

*

Twenty minutes later, after a refreshing shower, B.G. emerged from the bathroom feeling greatly improved. A greeting corroborated that perception.

"Man, you look a lot better coming out of the bathroom than when you first went in!" Irwin chortled as he saw B.G. walk between the buildings.

"Good morning, Irwin," B.G. said energetically.

"I think you mean, 'Good afternoon'. Morning already packed up and left a while ago. But whenever you're ready, I'll start the steak and eggs for you."

B.G. was astounded to learn that it was just about two o'clock and that he had slept nearly twelve hours straight. He had certainly been tired from the long days of driving, and that in combination with the large amount of food, drink and extended dark environment must have all contributed to his lengthy, peaceful slumber.

Realizing that it had been some time since he'd slept so long and so deeply, he was feeling better and better.

Although Irwin had already eaten, he shared some of the beef from the steak and eggs that were prepared for B.G. The fresh orange juice and toast added to the hearty breakfast, mid-afternoon style, which was enjoyed while they relaxed under the shade of the tall palm trees.

Not long afterward, as the two sat across from one another, a period of silence followed. While there were distant noises of traffic and planes and yes, even boats from the nearby waterway leading to the open ocean, B.G. noticed a sense of calmness he was experiencing as he came to realize there was no tension, no hurry, no rush, no stress, no need to do anything during this time they were sharing.

"Can you feel it?" Irwin asked a few minutes later, breaking the silence.

"Feel what?"

"The worry free lifestyle that's in the air. I picture it kind of like an invisible fog that quietly moves in and settles over you and visits for a while before it moves on. It comes and goes, but right here, right now, it's close by. I can feel it and for me, I know it's just what I need."

*

A bit later in the afternoon, Irwin brought out some more beer and potato chips. As they held their bottles, Irwin looked over at B.G.

"You know, I can't tell you just how much I appreciate your visit. And I didn't want to bother you with what was going on, but I really figured it was something that could be important to you."

"Well, I'm glad to see that you're doing well," B.G. answered. "And even though this whole new living situation is a bit out of the ordinary, I'm starting to see how it has its benefits, and it fits your lifestyle more than some upscale neighborhood would. Anyway, I'm here, and I'm rested up. Now, tell me about this situation, this important new development that you described on the phone and felt I should know about."

"Okay, I didn't want to lay too much on you all at once, before you'd had a chance to recover from the thousand plus miles you drove. But you seem to be ready to listen. So, here goes."

Irwin began to describe how he had been overseeing the storage facilities, and came to know that one of the units was paid for but always kept empty. Then he came to find out that such empty unit was actually one of two that were being rented in the name of Mr. Kurt Koppy.

Now, Irwin had known Kurt for well over a year, and he reminded B.G. that it was he who had given B.G.'s name to Kurt as a very capable attorney he could trust. Even though they were in Florida at the time, Kurt informed he had some business and friends up north and that he could use the services of an attorney in the states in which B.G. had been practicing. Irwin went on to inform that one of the storage units still held some of Kurt's belongings which Kurt had put there after his Florida warehouse burned.

B.G. nodded, recalling how the man January had described the incident when the two had met in Maine. Evidently, Irwin was quite familiar with the background and details of that occurrence.

"But that isn't what I called you about. What I felt you should know is that when I talked with him last week, he said he was real pleased with you and felt very comfortable that you would provide invaluable assistance, to handle things 'as you see fit.' Those were his exact words. And then Kurt said he wasn't sure if he should bother you any more, but he really hoped if and when it became necessary that you could help him with this new complication as well."

B.G.'s heart was starting to race.

"So, you're telling me that Kurt Koppy is okay, and he called you about a week ago?"

"Oh yeah, he's doing fine. But Kurt didn't call me. The fact is, he met with me right here before he asked me to store something else for him. Then he even offered to give the item to me if I wanted it."

B.G. was now leaning forward on the edge of his chair.

"Well-can you tell me what the item is?"

"Actually, I can do better than that. If you follow me, I'll show it to you.

212

CHAPTER THIRTY-FIVE

B.G. followed Irwin closely as he walked back towards another section of one of the storage facilities. Taking a set of keys out of his pocket, he stopped in front of one of the garage style doors that was identical to the dozens on all the other nearby units.

Unlocking the handle, Irwin then proceeded to lift the garage door upwards, as it started to roll into its overhead tracks. However, he stopped after raising the door just three feet. Then, he motioned for B.G. to bend somewhat to fit through the small opening and to follow him inside.

It was still too dark to see much, and it got even darker when to B.G.'s surprise, Irwin started to pull the garage door down and then closed it all the way behind them.

"I want to keep this shut for privacy. Stay here, and just as soon as I find the light switch, we'll be able to see fine," Irwin remarked.

A minute later, the room was filled with the light from an overhead bulb.

And what B.G. saw made his eyes grow wide.

Several feet in front of him was a compact, late model, silver motor home.

*

"I thought it would be a tight fit, but actually it fit in quite nicely. The unit is thirty feet long, and the motor home measures twenty-three, so there is plenty of extra space left where we walked in," Irwin was explaining.

B.G. still had not spoken.

"Overall it's in great shape. But there is something, some part of it, that is important for you to see. Come on over to this side."

B.G. followed Irwin over to the passenger side of the motor home, where Irwin proceeded to open the tall side door near the built in footstep.

As Irwin brought B.G. closer, he held the door open wide. The combination of the overhead light from the storage unit with the vehicle's interior dome light illuminated the interior well.

The inside was neat and clean. But Irwin's extended index finger which was pointing towards the floor drew his eyes to something that B.G. did not want to see.

On the light colored carpeting behind the front seats, about the size of a full sized bed pillow, was a large reddish brown stain.

And next to that was a heavy metal object about a foot in length, the kind seen in home gyms or fitness studios, with the number "30" on each end. By its size and number, it appeared to be a steel dumbbell used for exercising with a weight of thirty pounds. On its outside surface, B.G. saw that it bore some of the very same reddish brown colored stain as was on the adjacent carpeting.

"That's blood, isn't it?" B.G. said gravely.

"I wished I could say it was paint. But you're right, those are bloodstains."

*

Irwin was continuing to speak, but B.G. wasn't giving his friend his full attention. He heard the words, but did not fully absorb them. His mind was racing to other thoughts, which were not nearly as cheerful as was Irwin's tone.

Slowly, B.G.'s ears zoned back in, and he caught up with what Irwin was now talking about.

"Anyhow, the motor home is registered in the name of Kurt's sister. She and her husband bought it new a few years ago, and had made all these great plans to travel as soon as her husband retired. But then he was diagnosed with lung cancer, and just three months after he'd retired he passed away. His sister was so torn up by it, that she couldn't bear to look at it anymore, it made her so sad. When Kurt came to visit her, she offered to sell it to him for next to nothing, but on one condition...that he also take their big Newfoundland dog as part of the deal...Kurt agreed, and his sister kept it registered and insured in her name, but she had the vehicle's title signed and completed so it's all ready to transfer legally to the next owner...just needs the name filled out. Kurt thought that would be him, but due to some unexpected circumstances..." Irwin's voice trailed off.

B.G. was still staring vacantly at the bloodstains on the carpet.

"Anyway, I have a question for you," said Irwin. "Mr. W., can we keep it?"

The question brought B.G.'s attention back to the present.

"What?"

"The motor home. Now that you've heard the background, I want to know. So, tell me Mr. W., can we keep it?"

B.G. now looked directly at Irwin as he repeated the question, and focused his thinking completely on the man in front of him. And at that moment, instead of a middle aged, wealthy, successful albeit unconventional artist standing before him, he saw something quite different.

Now, in Irwin's blue eyes was the pleading, sparkling, hopeful entreaty akin to that of an eleven year old boy who was asking his parents if they could keep a stray puppy that had found its way onto their property.

Then, as if to confirm the accuracy of B.G.'s observation, came Irwin's one word, follow up inquiry.

"Please?" he asked enthusiastically.

*

An hour later Irwin was cooking burgers on the grill with B.G. sitting nearby under the tall palm trees. Irwin had told B.G. that he looked like he needed a beer, and at that moment B.G. couldn't have agreed more.

When it came time for Irwin to flip the burgers, B.G. was on his second beer and had started slicing the onions and tomatoes. Irwin brought over some fresh, thick slices of bread and when the burgers were done they put them all together and began eating.

They finished the burgers and beer in relative silence, enjoying the meal and at the same time collecting their thoughts.

Irwin then opened a new bag of potato chips and

offered up another round of cold beers.

"Kurt looked okay when you saw him?" B.G. broke the silence.

"Yeah, he was a little stressed out looking, but otherwise he was healthy and doing fine."

"So it's pretty clear that wasn't his blood on the carpet."

"That's right, the blood was not his."

"Did he explain the bloodstains to you?"

"Only very briefly. His feeling was that the less he told me the better it was, since he didn't want me to be involved in what happened previously. But he made it a point to say that it wasn't as bad as it looked."

"Did he tell you that there were news reports back in Pennsylvania about a dead body being dumped from a motor home that looked just like his?"

"He did mention that he felt he was getting some bad press about the whole thing, but that trying to give an explanation would only cause him major problems."

"Bad press!" B.G. exclaimed. "The police have a witness who saw a dead body being dumped from what appears to be the same vehicle. And now we see large blood stains inside the very same motor home. The cops issued a bulletin for that motor home, and it has been on the news virtually every night for the past couple of weeks."

"Well, I guess that probably explains why he wanted to get it out of circulation," Irwin pointed out.

"And I take it you don't know where Kurt is now?" B.G. asked.

Irwin shook his head calmly. "All I can tell you is that when I asked him where he was going to, he said 'it's a place called far away.' But actually, if you know

Kurt, to hear that wasn't really surprising."

B.G. was trying to understand Irwin's nonchalant demeanor. But then, he remembered, it was a rare occasion when Irwin would show signs of being upset at much of anything.

The two of them stayed quiet for another moment.

"You really don't think it's as bad as it looks?" B.G. then asked, with a hint of hopefulness in his voice.

"Nah, I know Kurt. He may be on the shady side, but he's no serial killer or anything like that."

"You're really pretty calm about this, overall," B.G. noted.

"Well, the way I look at it, it could be a lot worse," Irwin pointed out.

"But how so?"

"Well, let's face it, he could have driven here and stored the motor home in the storage unit with the dead person still inside. After that long ride, can you imagine the smell and how it would have reduced the value of the motor home? That sure would have been a lot worse, wouldn't it?"

Envisioning that possibility, B.G. had to grudgingly agree.

CHAPTER THIRTY-SIX

When the dinner hour rolled around, Irwin was preparing bratwursts on the grill. Along with that, the evening's menu was to include a large fresh salad, and a plate of boiled turnip greens topped with melted butter and salt.

"I know how you work, and you'll think better with a full stomach, Mr. W. Already, I can tell you're getting close to figuring out the best way for us to handle this," Irwin had told B.G. with encouragement.

To take a break from all that was weighing on his mind, B.G. told Irwin that he should really give Carol a call. To his suprise, Irwin quickly pulled out his own phone, dialed the number, and than handed the phone over to B.G. She was pleased to hear that he was enjoying Irwin's company and that he was getting a lot of rest along with plenty of food. When she asked how the matter involving Irwin's request for his visit was going, all B.G. could say was that it had gotten a bit more complicated. While he wanted to share his thoughts with someone, he opted to make no mention of the hookers, the bloodstains, or the fact that he was now sleeping in a dark storage unit. Even though his wife was compassionate and understanding, everyone had their limits.

"Oh, I'm certain the two of you will figure out how to handle it. Just be sure to take care of yourself, and don't forget to follow through on the distribution part of it as well. As I told you before you left, I think we'll both be really glad when that is all over with," she had told him reassuringly.

Hearing her make mention of the distribution, B.G. realized that he'd completely forgotten about the large amount of cash that still remained in the SUV. Yes, of course that would also require some more attention pretty soon as well, he thought.

*

After having several servings of the the bratwurst and requisite beer, the situation he was now involved with did seem to come into an improved state of clarity. As he and Irwin sat across from one another, the onset of nighttime seemed to invigorate Wumpkey.

Motioning for Irwin's attention, he nodded in favor of the offer of more chips and another beer, before snapping his fingers and making an announcement.

"All right. I've been giving this a lot of thought, and I think I have some ideas for how we should proceed," he began.

"Great!" was Irwin's reply. "I knew those bratwursts and fresh greens would help."

"To begin with," B.G. continued, "this is all heavy duty stuff we're dealing with. And I'm not even talking about what Kurt Koppy did or didn't do yet, I'm just addressing our role. I mean, there are a lot of things that we're in the middle of, and probably going to proceed with, which are illegal, to put it gently."

Hearing this, Irwin seemed even more intrigued. Clearly, B.G. was now talking his language.

"Okay, first of all the motor home. It needs to have us do a major renovation and cleaning. The carpeting, that steel dumbbell, it's all implicating. I mean, overall the vehicle sure is in nice shape, but it poses some definitely dangerous problems and risks as it stands."

"Like what, exactly?" Irwin inquired.

"Well, to start with it's a crime scene. And realize, this is a matter involving a dead body, therefore it is automatically seen as extremely serious. So, if we take steps to clean it up, right off the bat we're involved with tampering with, destroying and or falsifying evidence relating to a homicide. Then there is that dumbbell with the blood...that, investigators would likely conclude, appears to be a murder weapon. Added to that, there could be an umbrella of charges including aiding and abetting in Kurt's concealment, helping a fugitive, etc. Throw in the interstate travel and it gets even more involved. In short, there are more ways than I can come up with right now that our intended conduct would be breaking the law...And that doesn't even include the other separate matter that Kurt wanted me to handle when he met with me up north," B.G. added as an afterthought.

Irwin gave a slight nod, as if he knew all about what B.G. was referring to, before asking, "With all that in mind, now what do you suggest we do?"

"Well, practically, I don't see much in the way of reasonable alternatives. So, since we're in it this deep, and we certainly don't want to give trouble a cordial invitation to visit us, I say..." At this point B.G. paused, rose to a standing position, stretched out his hands for added emphasis, and then proclaimed, "Let the law-breaking begin!"

Irwin's eyes were now gleaming with excitement.

"I just knew it would be fun when you got here, Mr. W."

*

Their work to get rid of the evidence began the next morning after a late breakfast. B.G. still wasn't used to the total darkness in his storage unit turned sleeping quarters, but he had to admit the complete lack of light during his lengthy resting hours was making him feel very good.

When the two of them returned to the storage unit which contained the motor home, Irwin again took the precaution of closing the door quickly after they were inside. Irwin explained that there were a few other customers who sometimes came regarding their own items that were being stored, and he didn't want anyone to get a glimpse of what they were undertaking.

Once inside the enclosed unit, B.G. took a close look at the entire vehicle, starting with the exterior. As far as he could determine, there were no visible signs of any damage or impact on the vehicle whatsoever. That ruled out any chance that the bloodstains and dead body could have been the result of an act of vehicular homicide or the like. No, from B.G.'s untrained eye, the evidence indicated that the man died while inside the motor home.

That made the obvious facts weigh against Kurt even moreso.

This morning, their closer inspection of the interior of the motor home impressed upon them just how much blood that was there. They came to find blood spots and spattering outside of the main large stain on the carpet, going to a wider extent than previously noticed. The dumbbell too had spots of blood on more of its surface than just its top side, indicating it had been moving during the time the liquid was flowing.

B.G. looked at the carpet some more, then shook his head.

"Well, I mistakenly thought that the blood stains were in a more restricted area, but they are spread out more than I realized. And if you look closely, you can see how some of the blood trails toward the side door. That would corroborate that the dead body was in fact dragged and dumped from the vehicle, just as the police reported that their purported witness told them. You know, the subject of blood stains and blood spattering has developed into a science all its own, and frankly the prosecution can often use it to put together their own scenario, a reenactment of their own version of what they say must have happened, which is specifically designed to help them get a conviction."

Irwin was watching B.G. intently as he put these thoughts together.

"And Irwin, you may not know this, but the homicide investigators work with forensic teams, and together they can collect a hair or carpet fiber and then match it to show that in fact the victim was at a particular location before or during their time of death. And those distinctive fibers or hairs can be microscopic and not seen by the naked eye. By the way, this is just an overview of the basic steps they use to investigate a major crime, because they can use a lot more advanced methods as well."

"So what does all that tell you about what we're dealing with here?"

"It tells me a couple of things. The first is that there are many people doing long prison terms because they were convicted based on evidence that is not nearly as strong as what we're looking at here. And the second thing it tells me is that we need to do a major clean up of this motor home---remove the entire carpet, destroy it and replace it with new carpeting as soon as possible, and along with that we need to give the whole inside a thorough wash down, and be sure to get that dumbbell completely cleaned, and then maybe paint it. Later, we may want to get rid of it, but for the time being I suggest giving it a quick make over right here."

Irwin looked at B.G. with a serious expression, after which he was silent for a several moments.

"We can do all that," he then stated in a matter of fact tone. "And we can start right now."

*

The two of them worked all afternoon and into the nighttime. Along the way, Irwin recalled that there was some carpet and padding left in another storage unit by an older man who had a flooring company that had gone out of business. The man had never come to recover his materials, and his storage rentals payments were several months in arrears, so he obviously had no intention to keep the items.

The actual removal of the carpeting from the motor home was a bit more involved that it first appeared. Fortunately, it turned out that Irwin had once worked as a part-time carpet installer, which made the work go more efficiently. Still, it took a lot of time and effort, and before they were done Irwin had actually taken out the seats of the vehicle in order to completely extract all the carpeting along the floor.

As they pulled it out, they cut the carpet and pad-ding into small square sections,and then put those into black plastic garbage bags which they placed near the inside of the unit's garage door. They kept the section with the most visible bloodstains separate in a double bag with a piece of tape marking it on the outside.

After all the carpet and padding had been re-moved, the two of them made an interesting discovery. Hidden underneath the section of padding in the very back of the motor home, they found three license plates, each one from a different state.

Seeing these, they both figured that such were kept to help create the impression of another identity. Noticing that one of the plates had a "camper" desig-nation on it, B.G. further surmised that they may well even have been taken from other similar looking motor homes and kept handy in reserve, as a well thought out precaution if necessary to throw off possible efforts to flag or locate this particular vehicle. He told Irwin that it wouldn't surprise him if the license plates were from states that still had two plates for each vehicle, front and back. He knew of capers where this was done and the victims had not discovered for some time that one plate was even missing.

Irwin remarked offhandedly what B.G. was al-ready starting to realize.

"That Kurt, he's slick all right. And he'll really be hard to find if he wants to stay hidden."

*

After a thorough vacuuming, Irwin, with bucket, rags and mop in hand, next gave the vehicle's interior, including the dumbbell, a very meticulous overall wash-ing.

While they worked, B.G. was impressed to observe how determined Irwin was to help get the job completed. Although his previous carpet installing experience had been only in apartments and houses, he was able to carry his skills over to figure out how to do the same in the motor home.

It was already dark when Irwin had put down and secured the last portion of the new pad and carpet. Then they both lifted the vehicle's heavy seats back into the vehicle and fastened them back in place.

When they were all done, they stepped back and proudly admired their work. The old carpet, other than the bloodstained portion, had been in good condition. But the brand new carpeting that was now on the motor home's floor gave it a fresh, bright look that was most appealing.

With that part of their work completed success-fully, they turned to look at the black plastic garbage bags placed near the door.

"What about these?" came the question from Irwin that they were both thinking.

Exactly what to do with the bags would clearly require some more thought.

But rather than dwell on it right now, Irwin said he had a better idea.

"What do you like on your pizza?" he asked B.G.

CHAPTER THIRTY-SEVEN

"The guy who makes this pizza came down here from New York about twenty years ago. His place is close by, and he makes the best pie that I've been able to find the whole time I've been here," Irwin was saying to B.G. as they were walking on the sidewalk back to the storage units. They each held one extra large, warm, pizza box that if examined closely, could be seen to be just slightly steaming.

The aroma from the boxes was making B.G.'s mouth water. In their concentrated effort to quickly clean up the motor home, they completely overlooked how late it had gotten and that they had worked right through the lunch and dinner hours.

A half hour later they were finishing up their meal and enjoying their second round of beer. B.G. had to agree with Irwin that the guy from New York made an excellent pizza, and was pleased that in addition to the pepperoni and mushroom that even anchovies were available on the menu as one of the toppings he had selected.

Now with appetites satisfied, they relaxed in their comfortable positions on the outdoor lounge chairs. It was a calm night, with little if any breeze and they could see the moon poking through the palm fronds on the upper portions of the trees above them.

"Well, we accomplished quite a bit working together on that," B.G. remarked.

"Yeah, it went pretty smoothly considering all we had to deal with. And now that it's all cleaned up, what do you think we should do with those bags?"

"I was just thinking about that. My first instinct would be to personally make them disappear, maybe by burning them in a bonfire someplace. But from what I heard on the radio on the drive here, there's a drought in the state and there are alot of burning restrictions this summer. So that's probably not the best choice."

"I know somebody who might help with that, but he lives in the country and there's a lot of dry brush where he lives in the woods that goes on for miles. If he started a bonfire, it would probably attract a lot of attention, and even so it would be a bit of a drive to get there."

"My main concern is the one bag with the tape on it, that held the sections with all the big stains on it."

"You know, how about this. We could burn that one bag right now in a steel barrel I have. With it being dark, the smoke wouldn't be too noticeable, or if it is that small amount could be seen as just those guys cooking some more on the grill."

"What about the rest of the bags?"

"It's already after midnight. The garbage pickup is coming up this morning. And actually, the trucks come by here in about four hours. We could just stay up, I could cook a chicken," Irwin suggested.

"I like that idea. It probably is overly cautious, but I really would feel better if I actually see them get picked up myself. I would sleep better knowing that I saw those bags get lumped together with all the other garbage as the truck is driven away."

"Yeah, I know what you mean. Okay then, let's start to get the barrel fire and the grill burning together."

Doing it in small amounts, the contents of the bag with the largest bloodstained carpet and the pad that was with it still took quite a while to burn. Even though it ignited quickly from the help of a splash of cooking oil that Irwin poured on, the carpet seemed to get melted as it burned, and gave off a very thick smoke for an extended period. Seeing this, they were glad that they had chosen to do it at night and kept the flames contained just in the barrel.

Eventually, once the fire had transformed the carpet and reduced it to only a small melted lump which continued to slowly burn, Irwin put the chicken on the nearby grill.

*

As the two of them drank beer and ate chicken and potato chips, the hours passed quickly. They enjoyed watching the night sky, as the stars and planes came into view and then disappeared through oncoming clouds.

At ten minutes past four o'clock in the morning, the roar of a large engine was heard off in the distance on the roadway. Shortly afterward, the bright headlights of the garbage truck came into view, its identity unmistakable due to its size as well as its regular stops.

Irwin and B.G. carried the remaining black garbage bags containing the carpet and pads, along with two other bags that held food scraps, pizza boxes and household garbage out to the road and placed them on the curb. As the massive truck approached, the large lights illuminated both of them as they gave the driver and his assistant a friendly wave.

In a few minutes, all the bags had been tossed into the back of the truck, and became blended with the countless other similar bags and various types of refuse.

Watching as the truck proceeded down the road while making its successive stops, simultaneously they felt a combination of fatigue and relief sweep over them. Slowly, they headed back past the chain link fence and the gate that was now closed behind them.

"Well, I'll sleep better knowing we finished all that," B.G. said as they walked along.

"I'll second that for sure. Now it's time for some well deserved rest. Then, when we wake up, we'll be having western omelettes for breakfast."

It started to rain not long after B.G. and Irwin had bid each other goodnight and headed back to their respective lodgings.

Especially to those who aren't from the region, the Florida downpours can appear to be very heavy. B.G. had forgotten that when it comes, just how long and hard it rains in this area. The sound of the rainfall, under normal conditions can be very loud indeed. However, when one is under a metal roof, with limited interior ceilings installed, the sound of a such a deluge is greatly compounded and can upon first impression seem to approach a near deafening level.

Hearing this, it first startled B.G. as he was stretched out on his bed in the total darkness of the storage unit. Over time, though, the steady noise of the rain's rhythmic drumming on the sheet metal in combination with the protracted and strenuous activities of the long day, actually helped to lull him into a very deep sleep.

Not surprisingly, their breakfast didn't start until two o'clock the next afternoon.

CHAPTER THIRTY-EIGHT

Later the next afternoon, the rain let up and was followed by only some occasional drizzle. With the sky starting to clear, at B.G.'s suggestion, he and Irwin went out for a ride in the SUV.

Irwin understood the bit of regret that B.G. had from losing the Cadillac once it was damaged in the accident after the car theft, but he readily saw the ironic humor in the situation as well. As they drove along, he admired both the comfort and power that the ride in the SUV quickly displayed.

As they traveled, Irwin, assuming the role of tour guide, in short order was directing B.G. to a series of roads with which he was completely unfamiliar. After about twenty minutes, they had left the built up area and entered a region where the houses were spread out on larger tracts of land, and where occasional glimpses of horses and beef cattle could be seen.

Proceeding a bit further, Irwin then asked B.G. to slow down as they approached a long driveway up ahead on their right.

"You might want to pull in right over here if you'd

233

like," he then offered as a suggestion.

B.G. drove in a few car lengths from the road and came upon a driveway that had a substantial amount of broken pavement and potholes. The earlier heavy rains had left a number of the larger openings on the entryway full of water.

"What is this place, anyway?" he asked Irwin.

"It's a sad story is what it is. Take it real slow, but if you drive in about a hundred feet I can show you a bit more."

As he drove cautiously into the property, once he reached a certain point the thick trees and brush became cleared. In the opening, B.G. saw a cluster of several substantial buildings, with a barn and a board fenced pasture behind them. While such looked as though they had once been quite impressive, to B.G. now it all seemed more neglected. The lawn that hadn't been mowed, the driveway in disrepair, and the parking lot that had what appeared to be three vehicles, at least one of which could have been abandoned, didn't do much to add to B.G.'s initial impression.

"It was started as a center for the arts," Irwin was explaining.

"Seems like a wonderful idea for a place like this. What happened?"

"The guy who first set it up had just started to get it rolling, getting donations and support from some businesses and influential people who liked what he was trying to do. But then he got sick, and was out of the picture for many months. The assistant, a lady who was helping him set it up, then took over, and although the details are a little fuzzy, the end result was basically that the money and the assistant all disappeared. The first

234

guy contacted the authorities, but they never caught up with the thief. And the guy who was first setting it up, well his condition got worse and he died not long ago."

"You're right, that is a sad story. What a shame. So what's going on with it now?"

"Well, his daughter is trying to get the ship to sail once more, but it looks like that's not going to happen. There just isn't enough money to get it up and running again, and unless it gets on the right course, none of the former backers would even consider helping out financially any more."

"So why did you bring me here?" B.G. asked.

"A while ago I had thought of putting in some of my own money to help...but before making any decision I guess I wanted to know what your thoughts were."

B.G. took a moment to survey the property that he saw in front of him, before asking another question.

"Does anyone live here?"

"Yeah, the daughter I think is still hanging her hat in the main building there. And hey, I'm pretty sure that's her coming out of the barn in the back right now."

*

Her name was Amanda and B.G. was struck by the pure natural beauty of the woman. Her expression when he first saw her could best be described as guarded and pensive, but later when she smiled, everything at once around her suddenly seemed bright and wonderful. However, as he was to find out, she hadn't had much to smile about at all in the past year.

She knew Irwin somewhat, as it turned out that he had donated his time and given a couple of free beginner's painting classes before the center for creative arts had closed. When Irwin introduced B.G. as "my friend, Mr. W." Amanda tilted her head and said that he looked familiar. In reply, as such was often the case, B.G. merely smiled and said he hears that a lot.

Wumpkey was becoming intrigued by the whole scenario, and after a time of hearing Amanda and Irwin talk in general terms, he decided to ask a few questions of his own.

"How much land is included in this parcel?" he inquired.

"Twelve acres," Amanda replied. "It's a good parcel, and it has one thousand feet of road frontage, which my father always felt was valuable."

"I don't mean to pry, but what is the financial status right now?"

"How do you mean?"

"Well, Irwin told me just that there had been a problem with your father's assistant and the disappearance of money. With that in mind, I'd like to know the income, expenses or current debt load that exists on the property. That is, if you know it, and if you wouldn't mind sharing that information with me."

"Not at all. In fact, with the closing of the center and the tax lien and the article that was in the paper about the the stolen money, it's all been made pretty public anyway. So why don't you ask me some specifics and I'll try to answer them."

"Fair enough. You mentioned a tax lien. What is the amount and how far into the process is that?"

Over the next fifteen minutes, Amanda simply and directly provided an abundance of information. She was very well spoken with a knowledge about business matters, and B.G. found her command of the situation to be admirable, even though she put herself in a light that made it seem as though certain of the obstacles were overwhelming and out of her control.

"So, with that said, you should understand that it's not the running of the place that bothers me," she continued. "I know a bit about managing a business, and I could certainly handle this and make it success-ful. But right now, it's just a question of whether there is a way to get the operations functional again and the maintenance up to par, and at this time there simply isn't enough capital to do that."

Amanda paused then, and looked into the open field behind the house.

"Knowing all that, I was becoming pretty resigned to the fact that this dream of my father's to have a cen-ter for the arts had to die with him. But, can I tell you something?"

At that moment she looked expectantly at Irwin and B.G., and paused as if wanting some acknowledg-ment before continuing.

"Sure," Irwin spoke up.

"Well, like I said, I'd come to accept that this cen-ter was going to remain closed, and that I'd have to be getting what remained of our belongings out and leave the repairs and all to the next owner, whoever that might be. But then one night this past week, I had a dream. In the dream, I was watching while a person was over-seeing a crew of workers putting on a new roof, making a number of major repairs and doing all sorts of land-scaping. And then a big new sign with the name of the center was delivered by a truck with one of those loading and unloading motorized devices and it was being set in place near the entrance. It was such a happy dream, and it seemed so authentic and natural that when I woke up I really believed it was actually happening. Looking back on it, after all it was just a dream, but it struck me as being so real, like it was already accomplished...It's quite strange, isn't it?"

*

They took a casual walk around much of the property, with Amanda pointing out certain aspects of one building or another that needed repairs, or where additional maintenance or groundwork was necessary. Of the several structures, one had been used as an administrative office, another as an art gallery and workshop, and one was a small theater with a stage and seating for one hundred. However, it was apparent that a substantial amount of renovation work and landscaping was long overdue on most all aspects of the property. After strolling in more or less of a circle, they stopped in front of what appeared to be the walkway to the main building.

"Now, I think I have a handle on most of the financial state," B.G. began. "The tax lien is still in effect, and the property has not yet advanced to the tax sale date, but it is getting dangerously close. And you told me approximately what it would cost to catch up on the work that has been neglected, and to properly maintain it each year."

"Well, I'm glad that it's clear to you now."

"But there is one other matter. I imagine that with the financial problems of this magnitude as you described it, there must also be a lender, lien holder, or a mortgage in arrears on the property for a substantial amount. So, what is the..."

"I can stop you right there," Amanda quickly interrupted him. "Just to let you know, my father was very concerned about just that event occurring, so he took steps to avoid it."

"Is that so. Exactly what sort of steps?"

"Before he died, he made sure that the mortgage was paid off using his retirement savings. There is no mortgage at all on this property."

*

Amanda said she needed to check in the house on some food cooking in the oven, but invited them to look around. Just before she left, she stood close to B.G. for a moment, and looked intently at him. Then, her lovely eyes lit up as she smiled very widely. A minute later she had gone inside the house.

"I think she likes you," Irwin stated matter of factly as they looked out towards the long driveway.

"What makes you say that?"

"Well, the fact that she gave you all that information so readily. And then just now, even the way she looked at you."

B.G. let that remark settle over him.

"Anyhow, what do you think of the whole situation, now that you've learned a bit more about it?" Irwin asked.

"Well, the fact that there is no mortgage on the property is a great benefit and advantage. Clearly, it would take a lot of money to get this back on its feet, but since it's held free and clear, that makes the whole situation a lot more manageable. However..."

As his voice trailed off, B.G. then put his hand on his chin, which to those who knew him, was a well known position indicating he was close to reaching an important decision.

While he remained silent and deep in thought,

Irwin went on to describe aloud and in some detail the nature of his own current finances.

`"...And other than the smaller amount in mutual funds, most of my money is tied up in long term investments, bonds and other retirement accounts that give some kind of a penalty if early withdrawals are taken. But really, I'd be willing to take a hit if you think I should help them out here..."

B.G. was only partly listening, but he caught up with the last part of the Irwin's commentary and responded.

"No, I wouldn't advise you putting any of your own funds into this. There is the penalty for early withdrawals, which is usually substantial, and all of the transactions would be of record which may not be the best for this property at this time."

Irwin looked momentarily disappointed.

"But that doesn't mean that Amanda can't be helped," B.G. added.

*

In the next few moments, B.G. quietly posed to Irwin a few pointed questions concerning their mutual acquaintance Kurt Koppy, and precisely how much Irwin knew about what B.G. had been asked to do. In short order, B.G. was reminded that Irwin had been the one who had referred Kurt to B.G. and that Irwin was well aware that Kurt had wanted B.G. to clean up and put to good use some money he had unexpectedly come into.

"As you see fit, right?" Irwin had noted when they had finished their exchange of questions and answers.

That was all Wumpkey had wanted to know for now. He had figured that Irwin knew the general situation, but he wanted to be sure there was a common understanding between them.

"So, what are you going to do here?" Irwin inquired.

"I'm close to deciding. But right now, I think I'm waiting for a sign."

Exactly three minutes later, Amanda emerged from the front door of the main house. She was smiling, and looked especially lovely as she carried with her a large platter.

As she approached them, from a distance they saw that on the platter were small glasses of milk, and a basket covered with a cloth napkin in the middle.

"Here, for my guests. Fresh out of the oven, some chocolate chip cookies and milk," Amanda was saying happily in a loud voice while walking towards them.

"Well, there you go." Irwin whispered softly to B.G. "I think that's your sign."

And at that very moment, in fact a close examination would have noted that Wumpkey's eyes had suddenly become a bit misty.

*

The cookies and milk quickly served to relax everyone and put them in a noticeably good mood. For some reason which B.G. couldn't understand, while they talked Amanda kept smiling and looking fondly at him.

When they'd finished their mid-afternoon snack, B.G. decided it was time to get down to business.

He explained to Amanda that he was going to tell her something in a moment, but that he wanted to be sure that she kept it confidential and followed his instructions.

When B.G. left the two to continue talking among themselves, he walked over to the SUV and remained inside for several minutes. He emerged from the vehicle holding a shopping bag and walked back to where the two were standing before he addressed Amanda.

"This is to help you pursue your father's wishes, and, under your auspices, get the center for the arts back on its feet again. Pay off the tax lien right away, and use the remaining amount to complete the repairs, renovations and upgrades that you feel are necessary. Use it wisely and in small increments, being sure to do your best to stay away from banks or the like. If you are ever questioned, even by those who are well intentioned, my advice is to simply say that you are using a combination of your personal savings and some small anonymous donations from lovers of the arts. But don't volunteer any information. And along the way, you can start to offer your programs again to continue the good work your father started. Lastly, it will probably be in your best interest if you don't know much about me. So, let's just keep it that I'm the guy you knew as Mr. W."

He now looked at Amanda, who still had the same smile she'd worn when she brought them the cookies and milk earlier. She then replied in a soft but confident voice.

"Oh, you don't have to worry about all that, using small amounts and the like. Believe me, I know all about keeping a low profile with finances, especially after what my father went through. And even though I'm not certain exactly what is in the shopping bag, I have a pretty good idea... You see, it's because actually I do know you," Amanda said, looking directly at B.G. while still wearing the same wide smile.

This comment clearly caused an immediate curious reaction from both Irwin and B.G.

"I...I don't understand," B.G. finally got out the words. "What do you mean, you know me?"

"It took me a bit to make the connection. But then before I went in to get the cookies and milk, it was unmistakable to me. You're the man who was overseeing all the repairs on this property in my dream. It took a while to sink in, but then I recognized you for sure as that very same man in my happy dream. And now, here you are!"

*

Later, on the drive back to the storage units, they were both feeling in a very positive mood.

"You did a really good thing today, you know. And it's going to make a lot of people really proud and happy for years to come. Amanda was so pleased, and it's something I believe in, that whole bit about her seeing you beforehand in her dream and all...So tell me, how much was actually in the bag you gave her?" Irwin asked as they entered the highway.

"An even two hundred and ninety thousand," B.G. replied. In hearing himself say that, it gave him a real sense of satisfaction and accomplishment, knowing that he had now made such major progress in his ongoing distribution efforts.

"That's great, but you sure that's enough? It's a big property and there will always be more expenses that come up than people expect," Irwin remarked.

"Oh, I'm pretty sure that will be ample to get the place in good shape and back on the right track again."

"Well, let's hope so. And if it isn't, it's good to know there's more if and when it becomes necessary."

"More? What do you mean more?"

"Well, earlier today, while you were still sleeping,

and before we left, I found a briefcase that Kurt must have hidden in the storage unit when he dropped off the motor home, and I'm pretty sure I know what's in it. We can check it out after dinner if you want."

In contrast to his previous but now short lived feeling of accomplishment, B.G. was obviously a bit stunned to suddenly hear about this latest discovery. As a result, he drove for some time in silence.

"Hey Mr. W., I think you look like you could use another cookie," Irwin said calmly a bit later, as he reached into the basket on the seat between them.

CHAPTER THIRTY-NINE

B.G. chose not to check into the contents of the briefcase that evening, as he didn't want to be confronted with any new complications that might change his current upbeat state of mind. He and Irwin instead decided to have a good meal and enjoy the grand feeling of accomplishment that they both felt after meeting with Amanda.

After all, it wasn't every day that a person could say he had saved a promising center for the arts from permanently closing and at the same time brought joy to a beautiful young damsel in distress. And that didn't even take into account the basket of fresh chocolate chip cookies that they had received as part of the deal.

Later that night, after they'd enjoyed some juicy steaks on the grill, Irwin said he had to go back to his suite to get something, and he invited B.G. to come along. It wasn't dark yet, but the sun was starting to set through the clouds on what they could see of the horizon.

As Irwin opened the side door that swung into his

storage unit which was set up as his living quarters, he mumbled something to B.G. about the lack of lighting inside.

"What are you referring to?" B.G. asked him as they stepped inside, and a moment later the overhead light had been turned on.

"Well, I'm real comfortable here, but there is only one drawback that bothers me. It's the fact that there is no natural daylight inside. Generally, if it's early morning or late evening, I'd like to keep the door open for a while, just to look outside or get some sky-shine in here. But that's when the mosquitoes or other bugs seem to want to come in. And then sometimes, if it's raining, I'd like to look outside when I'm here under cover, but if I do it gets wet in here real quick."

B.G. studied the doorway as Irwin glanced around and located what he was looking for, which turned out to be a bottle of high alcohol content vodka.

"I think I can fix that for you," B.G. said after a moment.

Irwin was intrigued by the tone of confidence in B.G.'s voice.

"But how?" he asked quizzically.

"Easy," B.G. replied.

He then led Irwin over to the doorway to point something out to him.

"You see this is a thirty-six inch door. And it has its handle, its doorknob, on the left side as you face it. And when you open it, it swings into the storage unit."

"Yeah, so what?"

"Well, all you need is a thirty-six inch storm door that, like most, swings outward when it opens. It's a simple fix, Irwin. You just need to figure out what style you want, with a full view of glass or half a view. Then, you can also decide if you want to put in the screen that comes with most storm doors as an option."

"How do you know all that?"

"I know it because I've put in a few at the ranch over the years. It's an easy job, and if you like we can go to a building supply store tomorrow and you can pick out the exact color and style you want. We can bring it back here in the SUV and I can install it for you in about an hour, easy."

"Really?" Irwin said with genuine excitement. "And that would allow me to keep out the rain or the bugs and still have natural light here inside?"

"Whenever you want it. And maybe a bit of a fresh breeze now and then as well," B.G. added with a smile.

"You know, for all these months that I've been here, I never even thought of that idea. Man, a storm door, with a big screen or a glass. That would be great!"

And so, according to Irwin, with this latest and most positive finding, that night they had even more of a reason to raise two glasses of potent vodka in commemoration of what had turned out to be a very successful day.

CHAPTER FORTY

The next day, by mid-morning the two had traveled to a local building supply store. It didn't take Irwin long to decide his purchase was going to be a top of the line maroon colored storm door with a brass handle and lock-set. The door he chose had a large glass panel which could be replaced with a screen of the same size. In addition, because it was the highest priced model, it also came with a lifetime replacement warranty, which made Irwin especially pleased.

Two hours later, the door had been unloaded and was ready to be put in place. Before completing the installation, however, B.G. advised that he needed some weather stripping or caulking in order to insure a weather tight fit. While Irwin said he knew where some was located and went to get such, B.G. decided to give Carol a quick call.

However, before making the call, B.G.'s intuition made an appearance and sent him a flash of precautionary advice. Recalling that he wanted to keep as low a profile as possible in this matter, he realized that if he made the call using his own phone, it was possible that, should a thorough investigation ever come about, such could be used to confirm his visit to Florida. Locations of where calls were made from could be discovered by some technology using triangulation and advanced related practices. Thus far, he reminded himself, he had kept his travels more or less under the radar, and that made him feel more comfortable. Since Irwin had already made calls to B.G.'s number back at the ranch while B.G. was still there, more calls from Irwin's phone to his own would be in keeping with the prior activity, and not show any irregularity or link to B.G.'s visit if any check of telephone records were ever to be made.

It was a stretch, he knew, even to be thinking this way, but experience had shown him that sometimes overlooked little details ended up being the downfall of those who became targets in investigations and court cases. And he knew that later on these matters couldn't be changed.

He explained this all to Irwin, who was immediately understanding and agreeable.

What made their conversation on this topic even more interesting was when Irwin had revealed that for the past two months he wasn't even using his own phone, but instead had, with full permission, been using the telephone of the manager of the place who was temporarily away.

"The guy's still in rehab, and before he left he told me to use his phone as much as I want because he's got unlimited minutes on it," Irwin explained as he handed the phone to B.G. "Plus," he added, "The guy told me once he's out he's dumping that phone and getting a new one anyway."

Hearing that, B.G. liked the added complication,

and willingly accepted the offer to use a soon to be discarded phone which was currently in another person's name, to call Carol.

She was very pleased to hear from him, and informed that their children had just arrived back from their summer jobs the past afternoon. They were planning to spend about a week at the ranch, probably sleeping a lot, and then pack up and head back to their respective colleges.

It was a very enjoyable talk that B.G. had with his wife and two children. They missed him, but he assured them that he'd be seeing them all as soon as he was able to finish up some business matters here in Florida.

When Carol came back on the line after their son and daughter had returned to the matter of finishing their lunch, she asked how the work was progressing.

"Well, pretty slow right now, because I'm waiting for Irwin to locate some caulking or weather stripping."

"What are you talking about?"

"Oh, I'm installing a storm door on Irwin's unit, but before we do we just need to be sure the seal will be water tight," B.G. explained matter of factly.

When at last it became apparent to B.G. that Carol had no idea what her husband was talking about, he started to explain, but quickly found it was too complicated to describe understandably in a few minutes.

Carol finally helped out, by telling him that when she asked the question about how the work was progressing she was referring to the matter of the distribution.

That quickly jogged B.G.'s memory, enough so that he was able to tell her that he had just recently made some real headway in that department. Without going into too much detail about the amounts involved, or giving her too much to be concerned over, he did make mention of the fact that there had been a few surprises and complications along the way, but added that he felt things were moving along well and in the proper direction at the moment.

B.G. could tell that his optimistic tone relieved some of the anxiety she had been experiencing, while thinking about all that he was undertaking during his recent travels. Hearing her tone soften and become calmer made him feel better and he realized at once that making the call back home when he did had been a good idea.

Just as Irwin was coming back into view carrying a bucket full of supplies, B.G. told her that he was enjoying Irwin's good cooking as well as the combination of clear skies, very warm weather and the shade of some tall palm trees. Before they ended the call, she reminded him that he should try to visit the beach and enjoy the salt water during his visit.

*

The storm door, once the installation was completed, added an immediate warm and cozy quality to Irwin's lodging quarters, moreso than they would ever have imagined. Irwin was absolutely thrilled, and was already making plans on how he would rearrange his furnishings to accommodate the availability of this new natural lighting. B.G. too couldn't help but remark on how the addition of a simple storm door had served to transform the storage unit into something that seemed much more like a comfortable and welcoming living quarters.

While Irwin was deep in thought with his new ideas of interior decorating, B.G. felt it was a good time to follow Carol's suggestion and go to the beach. After getting the basic directions on how to drive to the nearest one, he changed into his bathing suit and a tank top and headed out.

Irwin's directions were so simple that before B.G. knew it, he was at the parking lot which bordered the walkway to the water. As he'd been told, the drive to the beach in fact took perhaps five minutes at most. After he'd parked, he followed the signs and arrows which indicated the direct way to the beach.

Once he had proceeded on the path in the wooded area as the arrows designated, as is often the case for those who are not accustomed to the view on a regular basis, the scene that soon unfolded before him caused him at once to stop in his tracks.

The palm trees which framed the distant view of the sand and open ocean beyond was so perfect it almost took his breath away. In combination with the few boats which were moving very slowly across the aqua colored water in the distance, the overall scene momentarily seemed to mesmerize him. He hadn't realized it, but now he knew it had been too long since he had been exposed to this.

Walking with his towel in hand, the feel of the sand on the beach broke anything that remained of the spell he had fallen under. Before he had reached this point, having previously taken off his slip on shoes and left them in the SUV, he immediately recognized his error.

On his bare feet, the warmth of the sand on the soles of his feet and in between his toes rapidly escalated until it was hot!

Really, really hot!

Too hot, in fact, to continue standing still or walking slowly on it.

B.G. quickly jogged to a spot of shade that was behind a garbage can which had been mounted on a permanent stand. There, keeping his burning feet in the area where the shaded sand was not nearly as hot, he rested while his feet cooled down.

Eventually, first moving rapidly and then with the help of a few more shady spots where he paused, and subsequently for a moment actually throwing his beach towel on the sand for him to stand on and get some relief, he made it to a spot near the water. He found the sand underfoot in that area to be a bit cooler, and after putting his towel down and piling some sand on its edges to keep the sea breeze from blowing it away, he had officially staked his claim for a spot on the beach. And then, he walked into the waves.

The chalk board near the life guard stand had written on it that the water temperature today was eighty-one degrees. Eighty-one degrees!

B.G. first dunked himself, and then proceeded to leisurely swim parallel with the shoreline. While doing so, his body was in conflict with his mind as the two could not seem to comprehend that he was in the water and the water was in fact as warm and inviting as it seemed. Although he had spent substantial time on the Gulf of Mexico's beaches in recent years, his overriding reaction from most of his lifetime in the north had instinctively led him to brace for the shock of cold water whenever he went to a beach.

But now, this was so refreshing, so pleasant, so welcoming.

He stayed in the water for nearly a half hour, after which he located his towel, immediately stretched out on his back and closed his eyes.

Waking up when some nearby beach-goers started packing up their belongings to leave, he turned over onto his stomach, and proceeded to doze some more, feeling the sun warm his back this time.

Later that night, after an enjoyable dinner with Irwin, who remarked that B.G. had gotten sunburned and was appearing a bit drowsy, by comparison from their prior schedules, after just a few beers they retired a bit earlier than they had in the past.

It was, B.G. acknowledged sleepily before he went to bed, just what a day at the beach should be. And in light of his extended exposure to the salt water and sun, with good reason his sleep was long and deep.

CHAPTER FORTY-ONE

The next morning, B.G. told Irwin that he wanted to prepare their breakfast. Irwin was a bit surprised, but since he hadn't started anything other than a large grapefruit which had been cut in half with each portion placed in two corresponding bowls, he agreed.

Quickly taking charge, while Irwin watched with curiosity, B.G. then went through Irwin's refrigerator. In a short time, he found just what he wanted.

Bringing the contents outside to where the grill was located under the large palm trees, B.G. told Irwin that he needed a large frying pan, preferably cast iron, two plates and a loaf of bread, along with some orange juice.

By the time Irwin returned with these items, B.G. already had the side burner on the gas grill ignited. Placing the cast iron fry pan on the burner, he let it warm for several moments.

Then, he carefully placed six pieces of thick sliced bacon into the pan. In a minute he started to hear the familiar sounds and smell the aroma of frying bacon.

When the bacon was cooked, he removed it from

the pan and placed three slices on each plate. Next, he took some fresh large eggs from a carton and began frying three of them in the pan.

"This next step," he confided to Irwin, "is perhaps one of the most important parts of the process."

Taking six slices of fresh bread from the loaf, B.G. then placed them on the plate. Nodding to Irwin, he then took a container of mustard and held it aloft to note its significance. He then spread a generous amount of the mustard on each of the slices.

He flipped the eggs and watched carefully until they were cooked to what could be called "over medium."

Next, he put one cooked egg on each of three slices of the bread. He then put two slices of the still warm bacon on top of the egg, and then covered the bacon with the other slice of bread. After he had repeated the exact process with the remaining ingredients, he made a formal announcement to Irwin.

"And here they are, prepared for your pleasure, sir. Three bacon and egg sandwiches, cooked, I might add, apparently to perfection."

B.G. then handed Irwin the plate, along with a tall glass of orange juice.

*

While B.G. then went through the same process again to prepare his own breakfast, Irwin ate the serving with obvious appreciation.

By the time B.G. had completed preparing his own bacon and egg sandwiches, Irwin was just starting to finish his third one.

"Man, I tell you what, that is some good," he said in a tone filled with respect.

"It really is a simple process," B.G. noted as he took a seat under the palm trees, before continuing. "But the combination of the bacon, the over medium egg, the fresh bread and the mustard...I tell you the mustard brings it all together...it really is very tasty."

"I'll have to remember this, so that I can include it on my weekly menu. Thanks for letting me know about it. And you know, right now, I could see it as a perfect fit for a breakfast or a lunch," Irwin added as he took his last bite.

*

With their morning meal finished, B.G. felt it was now as good a time as any to bring their attention to the matter of the briefcase that Irwin had discovered.

Walking back to the storage unit where the motor home remained, Irwin repeated the familiar steps to maintain their privacy, as he opened the garage door part way, turned on the lights, and then promptly closed it shut behind him.

When Irwin retrieved the briefcase from where it had been hidden behind some other items in the far corner, B.G. had a sudden flash of recognition. Seeing it, the briefcase appeared to be identical in size, shape and color to the one that had first been left up north in his law office by Kurt Koppy when this whole matter had begun.

Irwin placed it on a bench and then carefully opened it.

The contents were somewhat surprising. There was a substantial amount of cash, made up of several bundles of bills in large denominations. But it had nowhere near the amount that the other cases had contained. There were also about fifteen or twenty more gold coins, in plastic with cardboard jackets that had been stapled and taped in the same fashion as those he had seen previously in the cases that were left in his law office.

While the amount of valuables in front of them was certainly substantial, it was the other items in the briefcase that attracted more of their attention.

Secured in similar plastic with cardboard jackets as the gold coins, they saw five separate keys.

*

"What do you make of all this?" Irwin asked after they had been looking at the contents thoughtfully in silence.

B.G. held up one of the wrapped keys, and pointed to something on the back side of the cardboard.

"See that? It's a number. And there is a similar notation with a number or a combination of a letter and a number on the other cardboard wrappers as well."

"So, what do you think that tells us?"

"Well, I tell you what it looks like to me. It looks like our friend Mr. Kurt Koppy has some other valuables, hidden someplace that only he knows about. And I bet you that these are the keys to certain places, secured lockers, mail drop storage boxes, hidden closets or the like. But to you and I, the locations and the contents for such right now are a complete mystery. However, after seeing this, I do believe that Mr. Kurt Koppy may have more worth than I ever imagined... yet if and when we'll ever learn about it all, well that still remains to be seen."

CHAPTER FORTY-TWO

Early that afternoon, B.G. took a drive to the beach again. Although he knew he was a bit sunburned from his visit the day before, the feeling of calm and relaxation that his time there had provided was too much to resist. He knew that he'd have to be heading back north again soon, but in the meantime he wanted to sponge up a bit more of the salty air and ocean water from the Gulf of Mexico to keep the feeling fresh in his mind.

Although there were a fair amount of cars, he was still able to find a good parking spot in one of the shady areas. Being sure this time to wear sandals, he walked to the same area in the sand that he had been before, spread out his extra large towel to reserve his spot, and went into the warm water.

Later, after a relaxing swim, when he was stretched out on the towel he felt the warmth of the sunshine quickly comfort him. In no time at all, with the combined sounds of the gentle waves lapping the shore and the rustling of the palm fronds from the light sea breeze in the background, he was lulled to sleep.

*

When B.G. returned to the storage units, he saw that Irwin had an easel set up beneath the palm trees and was sketching an outline on the canvas in front of him.

"Just working on a new idea, and trying to get some thoughts on how I might eventually put it together," he explained.

As B.G. took a seat on one of the lounge chairs, Irwin handed him a cold beer that he had taken from a nearby cooler.

"Hey, by the way, I got a call while you were at the beach. You'll be surprised to know who it was!"

"By all means, tell me," B.G. said as he took a drink.

"It was Amanda. She said it took some work but she found my number in the older files from when I gave a couple of those beginning painting classes at the center for the arts before it closed. She was all excited and wanted to let me know that she'd already paid off the tax lien, and that she had a meeting with a roofing contractor who can start on some of the repairs next week."

"Wow, that was fast. I'm glad to hear she's making progress already."

"Yeah, but wait until you hear the rest. She said she didn't want to pry but that she wanted to be sure to get the message to you of how very grateful she is for what you've done to help. Not only that, but she said she had another dream where you were in it, and this time the center was all renovated and you were giving a speech to a group in the theater and you got a standing ovation!"

"Isn't that interesting," B.G. stated with genuine enthusiasm.

"And before I forget, she said that if I see you to please be sure to ask you to stop by again any time you're in the area... I think that because your identity is still quite a mystery is something she admires, and adds to her interest in you. But remember, I told you early on that I thought she likes you, even before you helped her."

"Well, I'm certainly flattered. If you talk with her again, be sure to tell her how impressed I was with her and that I will stop by sometime to see the improvements. But just between us, of course, it may not be for quite a while."

"Why is that?"

"I really need to get back to the ranch. There are still some things I have to complete with this whole distribution matter, and then I want to learn as much as I can before I consider my work all done."

Hearing this, Irwin sighed, and looked at B.G. with an expression of clear disappointment.

"Yeah, I understand. And I knew you'd have to be heading out sometime. But I'm really gonna miss having you around here, Mr. W."

"Well that's nice to hear. And please know that I appreciate your hospitality, especially all the good food and drink you've given me. I'm sure I've already gained a few pounds during my stay here."

"So then, the visit was a success."

"Oh, most definitely. And you know not only did we accomplish a lot, but it became clear that we work really good together as a team. I mean, think about all we did in just less than a week since I got here."

"I have to thank you for that," Irwin said sincerely. "Now that we've figured out that mess that was with the motor home, I feel a whole lot better. And I wouldn't have known what to do without your guidance."

"Well, time will tell, but I think overall it was the right thing to do, considering all that was involved. But there are still some answers that someday I want to try to find if I am able to."

"Yeah, it would be nice to know a bit more about what we were involved in, what with the motor home and all. Then again, maybe it's best at this time if we don't know all the details, at least for now...But hey, Mr. W., you think with what we did over these past several days, that when we work together we really do make a good team?"

"Oh, absolutely," B.G. said with certainty, as he raised his beer in a show of affirmation.

*

After telling Irwin of his plans to return north, it had been his intention to begin the trip the following morning. However, after some good natured discussion, Irwin was able to persuade B.G. to delay his departure for another day. Using Irwin's phone once more, he tried calling Carol but only got the voice mail. He left word that his latest plans were for him to try to be back in about two days.

CHAPTER FORTY-THREE

Carol had asked that B.G. bring back a few things from his stay in Florida, B.G. was recalling. These included several spices and fresh cooking ingredients that were rather difficult to find in the northern climes.

Late the next morning Irwin suggested that they take a ride together to some stores that would be of interest to B.G. Although Irwin had a newer car, it was not running well, as he was awaiting a part that was on order. So, with a spirit of adventure, they struck out again in the SUV.

Irwin directed them to a store that was unlike any other B.G. had seen. It was a vast supermarket, that had numerous ethnic foods, as were represented by its varied clientele. Among the huge aisles, the two came upon rows of extra large bags of rice of many various types. Back in the meat department, B.G. was impressed to see not only the standard cuts of pork, beef and chicken but variations that included more uncommon packages containing pigs feet and ears, chicken feet and beef tripe. And then he saw cuts of goat meat, lamb and rabbit as well. In the seafood area, there were large whole fish of various sizes with their eyes staring vacantly towards the numerous customers as they decided on their selections.

The array of spices was extensive, and included many which were not known at all to either of them. B.G. picked out some that Carol had wanted, and others which, he reasoned, they would come to learn about together.

The produce section was perhaps what was most impressive to B.G. Seeing so many varieties of fresh green vegetables and fruits, a large portion of which too were unfamiliar, was at first overwhelming. But in no time, B.G. had collected a basketful that he couldn't wait to bring back and try preparing back at the ranch.

Once they'd left the store and packed the purchases into the SUV, B.G. asked Irwin how far they were from a certain area of Tampa Bay. When Irwin replied with his estimate, B.G. smiled and said now he wanted to show him something.

*

B.G. made a few wrong turns and had to double back a couple of times, but he eventually found the particular street he was looking for. When he drove up to the restaurant he had intended to go into, he parked the SUV and walked up to the door.

But, it was locked.

Feeling disappointed, he drove to a parking area of a business that was just about a hundred feet away. Inviting Irwin to come along, they went inside.

The sign on this business said it had fresh baked goods, but that didn't tell the whole story. B.G. stepped inside and inquired of the clerk about the restaurant next door. The young lady told him that of late the owner was keeping irregular hours. It had been open earlier, but was now closed, apparently for the day. B.G. expressed his disappointment, explaining that he had driven here and was hoping to buy some good Cuban sandwiches.

Hearing that, she broke into a big smile, and then yelled something in Spanish to another worker behind the counter, who came over to join them.

"Well, then you've come to the right place. Because we also serve them, and as you will see, our Cuban sandwiches are among the very best. Please let this man take your order and then have a seat in one of the booths over there."

B.G. ordered two Cuban sandwiches, and they chose a booth by the windows in the corner that had a full view of the traffic on the busy roadway. Since no one else was in that area of the small restaurant, they felt comfortable to speak freely there.

A Cuban sandwich, B.G. had come to learn from his prior extended stays in Florida in years past, when properly prepared is quite delicious. Although there are variations among the different cooks, the basic recipe includes fresh Cuban bread, a type of Cuban ham, Swiss cheese and slices of dill pickle. Some of the varieties which B.G. had come across included a second layer of meat, sometimes sliced lamb or another cold cut, and some included a sauce and some sliced tomatoes or lettuce. In any event, one of the keys to a good Cuban sandwich was that they were pressed, that is squeezed in a hot press that packs the ingredients tightly and then warms them enough to melt the cheese.

"I've never been to this neighborhood. How did you know about this area?" Irwin asked as they settled back in their seats.

"Some years ago, one of the first times my family came here with me, we got lost driving around. It was a really hot day, we had no air conditioning in the car, and we stopped at that restaurant over there, that is closed now for the afternoon, just to ask for directions. It was extremely comfortable looking, so I had my wife and kids come in and we ordered some food. It was so good we did the same order again. That's when we had our first Cuban sandwich, and I always try to have another one whenever I'm in the state. But not all of them are prepared right. Let's hope that this place has the really good ones."

As they soon found out, it did. Because when their scrumptious looking order came soon after, they were not disappointed.

"Oh man, this is great," Irwin was saying as they started eating.

B.G.'s first bite had told him all he needed to know.

"Yup, they were right. This is definitely one of the best I've had," he said with a grin.

When they had eaten about half of their serving, the casual and private location along with the tasty meal made them relax and feel at ease. As a result, their conversation then proceeded to cover some of the important things that they needed to review.

"About the motor home...there are a few things I wanted to tell you," B.G. began.

"Good. Go ahead and you may answer what I was wondering about myself."

"Well, to start with, I wouldn't take it out on the roadway for at least a couple of months. Let's just see how things work out up north, with the details of that investigation and all. And maybe I can find out some things that will shed a little more light on the whole situation, but I've got to be careful doing it."

"Yeah, I was thinking, you know, and with all we did, it could get a little sticky. But I still can't picture Kurt as being a cold blooded killer. Then again, maybe someone else was involved who was. I don't know, I just hope it sort of quietly goes away on its own."

"Things don't always work out so simply, but we can be hopeful. In the meantime, the vehicle is still properly registered and insured in Kurt's sister's name for another seven or eight months, so if you absolutely had to you could legally operate it on the roads. And somewhere down the line, since the papers are all made out to have the title transferred, you can become the lawful owner. But I'd recommend that you just sit tight for a while. Of course, if no one's around, you can start it up to keep the fluids circulated, but I wouldn't do much more than that with it for now."

Irwin took another bite of what remained of his sandwich, then remembered something and posed a question to B.G. while his mouth was still full.

"What about that briefcase we looked at?"

This in turn caused B.G. to pause momentarily.

"Okay, this is what I recommend. Keep it under wraps along with the motor home. We could move it, but that might lead to more confusion. I think that it's pretty clear that Kurt felt in leaving it there, that he intends at some point to retrieve it. But I think he also decided that if for some reason he's never able to, that he's quite comfortable having it left under your authority."

"And yours as well," Irwin interjected.

"Yeah, you're probably right. Sooner or later he figured we'd come together over this. But yes, I'd say for now just let it be, covered and secure. And then sometime in the future, maybe we'll get a clear answer about how to proceed."

"I think Kurt would probably be very pleased with what you've done with, the distribution, as you call it, so far. And I think he'd be thrilled to have you continue doing it with more that he has as well. But that's a lot to consider, so for the next weeks or months let's just follow your plan to sit tight and see what happens."

"Sometimes that's that very best course of action. But sometimes, it's also the hardest to do," B.G. added.

When Irwin got up to visit the rest room, B.G. went over to the counter and ordered two more Cuban sandwiches, and then paid for the total bill.

He was very happy to tell the clerk that having just one of their sandwiches each, simply wasn't enough. As an afterthought, he also purchased two desserts.

CHAPTER FORTY-FOUR

By mutual agreement, B.G. was going to leave early the next morning.

With dawn just breaking, Irwin was already cooking their breakfasts when B.G. came out of the storage unit. By the time he had showered and shaved, Irwin had the food on a steaming plate waiting for him. After the sound sleep, the ham and eggs with fried potatoes along with a tall glass of orange juice made B.G. feel energized.

He had packed his few belongings, along with the multiple bags of fresh fruits, vegetables and varied spices into the SUV the previous evening. There was one box, however, which he felt might be appropriate to leave with Irwin.

"I bought these directly from the author who wrote them and they are really quite good. I kept some copies up north for myself and Carol, and she's already said how much she enjoys them. But I was thinking, why don't you keep this box here, and give it to Amanda? You can tell her that I said it can be the start of her new library collection when the center for the arts reopens."

Irwin in turn had something that he wanted B.G. to have, but he regretted that it was not yet completed. Leading B.G. back to his own lodging quarters, Irwin opened the storm door and motioned for B.G. to follow him inside. After he turned on a light, he asked him to take a closer look.

Although B.G. was well aware of Irwin's artistic talents, whenever he saw the quality of his work up close it always served to be a bit stunning.

Now uncovered on the easel in front of him, was a partly completed portrait. Sketch marks showed on the unpainted area of the canvas a scene that was immediately recognizable to B.G., although he enthusiastically waited to hear the artist's own description.

"If you look closely, this is the theater at the center for the arts. And although it's not completed yet, you can see that the seating is full to capacity, and standing on the stage is a great man addressing the audience."

Seeing it and hearing Irwin's words, B.G was struck with a wave of emotion.

"It's beautiful," he said somewhat hoarsely.

"That's the scene that Amanda described in her dreams, with you up there giving a speech...If you look closely, you can see that everyone there is really enjoying it. Now Mr. W., you know that I put a lot of stock in those things...And personally, I think that dream will come true soon."

*

Irwin promised that he'd keep working on the painting, and hoped to have it completed in another week. When it was done, he promised to be sure to let B.G. know.

With a last minute check to be sure he had all of

his belongings, it was now time to begin his long trip north. B.G. started the engine of the SUV, and turned it around so that it was heading in the right direction.

While letting the engine warm up, he got out and walked over to Irwin. They shook hands warmly while each promised to keep in touch concerning any new developments. They stated in unison that they were both very glad they were able to work as a team and were pleased with how the visit had turned out.

Irwin walked slowly down the driveway towards the entrance to the storage units. There, he went over to the chain link gate that had been closed and locked for the night, and proceeded to open it.

"So, what do you have planned for the day, other than working on the painting?" B.G. asked as he put down the driver's side window.

"Well, I plan to take a nap in the afternoon and then I'm going to put some chicken on the grill. Tonight, the ladies should be stopping by. And you know, I can't wait to show them my new storm door! You sure you don't want to stick around?"

Noting that he really had to head out, before leaving he asked one more question of his friend the artist.

"Hey Irwin, if I talk to anyone who asks about you, what do you want me to tell them about how you are and where you are living now?" B.G. inquired.

Irwin tilted his head as he thought about his response.

"Mr. W., you tell them that your friend Irwin is doing just fine and living happily in a very private, gated community."

CHAPTER FORTY-FIVE

Two hours into his drive, the rain started. It began as a light drizzle, but as he headed north on the interstate it increased into a steady shower. The rain continued as he crossed from Florida into Georgia. Once he hit South Carolina, the skies brightened at first, but then dark clouds began rolling in ahead of him, and he saw the first of the lightning.

Then came the thunderstorms. By the time he had reached North Carolina, the highway speed of all the traffic had slowed considerably, due to the heavy downpours and extremely high gusts of wind that accompanied these waves of severe storms.

About an hour before darkness fell, after topping off his fuel tank B.G. drove into a shopping plaza. There he parked in front of a large grocery store with signs that boasted it was always open. Next to the store, he located a small delicatessen, where he was able to order a sandwich, some potato salad and a piece of chocolate cake. Sitting at a table near the back, he watched the weather report on the big screen television and saw the ongoing severe storm alerts that seemed to cover his entire travel route.

After finishing his meal, while walking under the protected covering that ran the full length of the plaza's storefronts, as the rain continued he entered the large grocery store. There he wandered around a bit aimlessly, due in part to his curiosity but also because of his somewhat fatigued state which resulted from his many hours of driving. Ultimately, he made a purchase of a large bag of potato chips and a bottle of fruit juice.

Once outside, it appeared that the rain was now falling even harder than it had been when he had entered the store. Carrying his purchases under one arm, while avoiding several of the larger puddles he ran to where the SUV was parked and quickly got inside.

Looking through the vehicle's windows around the parking lot, B.G. noticed that darkness had already fallen. Even though the lights in the parking area were now on, the heavy rain seemed to diminish their normal intensity. He also took note that there seemed to be a lot of camping-type travelers now in the parking lot. He made a quick count, and came up with more than twenty camper trailers or bus type recreational vehicles spread out in various spaces around him. In about half of them he saw that the interior lights were on.

"I think they are thinking just what I am now thinking," he said aloud.

An hour later, B.G. was stretched out in the roomy back area of the SUV. Like many of those in vehicles whose numbers were still increasing in that parking lot, he soon fell asleep while the sounds of the heavy rain, winds and occasional hail pelting the roofs and windows continued throughout the rest of the night.

*

When he woke up the next morning, it took him a few moments to get his bearings. In his groggy state, as he blinked his eyes and looked around, he was soon able to realize that he was not in a darkened storage unit, but instead in the back of the SUV.

As the rain was not letting up, after stretching somewhat, he sat up and proceeded to climb into the front seat. Then he started up the engine, drove out of the shopping plaza parking lot and back onto the highway. Heading north again, he was pleased with himself as he noted that he had managed to do so rather quickly and without even getting wet.

Two hours later, he stopped at a restaurant where he treated himself to what the menu described as a southern style breakfast with large satisfying servings. B.G. was very pleased to find that their description was quite accurate.

*

Proceeding northward, his route took him first to Virginia, and then into West Virginia. All the while, the rain kept coming down. He listened to the radio, and found that every station seemed to have the same wet forecast for the next few days.

Once into the more mountainous part of the trip, while the rain persisted, it wasn't as heavy as it had been earlier. At the same time, the amount of traffic on the highway seemed to diminish as well.

With the decrease in the intensity of the rain and the lighter traffic on the road, B.G. was now able to relax moreso as he drove than he had previously. As he did so, his thoughts drifted to the past week and what he had accomplished specifically in relation to The Project.

First of all, he was pleased to note, he had taken his friend Henry's general advice to heart and followed it well so far.

No receipts, and nothing local.

Yes, his trip to Florida had been without any overnight stays at a motel or similar lodging facility. Instead, his travels had included respites in the SUV and at Irwin's extra storage unit turned guest suite. And so, if it were to ever become an issue should there at some time be any investigation of his conduct, just proving his whereabouts on a certain date or in any location would not be easily confirmed.

And actually, the same was true of when he had visited Maine beforehand as well.

That was good.

Next, he took a moment to review and update the actual amounts involved in his distribution efforts in relation to The Project.

After several minutes of going over each individual distribution he had completed, he came up with a number.

"Well, so far, if I have it all figured correctly, I should have just about five thousand dollars left from the three hundred and five or so that I started out with about a week ago...And perhaps most importantly, I can now feel reassured that what I distributed is in good hands, where it can be helping others to achieve some very positive benefits."

Hearing his words, as he drove along he looked in the rear view mirror and smiled at his reflection.

"You know, that was pretty good for a week's work," he added aloud with a note of obvious satisfaction.

Two hours later, he saw the "Welcome to Pennsylvania" sign.

CHAPTER FORTY-SIX

B.G. arrived at the ranch late in the evening, a little before sunset. The rain had stopped here, and through the clouds the sun was shining its last rays of the day. As he steered into the driveway, he beeped the horn several times to announce his return.

The timing was quite appropriate, for Carol and their children had just been gathering in the backyard and pointing to the sky over one of the property's large barns.

"It's a rainbow, and it just appeared about twenty minutes ago," his son Sammy and daughter Michelle were saying in unison as they each hurried to take photographs before it vanished from view. B.G. was also pleased to see that Jack quickly came over to join the welcoming committee, and promptly left a wad of his long black fur on B.G.'s pant leg as he happily brushed by. Clearly, the extra large dog had been accepted and was evidently very comfortable with his new surroundings.

Later, as he was unpacking various items from the

SUV with the enthusiastic help of his family, although fatigue from the long travel was settling over him, B.G. felt very glad to be home.

*

Over the course of the next week, B.G. accomplished several tasks.

Although he found that he still needed to take periodic naps to recover from the tired waves which would overcome him as a result of his travels, during his waking hours he kept busy and acted assiduously.

B.G. was pleased that the timing of his return allowed him to spend some time with Sammy and Michelle. He remarked that they both looked very well, and after hearing their plans for the upcoming year and beyond, noted proudly the ambition and energy of youth each displayed.

After his children had been packed and sent on to begin their respective college's pending fall semester, the following day B.G. took a drive over to see Shooter.

In short order, B.G. formalized his purchase of the SUV. He was eager to explain how much he appreciated the vehicle's comfort and roominess, while adding that Shooter had been right in saying that it would be a good fit.

After seeing Shooter, B.G. had also intended to have a visit with Henry. However, when B.G. stopped in at the tavern, he learned that Henry was currently away while enjoying a fishing trip in Canada.

B.G. also made periodic visits to his law office, and reassured his concerns by finding that the valuables he had hidden there remained just as he had left them, secure and intact. Of course, he knew that he still had to complete more in the way of distribution, but overall remained very pleased with all the progress he had already made on The Project.

B.G. also made sure to return a few phone calls from messages that were left during his absence. Most of these were of little consequence, asking if he would take a particular case in which he had neither the time nor the interest at the moment, and to which he politely declined.

However, he did make a return call to Merle, the unfortunate chap with the missing toe story. That call led to a short office conference, where Merle delivered some more of his medical bills for B.G. to review, and in which the two formally entered into a written agreement whereby B.G. would represent Merle in his efforts to receive compensation for his pain, suffering, and related losses. While B.G. made clear to Merle that this case was unusual in many respects and that no assurances could be made for recovery, he would do his best to try to help his client.

Merle was thrilled that he now not only had a lawyer, but one in which he heard had helped a number of people he knew achieve a good result from various legal entanglements.

At the end of their conference, while Merle was walking towards the door B.G. noticed that he was still limping from his injury. As they shared a handshake concluding their meeting, Merle made a passing comment.

"Oh, by the way, I've been curious about that whole matter with the dead body and the motor home. Just to let you know, from the bits and pieces I've heard at the bars and the like, it seems the cops are at sort of a dead end so far. I thought you might be interested, what with that guy I talked to outside your office the last time I saw you and all."

B.G.'s eyes had become narrowed and steely as he came to recall that Merle in fact had some knowledge which, while certainly limited, could be seen to have some connection to B.G. and those newsworthy events. Although B.G. said nothing his sudden change of expression did not go unnoticed.

Merle in seeing this reaction, was at once uncomfortable and a bit unnerved. Consequently, he wanted to immediately make clear to B.G. that there was no doubt that he was among friends.

"Of course," Merle added quickly, "I'm sure there must be countless motor homes out there, that happened to be in the area around that time which fit the description of the one the police were looking for. So, I think that any investigators or the like are going to have a real hard time trying to get anywhere on the whole matter."

*

One afternoon following a lengthy post lunch nap, B.G. took a drive to the nearby library. There, he casually went through the editions of the local newspapers which spanned the time he had left for Florida until the current date.

In doing so, he found that the coverage of the story about the dumping of the dead body and the mysterious motor home had clearly decreased. In fact, the only related stories were basically rehashing the information from the previous ones. Overall, this was a positive development, he felt, which indicated that nothing new in the way of critical evidence had been discovered so far.

The longer the matter remained an unsolved mystery to the authorities, the better.

Then again, B.G. mused, much of the matter still remained a mystery to him as well. Before long, he promised himself, he wanted to privately find some answers which would elucidate just what he had been involved in. Once he did, he had already decided, he wouldn't share it with anyone but a very few select persons, and would specifically be sure to exclude any authorities.

But until then, he concluded, in the meantime he would have to just patiently wait and see what else might develop.

CHAPTER FORTY-SEVEN

"Hey, you want to take a ride to Maine with me?"
B.G. was asking Carol one afternoon two weeks later.

Carol had tilted her head as she gave his question
some consideration.

"Well, yeah, I guess so. I've got the garden under
control, and the kids are all settled in back at college. It
would be nice to check on the cabin and maybe do a bit
of sightseeing. And you could certainly use a co-pilot
after all your travel alone over the last month. But tell
me, why so sudden---yet another trip?"

This conversation had taken place shortly after a
lengthy phone call that B.G. had unexpectedly received
from Irwin. During that call, some interesting, albeit
still inconclusive, news had come to light.

In the aftermath of his talk with Irwin, B.G. was
left with the following information:

Mr. Kurt Koppy had just made a brief call to Irwin.
He had informed Irwin that he was relaxing in a tropical
paradise somewhere, and doing very well, thank you.
Kurt had made clear that there were some details that

he wanted to divulge and share with B.G., and Irwin as well, but due to ongoing events, in doing so he felt it was necessary to use the help of a third party.

"So anyway," Irwin had told B.G., "That guy you know who likes seafood, well, if you want to, he could probably meet up with you soon."

*

They planned to make the trip and be back in a week or so. Contacting a neighbor who lived close by, arrangements were made for daily visits to check on the property, the bovines and of course Jack until their return. They had considered taking the dog with them, but ultimately felt he might be more comfortable staying in his familiar surroundings.

B.G. went to the office later that afternoon. He brought with him a large canvas book bag that was full of legal journals and related papers. When he left he had the same book bag, but this time underneath the top few papers it was full of something else.

While he had no reason to believe he might be under surveillance, his cautious rationale had led him to carry out this course of action. In entering the building, he had made sure to do so with a book bag that appeared to have the same items inside it as when he left. Were he being watched, he reasoned, to any observers whether casual or otherwise, there was nothing out of the ordinary in what he was doing.

And so, his work on The Project would continue.

*

Once back at the ranch, when he entered the house he heard Carol talking happily on the phone. When the call was over, she enthusiastically informed that her friend Anna had her guest room waiting for them if they could stop by for a visit. Anna lived in southern New Hampshire, and although her location was not on their direct route to Maine, it would still be a good place to stop and break up the long trip. The primary reason, though, was because Carol and Anna had been friends since grade school, and as they hadn't seen each other for over a year, they felt a visit was long overdue.

"It seems whether you go alone or with me, that there is always a sense of rushing on these trips. Let's try to slow down and relax a bit more, and make it more enjoyable," Carol had said while noting that she was really looking forward to the travel.

As B.G. nodded in agreement, his thoughts wandered to the possibility of looking up an old friend who he believed still lived in that part of New Hampshire as well.

*

Since they didn't have as many miles to travel in light of their planned stopover, they got up and had a leisurely breakfast before beginning their trip.

It was enjoyable for the two of them to be traveling together, since on his last two trips he had been alone. Carol marveled at the comfort of the vehicle, and when B.G. suggested that later on he might want to stretch out and rest in the back, she said it would give her a chance to get a feel for driving the SUV on the highway.

A few hours later, B.G. pulled into a truck stop. There, he went inside and used a pay telephone to make a call. It was the same phone he had used more than a month ago when he had first tried to arrange a meeting with the mysterious contact. Without mentioning any names, he left a message on the voice mail informing if they wanted to have some seafood together, mid afternoon in a day or so might be convenient.

Then, as an afterthought, he also made one other call. He left another message, this time leaving his name and that as he might be passing through his area soon he just wanted to let him know he was thinking of him, on what he believed was still the number of an old friend. If it wasn't the correct number, the listener would be really puzzled, he thought as he hung up.

Once he'd left the messages, after a fuel fill-up, this time Carol got behind the wheel and B.G. prepared to take a leisurely nap in the back.

Some time later when he woke up and crawled back into the front passenger seat, he was surprised to learn that they were already in New York and approaching the Connecticut border. His nap had been a lot longer than expected, but he was feeling more and more refreshed as he became fully awake.

Some hours later, with B.G. now back behind the wheel, they approached the New Hampshire border. A few miles further on, they pulled into the combination rest area and state run liquor store and were able to find a parking spot in the crowded lot. Inside these large stores, (that New Hampshire, which has no state income tax and in turn by setting up these stores benefits greatly from), is found a wide selection of various wines and liquors that are sold at much lower rates than conventional merchants. They bought two bottles of wine to give to Carol's friend and then continued on their way.

When they arrived at her house, which was a beautiful and contemporary energy efficient structure, Anna gave them a warm welcome. It was evident that she and Carol had a lot to share and talk over, much of which related to people and places that were unfamiliar to B.G.

Once Anna informed that they would be having dinner around seven tonight, B.G. realized that they had made good time on their travels. As it was now only four in the afternoon, he told them he wanted to take a ride and explore some of the countryside where he had once spent time, with the assurance that he would be back before dinner.

*

He drove north for about a half an hour. This part of New Hampshire, like much of Maine, he remembered from his college days, law school and attorney work which had often led him in or through this region, showed that such was still a land of contrasts. While his travels here might bring him by a grand resort hotel or a large home with a mountain view, there were also ramshackle houses and trailers which housed a substantial portion of the year round population.

It was the woodpiles though, those indicators of hard work and survival, stacked high and handy to most of the dwellings, that were the common thread which most all of the buildings kept nearby, and which told the same story. Winter, the great equalizer, often made the need for supplemental heating readily apparent to all of those year round residents in Maine, New Hampshire and Vermont for those dark frigid days, when an ample supply of aged firewood could bring a welcoming warmth to any home.

The little town that he approached hadn't changed much since he had last been here seven or eight years ago. It did sadden him to see that a small diner which used to serve fine breakfasts was now closed and boarded up, with a weathered for sale sign on its door.

About a mile past the town office, he turned right on a gravel road, and went up a steep incline. He thought this was the road he was looking for, but it had been a long time and he wasn't quite sure. He continued on that road as it wound its way to a higher elevation, with thick mature woodlands on both sides. Periodically, a medium sized mountain stream would come into view alongside the roadway. Then, when he came to a very small bridge which crossed the stream, he recognized the area.

The place he was looking for was the second driveway on the right past the bridge. Slowing down the SUV, as it came into view he turned into the narrow dirt lane.

His name was Preston Price. His nickname was "Priceless," due to his well-earned reputation that to those in need, as a friend he was without peer.

*

Getting out of the vehicle, B.G. took a long look around. In the yard, he saw an older rusty pick-up truck, a couple of lawnmowers that were disassembled, and an automobile that had four flat tires and no hood. A large black and white cat was sitting motionless atop an old refrigerator that was under an apple tree. Weeds in the yard had grown to a height that was knee high.

Beyond that, he observed the small building that had a broken front window pane, a bowed roof line which was missing many shingles, and siding that was in desperate need of paint. The front door was wide open.

The place hadn't changed.

And he knew very well that what he was about to

do wasn't going to be easy.

Nonetheless, after squaring his shoulders, B.G. took a deep breath and strode energetically toward the door.

*

About thirty years ago, B.G. had first met Preston. B.G. was a financially struggling student trying to make ends meet at the time, returning from a visit with a girlfriend named Carol who lived about three hours away. On the way back to his class, B.G. had experienced a car breakdown, was unable to afford the repairs, and needed to get to his courses over the next two weeks in order to complete that semester's exams.

Preston had offered immediate assistance, which, B.G. later came to learn, was what Preston did. Offering the use of his own vehicle, Preston had provided free room and board to the young man in need for three weeks. It was December, and winter had arrived, which made the whole experience more difficult in this rugged mountainous environment. B.G. had stayed at Preston's while he studied for his exams, slept on the floor in front of Preston's wood stove, passed his courses and eventually went on to graduate and receive his law degree. And for this hospitality he remained forever grateful.

Years later, when B.G. had opened his own law practice, there was a time when a client of his needed a place to stay to start a new job, when a settlement from an accident case was repeatedly delayed. The client didn't have any funds, but would be able to afford his own place if he could just work for a month or so first. Once again, when he was contacted, Preston extended the welcome mat and provided a warm place and good food to boot for the appreciative client.

The problem was, that Preston would never accept anything in return for his kindness. B.G. had come to learn that he was just one of many people on a long list for whom Preston had given similar assistance over the years, but all of them were unable to get Preston to take any sort of gift or payback.

"Hey!" a voice came from behind the front door as B.G. approached.

"Hey yourself," B.G. said cheerfully as he saw his old friend and they warmly shook hands.

A few minutes later, B.G. was seated at the kitchen table, while Preston was bringing out plates and silverware.

"I got your message, and I made your favorite," Preston was saying as he proceeded to set the table.

"What do you mean my favorite? And how did you even know I was coming over? All I said on the message was that I was going to be in your area and I'd be thinking of you."

"Oh, I knew you'd be stopping by. That's why I went out and bought your favorite meal. It's all cooked now, ready for us to start."

"What is it?" B.G. asked as he followed his friend over to the stove.

"A turkey dinner. I bought a fresh one right after I got your message, and it's been in the oven cooking slowly all afternoon. And over here we have the mashed potatoes and gravy, turnips and cranberry sauce and a fresh salad. Ready to start?"

Of course, B.G. had to eat with his old friend, and of course, it was all absolutely delicious.

Midway through their dinner, B.G. noted that

Preston had glanced out the window that was behind where B.G. was sitting. Then, in a casual movement he had gotten to his feet and walked towards where some of the side dishes were cooling near the stove. While he was taking a large bite of a turkey drumstick, B.G. heard a slight scraping noise in back of him...and then after two seconds of silence, something more memorable.

The sound of the explosion just a few feet away on the doorstep was ear splitting and it occurred just as B.G. was starting to pour more gravy on his mashed potatoes. It startled him to such an extent that he dropped the gravy boat, but fortunately it was close to the tabletop and did not spill.

Before he could react any more, Preston came back into view, holding a shotgun which still had faint wafts of smoke emanating from its barrel. After ejecting the shell, he put the shotgun on a rack behind the door, and then returned to his seat at the table.

While quietly resuming his eating, Preston looked up at B.G. and in response to the startled expression he saw staring back at him, mumbled six words with his mouth half full and a cheerful nod.

"Woodchuck---eating my garden...Got him!"

*

Having the rest of the meal together without gunfire relaxed them both, and in no time they were exchanging jokes and stories as they always had in the past. But B.G.'s visit this time was more than a social call, and before it came time for dessert, which was a bread pudding that Preston had made, B.G. felt he needed to get down to the business that had brought him here.

"So Preston, what have you been up to lately?"

"Well, a lot of the same projects, always something

to do, you know. And I was trying to make some more progress on the big house in back, but it all takes time. I was helping out a guy and his girlfriend this spring, they needed a place to stay for a while after he lost his job, and her being pregnant and all. So, they stayed there in the big house for three months, and he got another job, they found an apartment, and it all worked out for them just before the baby was born."

"That was really nice of you. Tell me, did you charge them for staying here?"

"Charge them? You mean money, or rent? Why of course not. That's the whole reason I wanted them to stay here, so they wouldn't have to pay anything while they got back on their feet."

"See that's kind of what I want to talk to you about. But before we do, you mentioned the big house. How's that project coming?"

When Preston had bought the property more than thirty years ago, it had the run down building in the front where they were sitting now, but it also had the shell of a much larger, beautiful house out back behind it. The location of the "big house" had been well planned by the prior owner, as it overlooked the valley below in a panoramic view. But the prior owner encountered financial problems, and had ended up selling the property before he ever got around to finishing it. Preston had bought the parcel, which had seventeen acres and bordered the mountain stream.

"Geez, I have to tell you that I haven't done much in that way. Last summer, before the couple moved in, I did paint the front door. But mostly, it still is unfinished."

When B.G. asked if they could take a walk to see

it, Preston was more than willing.

Seeing the house, unfinished as it still was, was quite a contrast to where they had just been sitting while enjoying their turkey dinner. It had large windows that let in the sunlight while showcasing the view of the valley in the distance. But although he couldn't be certain, it didn't look much different than when B.G. had last seen it years ago.

"What does it need to be completed?" he asked as they walked past the still uncovered wooden framed open walls.

"Well, the electric was roughed in years ago, and the plumbing is up and running, although I drain it every winter so it doesn't freeze. But it still needs insulation and drywall and the finish flooring and a full kitchen. As far as heat goes, I planned to use wood stoves, since I've got this woodlot right here."

"It's a beautiful property. I'd really like to see you get it all finished. In fact, that's one of the things I want to talk to you about."

When they returned to the kitchen table, B.G. studied his friend for a moment. He had aged very little, but B.G. knew he was getting up there in years. He was of medium height and weight, and still had the habit of moving quickly in nearly everything he did.

"Preston, how old are you these days?"

"Just turned eight-one," came the reply.

"Eighty-one! You could still pass for someone in their fifties!" B.G. exclaimed.

And he meant it.

B.G. finally got around to the subject he wanted when the bread pudding made its appearance. Somehow, it seemed B.G. was able to do his best work when dessert was close by.

"All right, Preston, now listen up. It turns out that I have some money that needs to be put to good use. I want you to have some of it. It's not my money, but I've been asked to distribute it as I see fit. And I want to give some to you."

"I won't take it."

"I think you should."

"I don't need it."

"I think you do. And besides, over all these years that I've known you, you've done all these favors for other people, and yet you never want to take anything in return. So I say it's about time, and you can just think of it as getting some payment on the many loans you've given out."

"All right. I need a tire for the truck. I'll take thirty dollars to buy the tire."

Clearly, this was a major concession for Preston.

"But a new tire costs a lot more than thirty dollars, especially a bigger truck tire."

"Who said anything about a new tire? I get my tires used down at the junkyard, and I can get a good one for thirty dollars."

And so it went. Somewhat later, once the serving of bread pudding was finished, the heavy negotiating began.

"Listen, I'm talking about a substantial amount of money that I want to give to you, because you deserve it and you can use it."

"Did you rob a bank?" Preston asked pointedly.

"No, I did not rob a bank," B.G. replied.

"Well, in a way that's a shame, because if you had robbed a bank I think I'd take the money. I don't like banks."

B.G. paused, then boldly pressed on.

"Let me put it this way. There is a lot that could be finished around here to make your life more comfortable. You yourself told me all that needs to be done to complete the work on the big house and we both know you've wanted to do that ever since I first met you. With the money I give you, you could have some people finish all that and you could be moved in by winter time, all warm and comfortable and enjoying that great view of the valley out your windows every day."

"I don't know about all this..."

Hearing these words, B.G. sensed that he might actually be making some progress, so he continued as persuasively as he could manage.

"Well, let's start even closer. Look around you here where we are sitting. I can tell you right away that there are lots of projects that could be done that could make things easier and more pleasant for you right in front of us."

"Like what?"

"Okay, how about that dripping faucet at the sink. Or the broken window, or the roof repairs. Even if you do move into the big house soon, you still might want to get this place in nicer shape. It could be your guest house, where you could let friends or anybody who needed a hand to stay in. But it could use some work, couldn't it?"

"You're right about that part. This place could use a lot."

"Okay then, even in the winter, I bet that there are things you wish you had done to make this a little better right? Things that maybe would make this place a little warmer, a little more comfortable when it's really cold outside. Maybe it could use some insulation, for example."

This got a quick reaction from Preston.

"Insulation? Are you kidding? Well, let me put it this way. The insulation in this place is so bad that here, in the wintertime, when the cat wants to go out, I don't have to open the door."

Some time later, finally, their conversation had gotten to the point where they were talking about numbers. Ordinarily, B.G. would have avoided that and just left a package without explanation. But he knew that Preston was almost of a different species, and might be inclined to dispose of or destroy something which he didn't fully know about or want. Plus, B.G. really wanted to improve Preston's lifestyle in his later years, and to do so he'd have to reach something approaching a common understanding.

"All right, here's what I'm thinking. I want to give you sixty thousand dollars in cash, with the understanding that you can't tell anyone and you won't put it in a bank account."

"Well, I wouldn't tell anyone no matter what amount you gave me if you asked me not to, and of course I don't deal with banks if I can help it."

"Okay then, it sounds like we have an agreement." B.G. was getting giddy.

"Not so fast young man. There are a few things we have to get straight first."

"Like what?"

"How about seventy thousand dollars?" Preston asked.

This question puzzled B.G., but not enough to cause any major concern.

"That could be arranged. But let me ask you, why that amount all of a sudden?"

"I read in the paper that a big old church a few towns over needs a new clock and steeple as well as a roof and they need to raise seventy thousand dollars to cover it so I was thinking..."

"No, no, no! That's the whole point. I want this money for you alone, to do things only for you, personally. Then, once you've made these improvements for this place and the big house, or if maybe you want to get another truck, well afterward if you have anything left over, I suppose you could give that away."

"That truck has over three hundred thousand miles on it. When I go in town, it belches blue smoke and I have to remember to check the gas and fill it with oil."

It was a long struggle. However, more discussion and another serving of bread pudding seemed to pull the loose strings of the negotiations closer together.

At last, just when B.G. felt he was getting Preston to the point of an agreement, the spry older man brought up another point.

"I tell you what. I'll accept your seventy thousand dollars, but on the condition that you have to accept something from me in return. That way, I can think of it as a trade, and I'll feel better about the whole thing."

While vaguely feeling that he might be getting set up, nonetheless B.G. warily asked the inevitable next question.

"Well, what would I have to accept?"

"That, my friend, is entirely up to me."

It took another round of negotiations, but eventually they found a topic which could be mutually acceptable.

"I have a tire that will fit your SUV over there. I got it in a trade, and it won't fit my truck. I thought it would fit, but it's the wrong size and it makes me mad to look at it. It's been cluttering up my living room and I don't want it. So, you have to take that tire."

"Is that all? I just take the tire and then I can give you the cash and you'll use it to make your life more comfortable and finish these projects and maybe even buy another truck for you? I want to be sure we have a deal and that we are both clear on all this," B.G. said slowly and in summary fashion.

Preston paused thoughtfully, and then nodded his head decisively.

"Young man, if we shake on it right now, we can call it a deal," he said to B.G. as he extended his hand.

About fifteen minutes later, when B.G. returned from the SUV and brought in a brown paper shopping bag that showed some signs of weight, he was very pleased to place it on Preston "Priceless" Price's kitchen table.

And Preston was equally pleased to get the tire out of his living room.

As he drove away, B.G. smiled as he thought of how Preston would react when he realized the bag contained seventy-five thousand dollars instead of seventy. Knowing Preston, he had decided that a little extra would insure that the kindly gentleman spent more on himself before he would give any of it away.

And after all, it was a pretty good tire.

*

He was late getting back to Anna's house and they had been waiting patiently for him before starting their meal.   It was a bit of a challenge to eat another entire dinner after his previous one, but rather than trying to explain his recent activities, he was able to manage it quite well. Still, he noted that all the food made him feel overly tired and he felt his eyelids getting heavy early on. Turkey, he seemed to remember, supposedly had soporific qualities.

That night, as they went to sleep in Anna's guest room, Carol asked her sleepy husband what had taken him so long in returning.

When he told her in a groggy voice that he made a trade for a tire, it piqued her curiosity.

"A tire? What did you trade it for?"

At first he made no reply, but when a moment later he mumbled something that sounded like seventy-five thousand dollars, she felt he must have been talking in his sleep.

CHAPTER FORTY-EIGHT

By noon the next day they had arrived at their cabin in Midcoast Maine. Before their departure, the early breakfast that Anna had prepared was a delightful one of blueberry pancakes and sausage patties, and it had served as ample fuel to give them energy to easily complete the last leg of their journey.

It was a warm, sunny day, but a hint of autumn was already in the clear, crisp air. Once they had unpacked, Carol began busying herself in the kitchen with lunch preparations. B.G. stopped her before she got very far, with a reminder that they were going to have seafood at the lobster pound this afternoon, where at the same time B.G. was hoping to reconvene with a certain person of mystery.

They rested in the cabin for over an hour, before getting back in the SUV and heading into town.

*

It was two o'clock when they drove down the hill to the waterfront where the lobster pound was located. The parking lot wasn't very crowded, not even half full, which was a good sign to B.G. as he wanted to get a table with some privacy in the event the meeting took place.

When they got in line to order, Carol was immediately recognized by an old friend, who was having lunch there with her daughter. They struck up a friendly conversation, and before long Carol and B.G. had been invited to join them at their table.

That turned out to be a good thing, because shortly after they picked up their order, B.G. saw a familiar face walking towards him from the parking lot. He escorted Carol to the table with her friend, and then excused himself, being sure to take his own plate of food along with him.

By the time B.G. had located and sat down at the same table on the outdoor upper deck where the last meeting had occurred, the man who he remembered was already walking towards him and extending his hand.

"Mr. Wumpkey, glad you could make it."

"Mr. January, nice to see you again," B.G. said after their warm handshake.

"Please, just January is fine," he said with a friendly smile.

"Well then, just B.G. will do as well," came his reply while quickly adding, "Now, may I treat you to a lobster roll?"

*

Once they each had their respective lobster rolls, they ate in silence as they watched the various boats in the harbor. As it was already later in the season, the number of vessels either moored or passing by was less than the last time they had been there. But to B.G. the warm sun and good food made the occasion just as enjoyable.

When they had each finished their food and drink, it was January who spoke first.

"Okay then, here we are. Well, I have some information for you, and our friend wanted me to give you all the details so here goes. Maybe it'd be easiest if I just tell you all I've got to say, and then if you have any questions you can ask them later. That way, I'll be sure to tell you everything without forgetting any of it."

By way of response, B.G. nodded in prompt agreement.

This was what B.G. had been waiting for, and he leaned forward to be sure he heard every word. B.G. noticed that before beginning, January had looked again from side to side and, noting that the tables on the upper deck next to them were all empty, seemed to at once be more at ease.

"After Foto--Kurt--saw you, when he later left that second briefcase, he was in a hurry. And for good reason. He still had a lot more money in the motor home, along with a couple of guns."

January paused and looked out over the water.

"But there was more in the motor home. Lots of fresh blood on the carpet. It wasn't his."

The pace of the information B.G. was hearing was coming very slowly, and it made him want to interrupt and ask questions at once. But, he restrained himself, kept silent, and waited as he listened attentively.

"The witness was right who said that a dead body had been dumped on the side of the road in a spot where vehicles pulled off to park."

January now turned to look at B.G. directly.

"It was Kurt who did it."

B.G. gulped. In his mind, his own voice was now

screaming with the questions about what and how and why. But again, he kept quiet, and after taking a deep breath, he just listened.

"Kurt had spent the night in what he thought was a somewhat remote area. He had just pulled off on to a dirt road that led to a spot by a river where it looked like people came to party or go fishing now and then. It wasn't posted, and there were some fresh tire tracks, scattered beer cans and remains from a campfire, but no one was around. So, he just drove the motor home in, parked it in a spot where it was heading out for when he left the next morning, and went to sleep.

The next morning he got up early, and cooked himself a little breakfast. Then, realizing he still had some time before he was planning to run some errands and later arrange to see you, he took a walk along the trail that followed the river. He said he was probably gone about forty-five minutes or an hour."

January paused as two seagulls squawked over some shells that were left on the large rocks that bordered the water nearby.

"Kurt felt good after the walk. He returned, got behind the wheel of the motor home and drove out the dirt lane back onto the main road. A couple of miles down the road there wasn't any traffic, and he says he was going about thirty-five or forty.

All of a sudden he senses something. He quickly glances to his right and sees that there are hands reaching for him. Two very large hands, and then he realizes they are just starting to grab his throat.

Kurt yells, looks in the rear view mirror and sees a big guy standing there. Immediately, Kurt doesn't know why, but he just floors the gas pedal.

Even though it's a small motor home, it has a powerful engine, and the acceleration is very sudden. At the same time Kurt swerves on the empty road. Then he slams on the brakes really hard. And then he floors the gas pedal again.

These sudden changes cause the guy to lose his balance and he first sways but then slips and falls down, hard.

Just as he falls, Kurt hears a sickening crack. The guy's head hits straight on to a heavy dumbbell that was on the floor. The dumbbell was owned by Kurt's sister's late husband, who called it his portable gym, and used it to work out before he got sick and died. The dumbbell was kept for sentimental reasons by his sister, but they came to realize it served a very useful purpose as a weight for the pull out canvas overhead tarp and sunshade that is built in on the recreational vehicle, to help hold it down on windy days.

Anyway, Kurt sees this guy bleeding badly, and he has no idea what to do.

He turns around, drives back to where he had spent the night. He gets out of the motor home and quickly walks around the area. In the opposite direction from where he took his earlier walk, he sees on the ground a sleeping bag, a ratty pillow and some food containers. He looks closer, and he realizes that the food containers are from his own motor home refrigerator.

He figures out that the guy was sleeping there overnight, and after seeing that Kurt went for a walk, he went into the motor home and stole some food. The guy must have eaten it and come back for some more when Kurt returned. He stayed hidden in the back and when the motor home was driving away, he came up front and started to grab him.

But here's one other thing. Kurt goes back into the motor home and he sees that some of his cash has been taken out from where it was hidden. So the guy was rummaging through, had found some money and was preparing to take that as well, just when Kurt returned from his walk.

So now Kurt checks on this guy, and sees he has no identification on him at all. And even though he has no experience in such matters, he sees the skull is caved in and he can tell that the guy is stone cold dead. The guy is real big, real dirty and Kurt takes him to be a homeless bum by all appearances.

He doesn't know what to do. He realizes as he's driving that none of this looks good. Here he is, a stranger from out of state with bags of cash and unregistered guns, and now on top of that he has a dead body in his motor home. Explaining it would be difficult, to say the least. So, he drives about twenty miles away, and then pulls over into what he thinks is a spot with nobody around, and he tosses out the dead body. Of course, it turns out that somebody, apparently an early morning jogger on a trail in the woods, gets a glimpse of this before Kurt drives away.

And after that, Kurt does what he is really good at. He very quickly disappears."

*

Most of the questions that B.G. could think of had been answered by the time they had finished their second lobster roll. Some, including any that had to do with Kurt's current whereabouts or plans, truly seemed to be unknown territory for January, and his reply that he really didn't know, was believable.

They parted on friendly terms. This time, it was evident that January had learned a lot more about B.G. since their last encounter, and a feeling of genuine respect and admiration was passed his way. This impression was confirmed when, as the two shook hands in parting, January politely asked if he could contact B.G. if he ever needed some help.

B.G. and Carol stayed there for a while longer after both of their acquaintances had left. Eventually, as the sun started to get lower in the sky and the sea breeze grew cooler, they bought three pounds of clams and took them back to the cabin.

CHAPTER FORTY-NINE

The remainder of the week which B.G. and Carol spent at the cabin was one of the most relaxing times they could recall. With nothing more on their schedule, they slept late, did some sightseeing and would sit comfortably on the porch as the sun went down. And of course, each day they ate more fresh seafood.

Along the way, in the privacy of their cabin in the Maine woods, B.G. shared with Carol all the actions and developments that had ensued since his very first encounter with the mysterious Mr. Kurt "Foto" Koppy. Hearing himself tell it, his detailed description of the story's inception from the law office in the small city in western Pennsylvania, to midcoast Maine, then to the west coast of Florida, and back north again was even more complicated than he had remembered.

Still, it did him a lot of good to bare his thoughts, especially when he now had an explanation of sorts with which to rationalize much of his own actions that he had taken. The part about the bloodstains and the destroying of evidence, along with the discovery of yet

311

another briefcase leading to more questions, left Carol wide eyed and speechless. But in the end, after hearing of the hows and whys about the dumping of the dead body, as well as the indications that there were even more valuables involved and still out there, it all seemed to be understandable, as convoluted as it was.

As things stood now, they agreed, providing that no new leads or evidence were revealed, it seemed that this might remain a cold case for which the authorities placed it alongside others which had more questions than answers, and which might eventually be considered closed.

In support of that possibility, to his knowledge the body had yet to even be identified, and that fact alone might keep the entire matter suspended indefinitely.

In the meantime, B.G. still wanted to see his distribution efforts on The Project through to their final phase. And, looking back on it and sharing the breakdown of his efforts to date with Carol, when they tallied up all the numbers he realized that he was already close to accomplishing that result.

*

At eight-thirty on the following morning, they began their travel from Maine back to the ranch. Since there wasn't much to pack, it didn't take them long to get started.

About ninety minutes after heading out, they drove through a town where they had planned to stop at a small diner where tasty breakfasts were well known to them. However, they were quickly disappointed when after driving into the parking area they saw that the place was temporarily closed for remodeling, and wouldn't reopen for another week.

Continuing on, they decided to wait until they stopped for gas in the southern part of the state and then have a late morning repast. And so, they proceeded in their travel while leisurely taking in the sights of the early morning in rural Maine.

*

Just over an hour and a half later after they had purchased fuel, their appetites were increasing noticeably.

As they drove away from the main highway, even though it was a busy commercial area, it became apparent that there was little in the way of diners or restaurants in the vicinity. Turning around, as they retraced their route they came upon a sign that was just being placed onto the front lawn of a sprawling building by a middle-aged woman. The sign said "Lunch Today," and without giving it any further thought, B.G. pulled into the parking lot.

Upon looking into the building, it was their first impression that the meal was a church sponsored luncheon of some sort. The room was very large and by the way it was set up with large tables and chairs and smiling people serving meals on trays to the growing line of guests, it resembled a cafeteria.

Looking at one another, after his remark that the food smelled good, and giving a shrug that seemed to say that we're here so let's eat, they walked in.

Taking a place in line, B.G. and Carol approached the first counter where the trays, plates and silverware were stacked.

Reaching for his wallet, he asked the man behind the counter how much the lunch for two would cost.

The man's eyes grew wide with curiosity, but

quickly changed into a smile. Then, his explanation told them why.

"Your first time here, I take it?" he asked.

"Why yes," said Carol, "We saw the sign and ..."

"Yeah, I kind of figured that," he said, looking quickly at B.G. "It's okay, though, just put away your wallet, mister. You see this is a soup kitchen, where the local community and several organizations give a free lunch twice a week for anyone. Even though it's designed for folks who need a helping hand, we get people from all walks of life who come in here. In fact, today a Congressman is supposed to show up, although they say he likes to come incognito and just blends in like the rest of us so you may not notice him. Anyway, the most important thing to keep in mind is, simply, that everyone is always welcome here. And by the way, we don't like leftovers, so be sure to eat as much as you want."

"Well, thanks, that's very kind of you," B.G. replied with genuine appreciation.

*

Taking this invitation to heart, B.G. was on his second trip back from the food line when he noticed a man who had just come in and was sitting alone at a table in the corner of the room. The fact that some of the workers seemed to recognize the individual, and went so far as to bring a tray with plates full of food over to him, made his appearance a bit intriguing.

"See that guy over in the corner?" B.G. quietly asked Carol as he returned to his seat with another tray full of food.

"The man sitting alone, with the silk shirt? Yes, I see him."

"How do you know it's a silk shirt?"

314

"Oh, while you were in the line I walked right by him when I went to the ladies room. I'm pretty sure it's one of the very expensive lines but it really doesn't go with the rest of his outfit. But anyway, what about him?"

"I was noticing that he's acting a little different, purposely staying out of the way and all..."

"Ah, now I see. You think he's that Congressman that the man was telling us about, who is coming here but doesn't want to be recognized..."

"I suppose it could be..."

"Well, instead of wondering, why don't you go over and talk to him and find out? I tell you what, if you do, I'll get us some desserts and have them waiting here when you come back. "

"The man did say they hate leftovers."

*

Five minutes later, B.G. was sitting across from the man in the corner, having a casual conversation. What struck B.G. was that the man spoke in sweeping generalities, without being very focused. Still, the man seemed amiable enough, and as B.G. listened, he observed that the shirt the man was wearing was indeed of an unusual styling and material. It was one particular comment, though that seemed to give B.G. the key to the man's identity.

"That's the main problem now that is keeping us from getting things done in Washington," the man was saying to B.G. in a confidential manner.

"Really...Well, you sound as though you have some experience in the matter," B.G. commented.

The man leaned in closer to B.G. and his eyes sparkled mischievously.

"I could tell you things that are going on, that

people don't hear on the news and that you'd never imagine...Meanwhile, the amounts of money that are being wasted is almost beyond comprehension!"

They spoke for another ten minutes or so. During that time, B.G. learned that the political climate was currently in such a state of disarray that it was extremely difficult to get anything positive accomplished, no matter which party brought it up. And, he was told, the big money people, they carry their influence no matter what party happens to be in office.

"Well, it's certainly been a pleasure talking with you. And this is really a great place and probably gives you an opportunity to get a feel for what's going on back in your home district. Do you come here often?"

"As often as they let me," the man said with a chuckle, while adding that "It's important to stay in touch with your roots. And the food and atmosphere in this establishment always makes me feel so comfortable. That's why I'm doing all I can in my own humble way to make sure it gets the funding it deserves."

Just as B.G. was about to stand up and say his goodbye, the man looked over toward the entrance door and nodded to someone. Then, he too got to his feet and stated the following in parting.

"Oh, but there's my ride. I enjoyed our little chat. Perhaps I'll see you here again soon."

And then he was gone, heading to the door where a uniformed police officer was standing.

"So, did you have your question answered?" Carol asked B.G. as she handed over a plate with a large slice of chocolate cake and pushed a glass of milk across the table towards him.

B.G. looked at the dessert with obvious approval.

"Well, he didn't give me much in the way of specifics. But I learned a lot and yes, as soon as he started to
tell me about his time in Washington it was pretty clear
to me that he was who I thought."

With dessert finished and their appetites satisfied,
B.G. wanted to have a word with the manager. When
he asked one of the ladies in the serving line, she said
he'd be back from the kitchen shortly.

A moment later, B.G. and Carol were face to
face with the same man who had met them and kindly
invited them to join in the meal. B.G. thanked him for
his kindness, and then asked if they accepted donations.

"Oh sure, we take canned food, flour and fresh
vegetables over there. But we get a lot of our donations
including hamburger and turkey, you know, from the big
grocery stores, the chains and such. While that keeps
us afloat, there are still the matters of the utility bills to
try to keep up with...you know, heat, electric, water and
sewer...right now that's our biggest challenge because for
a building of this size, well, they can be quite substantial,
all right."

"It sounds like you'll be getting some grant
money, though," B.G. added.

"I'm not sure about that...We deal with a lot of
volunteers and charity. What do mean?"

"Well, if what your friend the Congressman has
to say means anything..."

"I wouldn't count on that...My experience has
been that the politicians give a lot of talk and a little
action. Just by way of example, the aide to the Congressman called a little while ago and said he wouldn't
be coming after all. That makes the third time he's
canceled. It makes a good photo op, so maybe he'll

finally show up when election time is near. But so far, he's another no-show."

"But that man I was talking with seated over in the corner, the one who was telling me about his time in Washington..."

The manager got a goofy look on his face, and then broke out into a howl of laughter.

"Him! You mean Silly Simon? The guy's a nut case. He lives in a refrigerator box under the bridge in the next town."

"But he spoke about Washington like an insider..."

"Well, the bridge where he calls home crosses Washington Street, if that helps out any."

"Yes, but he indicated the officer was his ride..."

"Yeah, his ride straight to court for some other charge, I'd imagine. Listen, the guy's basically harmless, and he speaks quite well, but he's a looney. Still, we always do take note of the fact that for a guy who lives in a refrigerator box under a bridge, whenever he comes here he somehow always manages to dress in really nice clothes."

With all that now settled, B.G. told the manager that he would be back momentarily.

"I told you that was an expensive shirt," Carol was telling B.G. as they proceeded towards the door.

*

"I have to give them something," B.G. was saying to Carol as they sat inside the SUV. "They are doing good things to help people, for free, and they deserve it. By the way, the lunch was really tasty, wasn't it?"

"Yes it was, and frankly, although I was a bit uncertain, I'm glad you stopped here after all. And I think a donation would be a wonderful idea, looking back on how we came upon the place."

"All right then, and especially because the whole thought of the supposed Congressman getting them funding is out the window, now I feel especially obligated."

In the back of the SUV, B.G. was able to locate some food supplies that he'd kept from his earlier travels as emergency reserves.

Just under an hour later, B.G. and Carol were back on the interstate highway, once again heading south.

"Well, now that we're on our way, I want to know the details about your donation. So come on, tell me exactly how you did it and what you gave to the place in that triple layer of plastic bags that you tied up so securely when you were in the back of the SUV?"

"Oh, it was nothing special, really. I just went in and left the bag on the table where there were a number of other varied containers of food, and put it next to a large carton of macaroni and cheese. Inside, my donation had just a big jar of roasted peanuts, a couple of cans of sardines in mustard sauce...and twenty thousand dollars in cash."

CHAPTER FIFTY

It was now several days after B.G. and Carol had returned from their time spent in Maine. Back at home, the ranch in western Pennsylvania was looking at its best this time of year, with the garden in full production, the apples ripening on the trees, and the pastures with the beef cows grazing were lush in their summer greenery.

And yet, one morning as he sat with a mug of coffee on the back porch looking over the pastures, he noticed on the treeline behind the far fence row, that some leaves were already starting to change color.

The summer had passed quickly. He had been deeply absorbed in The Project over most of it, and all of a sudden he realized it was nearly autumn.

*

Later that morning, he led Jack outside and had him hop into the back of the SUV. B.G. was enjoying the friendly demeanor of the huge dog more and more, along with its ever present willingness to enthusiastically partake in most any activity. Taking a ride, they soon were exiting the vehicle and entering B.G.'s law office.

He had been spending less and less time in his office over the past year. That was an indication that his interest had been consistently fading from the business of the practice of law. In general, he didn't like it much anymore, especially the tedium of courtroom work, where the selective application of certain time limits, document requirements or the like, which he periodically saw, became hard to accept. He had come to find much of the court's procedural guidelines unnecessary, and saw this borne out when police misconduct was overlooked or when he had observed judges time and again choose not to apply the rules to a prosecutor in a criminal matter or lawyer in a civil case who happened to be in their golf foursome, or who had been instrumental in getting that particular judge their job on the bench.

Furthermore, the weight of having many other people's problems placed in one's lap, which while initially legal, seemed to always end up encompassing their personal difficulties as well, over time became a burden that was simply unwanted. Although his skills were in demand, B.G. had refused more cases than he could recall over the past few years, simply because he didn't want to be caught up in the morass of paperwork, delays, and often time lies built upon lies accumulated from parties, witnesses, opposing counsel and even the courts.

Consequently, this most recent legal matter with Mr. Kurt Koppy had been different all right, and that may well have been why it appealed to him. Certainly, it had concerned some unusual matters. It had required substantial travel. It had led to his own involvement in events that clearly proved to be illegal, which had been more or less a first for B.G. over his decades of practice where in the past he had previously and steadfastly tried to follow the rules.

In this case, he had acted much differently. He had set up his own course of conduct, with only passing concern for the legality of such. And looking back on it all, in doing so, it had been lots of fun.

*

With Jack sleeping peacefully on the carpet in front of his desk, B.G. went over to the front door and double checked that he had locked it from the inside. After that, he closed the shades on the windows.

He then took some time and located the hidden briefcases which had given rise to this entire matter. Carefully, he observed their contents, and without making any precise count, he immediately noticed how much lighter one of them was, and thus how much less in the way of currency they contained in light of his distribution over many states.

He had done what his client had asked him, and then some. He had done it well. While there was still some distribution work remaining on The Project, the bulk of it had been successfully accomplished.

Now, he thought as he looked at the straps of currency and gold coins before him, he felt he could properly direct his thoughts to the happy subject of legal fees.

His client had made very clear that one-third of the total was to be for his attorneys fees, and had done so repeatedly. That was a certainty. Therefore, while he had separated his portion roughly some time ago, soon it would be time to precisely count each and every dollar of his share.

B.G. giggled aloud at the thought. It was becoming a rare event indeed when you could do that today, actually count out large amounts of cash for yourself, in this world of strict record keeping and documentation of checks, wire transfers and the like.

And yet, he paused as the term stuck with him for a moment.

Legal fees.

His legal fees.

He stopped to analyze the words for a moment.

They were fees. And they were his, according to his client's specific instructions.

But what about the legal part of it?

Were they legal?

Not that it mattered at this point, because B.G. had long ago decided that he was going to pursue the matter regardless of the possible consequences. And for the foreseeable future at least, if not permanently, while keeping in mind the well-being of all involved, he was altogether overlooking any such details relating to tax reporting, which rules of disclosure he knew created even more risk and complications.

But getting back to the basic terminology, he continued his analysis.

Well, he was an attorney, attorneys did legal work, and those were his fees for the work which he had been hired to do...so in that sense they certainly were legal fees.

But setting aside the fact that the fees were for the payment of a lawyer for his legal work, his contemplation of the question persisted.

Were the fees legal?

From another perspective, in many respects, since they involved his own participation in unlawful activities, perhaps they were not.

Also, going back further to the source, if the information he received had been accurate, the loot, if you will, all came from illegal activities, in several layers. Initially, the fees reportedly had been part of the profits from illegal drug dealing. Secondarily, that same loot came into Kurt's hands when he stole it from the warehouse rented by the since deceased drug dealer who had owed him rent money, just before Kurt set that warehouse ablaze.

The more he thought about it the more perplexing it became.

Letting out a big sigh, B.G. smiled.

"You know," he said aloud to the briefcases before him, "you would be a great subject for a discussion by a group of individuals with advanced philosophy degrees."

And then, realizing that he had more than enough reason to continue on his set path, he closed the briefcases, and while patting one affectionately he said gently, "Don't worry, I'll take very good care of you."

His decision was firm. The designated amounts were clearly his own legal fees.

Overall, he had taken steps to make the lives of many deserving people much better. And so...

He was an attorney, according to his client they were his fees...and that was that.

B.G. Wumpkey was now following his own set of rules, and knowing that, he had never felt better.

CHAPTER FIFTY-ONE

Three days later, Irwin called. Very happily, he informed that even though it took longer than expected, he had now finished the portrait showing a likeness of B.G. addressing a large crowd in the art center's theater. Irwin indicated that he was very pleased with the final product, and believed it was one of his better works. He said that he would hold it until B.G. came back again to pick it up, unless advised otherwise.

After that, in more cryptic words, Irwin informed that from what he understood in talking with people familiar with the subject, what he had would allow him to properly transfer ownership of a certain item if and when he decided to do so. Tentatively, he wasn't looking to do so until next spring, when he might be making a trip up north and could visit him at the ranch.

While B.G. told Irwin that he had seen the certain gentleman and shared some seafood, he kept the conversation more general. In essence, he let Irwin know that it seemed he had been right about their friend, and thought the situation was heading in a more positive direction, adding that the longer that it remained a puzzle the better. He figured that Irwin would understand, and based on Irwin's brief but upbeat reply, the message was received. Irwin then expressed warm greetings and sent an open invitation that the guest quarters would be reserved for him alone or with Mrs. W., if they wanted to visit when the cold weather arrived.

He ended the conversation, however, with a closing comment that left much room for speculation.

"One last thing, Mr. W. I didn't mention this last time we spoke...I figured you had enough on your mind already...but when I got that call from our friend before you went up north...he did request that I let you know that if you're interested, he may want to talk to you about a few keys, maybe sometime next year."

*

Later in the week, B.G. got a message that Merle wanted to meet with him.

They set up another late morning conference, and at the arranged time Merle promptly showed up carrying a bulky envelope.

In response to B.G.'s inquiries, Merle was more than pleased to give a detailed account of the pain he had first endured and the after effects. Starting with the ordeal of having the cat push the drywall trowel over the counter which caused the cutting off of his baby toe and the further trauma of watching the dog come in from the next room and eat it, B.G. thought he heard Merle's voice crack as he relived the events.

When Merle said it bothered him that a lot of the people at the bars were still laughing about it, B.G. couldn't help but chuckle himself as he envisioned just how the unusual sequence of events took place.

Merle informed that the pain still persisted, and that as a result he was unable to wear some of the shoes that he had in the past.

"It's surprising, and I never would have believed it, but that little toe is pretty important. I mean, just to try to go up on the balls of my feet hurts like crazy, and not having a toe anymore on the edge of my foot has an effect on my balance as well."

B.G. said that he understood and would do his best to try to help. Merle then brought out more bills and noted that he had some past due notices on a few of the earlier ones already. Next, he took out some photographs, which struck B.G. as to just how much of an impact the injury had on him.

The first photo had been taken from the phone of the lady who drove him to the hospital. It showed in vivid detail, the open wound and the still bleeding area on the foot.

Seeing that, made B.G. wince.

Next, he brought out several other photos. These were more uncommon in their nature.

One by one, Merle had taken the time to review pictures starting from his youth, which happened to show him with bare feet or wearing open toed sandals.

"As you can see, it was a pretty good looking toe, as toes go. And now, even though I really like to go barefoot in the warm weather or if I go swimming, I'm going to feel like a bit of a freak if I have that part of my foot on display. And I hate all the jokes about me being really stupid, too. So I won't want to go barefoot, or wear sandals in public... And it's all because of that silly cat and the dumb dog..."

Merle's voice then trailed off as he went silent.

Suddenly, to B.G.'s amazement, he saw that Merle was crying.

As his shoulders shook, he sobbed visibly for several minutes, while B.G. watched and then started to better understand what this man had been going through. Previously, he had regarded it all somewhat lightheartedly, which was easy to do for there was certainly real humor in the situation. But now, right here seeing him overcome with sadness, there was a sense of compassion which entered the room.

"I'm sorry, Mr. Wumpkey," Merle was saying as his tears continued. "It's just that I've never really been good at much of anything, and lots of what I tried over the years just didn't work out...Work, relationships, it all ends up on the negative side...And now being injured, I can't do the drywall stuff for now, and my rent just went up and even though I think I have enough savings to last for a while..."

Merle paused and took a handkerchief from his pocket and wiped his eyes.

"Anyway, all I want you to know is that I think you're a really good guy and a good lawyer, and I sure hope you can help me out."

In his mind, B.G. quickly went over the facts of Merle's case. Unfortunately, he couldn't sue the cat or the dog, and whether there was homeowner's or other insurance involved was speculative at this point. Still, he wanted to help his client, and felt that perhaps even the owner who had hired him might be more than willing to help him out informally if approached properly.

After considering these factors in his thoughts, B.G. then explained that he would try, but that he wanted Merle to know it was an unusual case, and there were complications involved in his working under the table and all, and that these things often take longer than you would like.

Merle blew his nose and then put away his handkerchief before he said anything more.

"I understand, Mr. Wumpkey. And I trust you, that you'll do the best you can for me, and if you can get me some money it's okay, but if you can't, well I'll understand. Just as long as you handle my case as you see fit."

B.G.'s eyes suddenly looked up from the papers on his desk.

"What did you just say?" he asked sharply.

"I was just saying that if you can get something out of the case for me it's okay, but if you can't I'll understand. And then I said, just as long as you handle my case as you see fit."

The last words hung in the air.

Without realizing it, B.G. repeated them aloud.

"As you see fit..."

"That's right Mr. Wumpkey. Handle it as you see fit."

All at once, Wumpkey realized that everything was related, and that somehow it all eventually worked out. He pictured one of the briefcases clearly in his mind, and then he smiled broadly.

"You know Merle, in this matter, you could say, 'handle it---as you see foot'," Wumpkey said in a tone that made them both start to laugh out loud.

They laughed at that for several moments, and it was a good thing for both of them.

Later, with their conference over, B.G. accompanied Merle as he limped toward the door. Extending his hand, Merle expressed his thanks for the meeting.

Before he opened the door, B.G. wanted to be sure that Merle left on a positive note. He thought of the briefcase again, and a smile came over his face before he spoke.

"You know Merle, let me tell you this. One way or another, I feel confident that we'll be able to get you a result that will make you happy."

That was even more than what Merle was hoping to hear. He looked gratefully at B.G. and seemed to suddenly stand taller and prouder.

"As you see foot?" he asked with a grin.

"Yes Merle," B.G. replied. "As I see foot."

And after that, B.G. Wumpkey, Attorney at Law, gave a friendly wave as he watched his newest client walk very carefully down the sidewalk.

*

THE END

EPILOGUE

In the preceding story, the situation in which B.G. Wumpkey found himself was in many ways, a precarious one. Of course, deciding upon the best way to handle the matter of apparently tainted loot, a suspect on the run, a dead body and a crime scene each on their own would present to most a substantial dilemma. And to an attorney, such problems and considerations become compounded for a number of reasons.

But what about that loot, the large amount of monies from a questionable source?

In having to deal with a very unusual matter, he used his own methods to carry out his client's very unusual requests. And from that, he achieved what he considered to be a successful outcome, while something extremely positive with far-reaching benefits resulted to numerous parties. Had he instead chosen the more conventional route and dealt with the authorities from the onset, his overriding feelings were, and rightly so, that any valuables would have quickly fallen into greedy hands and then disappeared with no lasting or wide-spread benefit whatsoever.

And so, while weaving his way through a complicated and dangerous scenario, B.G. Wumpkey found his own solution. Now, while looking back on it, he has a simple question for his readers.

What would you have done?